# THE SECRET PLACE
*And Other Cornish Stories*

# THE SECRET PLACE

*And Other Cornish Stories*

DENYS VAL BAKER

WILLIAM KIMBER · LONDON

This collection first published in 1977 by
WILLIAM KIMBER & CO. LIMITED
Godolphin House, 22a Queen Anne's Gate,
London, SW1H 9AE

© Denys Val Baker, 1977
ISBN 0 7183 0285 0

Photoset by
Specialised Offset Services Limited, Liverpool
and printed in Great Britain by
Redwood Burn Ltd, Trowbridge and Esher

# CONTENTS

# I

## In the Words of the Prophet

Madoc the Prophet was from the bleak moorlands of Penwith in West Cornwall, a great tall man with a red beard and flowing red hair all around his shoulders and always wearing the same long black robes with a silver cross hanging down the middle. From the time he was a young man and first heard the call he wandered about the Cornish countryside and wherever there was a village or even a handful of farm cottages he would take his stand at the roadside and preach his message.

A striking sight he was, with his waving hands and his fiery eyes and his high, strong voice booming out all over the place. Some people used to laugh and make fun of him, and those that were set on the more proper-like routines of chapel life would go so far as to make protests and speak of blasphemy. But others listened despite themselves and were impressed. For there were times, with the sunlight glinting upon the tips of his frothing red hair, when Madoc took on the very look of a mighty ancient prophet. That was how he thought of himself: 'Listen, ye sinners and doubters! Listen to the voice that has been sent to warn you. Take heed, before it is too late! A time of reckoning is at hand!' Let them beware, he cried, for soon there would come to pass again the miracle of Mary of Nazareth, of the Virgin Mother.

But like all prophets, Madoc found his warnings unheeded, his voice the lone one in the wilderness. The years went their hasty way; his feet grew hard and sore from tramping dusty roads or scaling sharp moorland tracks, and he felt his heart heavy with the burdens of disappointment and disillusionment.

Oh, it was a weary business, wandering through the hotness of a dusty day, the frayed ends of his black robes swirling the dust, fraying still more. How hot and dried up his body, how parched his tongue! With what eagerness would he await the sight of the straggling cottages marking the next village – knowing that at least in one, usually the largest of the buildings, he would find a welcome seat, a still more welcome home-brewed beer. What true blessing it was to tilt the glass back, to let the cool liquid trickle across his tongue and into the arid cavern of his throat, to feel the dried up pores opening, the dust washed away, the whole blood and bones of him revived, become alive again. How fortunate he was to have discovered this secret spring of life, without which he would long ago have drooped and faded away into no more than the dust he trampled on each day. For there was something about a glass of rich dark ale that pulled a man together, even a prophet, that made him more himself. After that, it required but little experience to discover that there was something still more about two glasses, while three, or perhaps four or five glasses, were likely to have the most amazing effects. The body glowed, the mind sparkled like a clear crystal, your very soul swelled and wanted to burst goodwill all over the whole world. Disappointments and disillusionments were exposed for the threadbare things they were – in their place sprang up sturdy saplings of new faith. You were confident, once again, that the world was bulging with potential miracles.

It was one pleasant autumnal evening, after reviving himself in this manner, that Madoc made the encounter which confirmed him quite surely in his faith in his role of prophet, sent to bear a message. He had walked some way out of the village, following a narrow lane that wound among moss-covered stone walls. It was as he came up towards the top of a rise in the lane that he saw a sight to make him gasp and stop in his tracks. Directly ahead of him, sitting on the wall was a little girl. There was a bright early moon peeping from over the mountain's shoulder, and the silver of this seemed to fasten around the shadow of the little girl's head and shoulders, and even to encircle them. Madoc knew it was a halo the moment he saw it. What else could it be but a halo, the sign for which he had waited all these years? He ran up the lane brandishing his arms in welcome, crying out a babel of his preaching words.

The little girl was dark and pale, a very slight creature, with big brown eyes that fixed on Madoc the Prophet a look of fright. There were red flushes all around her eyes and stains down her white dress front, like there had been a storm of tears. She looked forlorn and pitiful as if she had suddenly been abandoned to her fate by those that should have loved her.

As the strange torrent of words streamed out from a space in the forest of red hairs, the little girl began crying again.

'Oh, man with the red beard,' she cried. 'Oh, please sir, help me. I am all alone … I have nowhere to go.'

Then Madoc dropped on one knee, and took one of the tiny hands in his own.

'Fear not, child. I am Madoc the Prophet, who has been put into this world to give warning of what is to come. Now is my reward, this lovely silver evening – now my tired, weary feet have at last brought me to you. Fear not, I know who you are – Mary!'

'Sir, my name is Karenza,' said the little girl, brushing away a tear and pouting.

'No, child,' said Madoc firmly. 'Your name is Mary. The Virgin Mother is with us again. Hallelujah!'

Then came a great change in the life of Madoc the Prophet. At first it was in his mind to parade his new discovery through the length and breadth of Cornwall, aye and other countries too, to prove to the world that a miracle was abroad. But after one or two try-outs, notably at a market town, near the Lizard where he was pelted with potatoes by shocked housewives, he came to the sad realisation that the time was not yet ripe. His purpose must no longer be to scour the country with his message, but to settle back in some quiet spot and rear the girl Mary in preparation for her great revelation. Accordingly, the black robed feet turned themselves away from the familiar paths, down towards a remote moorlands village. There, with his small savings he secured a cottage, a portion of grazing land and a few head of sheep, and settled down to the two tasks of shepherding his sheep and shepherding his protégé.

At first his neighbours were alarmed by Madoc and his great red locks and flashing eyes. But they were a kindly lot and after a while grew accustomed to his eccentricities. Perceiving that Madoc was rather a poor one at sheep-rearing, some of the neighbouring farmers occasionally called over to give a helping hand. And sometimes their wives cried out, 'Heavens, I don't know how that Madoc manages all on his own with that little girl' – and over they bustled with their plates of cold lamb, or a basket of apples, or an old biscuit barrel filled with fruit cake and pasties.

Of the little girl Karenza, or Mary – upon my soul, how could you know which was right? But, anyway, they plumped for Karenza as a good old Cornish name – well, of Karenza they grew very fond. And who would not, indeed, for a pretty little thing she was, with her long pigtails and her bow of blue ribbon, and her plump cheeks with always a spot of healthy colour in them. You couldn't be sure quite how old she was for she didn't seem at all sure herself, but it was reckoned that she must have been about seven when she first came. But she was always well developed for her age, you could see that. Indeed, there was quite a lot puzzling about little Karenza. She seemed a little apart from the other girls in the village. Mind you, she played like all the others, and was popular with them, and often the leader of their pranks. Yet she was sometimes different from them even in playing, for more than once you could see her wandering off over the moors, miles and miles away, without seeming to be feared at all. It was difficult to say quite what it was, but somehow Karenza was always restless, always a bit of a wanderer. You felt there was some part of her belonging elsewhere, so that she was just a little bit of the foreigner.

For a time Madoc kept his tongue quiet and himself to himself. But as his sheep-rearing, with the help of more expert neighbours, began to bring in some money, he found himself better equipped for attending the snug parlour of the Miner's Arms in the village. Every one among the village men, with the exception of John Hosking the postman who was teetotal, was fond of calling in at least once an evening to the Miner's Arms. At first there was a little surprise to see Madoc there, for, though he wasn't exactly like a proper preacher – well, you rather expected that he would be in the tradition of ministers and their like, professing a holy abstinence from strong liquids. Still, that was his own business. So long as he liked to come, he was welcome.

It wasn't long before there was his own special seat for him, and you could time his arrival like clock-work – a little while after the time that he had tucked the girl Karenza safe and snug into her bed. By then, his throat was dry, indeed, and he was glad of the old relief of wetting it, and wetting it again. And then, sure enough, he would feel the fire surging back into him, his long red tongue would become fine and free and loose again, and in no time the rich voice would boom in and out of the crooks and crannies of the old pub.

It was a good strong voice, pleasant music, and the villagers were as glad to listen to it as anything, especially if old Madoc could be prevailed on to read passages from the Book. But sometimes Madoc forgot where he was, thinking he was back on some fargone roadside pulpit, and then his voice became shrill and worrying, and you began to get a little fed up with it. Especially when he got on to this fanciful story about the little girl Karenza and her being who she was, and all that stuff. It was not right, really, you know, and those who felt more strict than others about their chapel duties felt that old Madoc was over-stepping himself, even making allowances for the fact that he was a little queer in the head as you might say.

So, though no one liked to be too rude and speak outright to Madoc, there was a general agreement that he should always be guided away from the dangerous subject so much in his mind. When his voice persisted in venturing into such blasphemous regions, the only thing was to leave him alone and play some darts or have an argument, or go home.

So that was how it came to be, and it was a hard blow for

Madoc, who had thought the prophet to be due for his recognition at last. But no, all those years, one and two and three, and right on, those growing years of the girlhood of the dark-eyed Karenza, there was no one who would listen much to the prophet, who had seen the little girl with the halo. Ah well, that was the hard way of the world. The red hairs bristled, the shaggy red eyebrows raised; there was a snort and a splutter, and Madoc wriggled his nose disdainfully. His triumph would come, the words of the prophet would be justified. He was content to wait.

But waiting takes time. And time went by fast, spring sowing and autumn reaping, savage winds of winter, howling over the moors and hills, sudden quiet summer days with not a ripple on the sea, fishermen out crabbing. A sheep caught in a disused mine shaft, a marriage of a farmer's daughter, the annual whist drive, some holiday makers staying at the Miner's Arms, a trip to Falmouth and another one to Newquay – that was how time passed, filled with its little events. And pacing it all, there was Madoc the Prophet's girl Karenza, spreading out like a flower, first the tall legs growing into white stems, then the neck deepening and the features of the face filling out, then the whole of her suddenly swelling slightly, like plants after a sudden storm – at last the flat-chested school girl was disappeared and lost in the depths of a new, softer whiteness. This was now Karenza, the big warm girl with legs bare brown to the wind, with her firm tweed skirt, and bright blue blouse, and her tidy brown overalls to keep them clean, helping Madoc with his sheep and his house and his living.

And now Madoc took to sitting by the fire in the evening, with the Book beside him, staring long stares across at Karenza curled up in the other chair. There was a sudden maturity about her that he had hardly noticed before. He felt old excitement flooding through him ... surely the time was drawing near? They had been long years of waiting, but they would all be justified. Then he smiled across at Karenza whom he thought of as Mary, and she smiled back for she was grateful for all his care and love.

But Madoc the Prophet was no longer a young man, and no longer just an elderly man, but a very old man. The red in his hair was faded into grey and then white, and there was even some of the strong hairs turning dry and falling away. He was aware of a weariness in his bones, sometimes the cold, too, and he felt a great sadness to think of how short life must be for one like him. So it was not surprising that he took to worrying and fretting towards Karenza, as if in some way he could hasten her into performance of the long awaited miracle.

Karenza, for her part, at the turn of eight-and-ten years, was in full bloom, the world opening out in full luxuriance. She felt within her great strength and vigour, the unquenchable power of youth. She saw Madoc as the old, old man he was, and with her heart filled with love for him and his kindness she began to look after him with all the fuss and bother of which women are capable. Earlier to bed it was to be for Madoc, not so many visits to the Miner's Arms; and he wasn't to bother so much about fetching in the sheep – Daniel, the next door farmer's man could give a hand, or if necessary Karenza herself could manage on her own. But there would be compensations. Madoc should have meals regular and fine and tasty as he could wish, he could have the Book read to him in bed an hour every evening before he fell asleep, and there would be home-made treacle toffee when he wished – oh, and lots of nice things to make up for growing old.

Now, with the old one tucked early into bed, and the young one blooming with life and curiosity, there was the time come for Karenza to begin thinking about capturing the favours of handsome princes and their like. You might have thought that she would have had plenty of interest to show in some of the village lads: there was Joseph the farmer's son, and there was James from the big house by the sea, and there was Mrs Tregonning's son Marsden, and the good-looking boy from St Just who was courting Loveday Pengelly, but probably wouldn't be averse to a change.

Yet, fancy, with none of these did young Karenza bother, not at all. But then, perhaps it was because she was not quite the same as the village girls. There was in her a strange restlessness, an eternal desire to be wandering away, just wandering and wandering; something trickling through her very blood, the itch you might call it. She had always felt it, no doubt, only now she was growing old enough to feel it proper.

Perhaps it was this really that took her off on the old tiny bus into Penzance one sunny day, and then sent her wandering down a side street to where there was the swing and jingle and the coloured tops of a real old-fashioned fair. Have you ever seen a travelling fair, with the streaming red-and-white banners, the gold braided coaches, the little caravans dotted about the field, the dirty marquees – and the sight of brown horses, the smell of the lions and tigers?

Oh, it was exciting to Karenza, wandering round with her eyes wide and bright and her black hair tossed back and fluttering at the ends in the breeze, a sparkle upon her all over. You couldn't miss looking at Karenza that day, for she was quite alive and beautiful, and moving as graceful as the silver tiger itself. There were many eyes feasted on Karenza that day, and many who wished they walked beside her. And her? Well, strange, she felt as if everything had once been familiar. Like for instance, when she stopped by the little tent with the gold-and-silver sign, the tent of the fortune-teller, Madame This-and-That, call her what you will, the stout old gipsy lady with dark curls and a rainbow-coloured scarf round her head. When Karenza sat down and looked into the crystal ball she saw the old lady's face clear and round and familiar, like her own, and she was startled and looked up. The old lady smiled in the queerest fashion, and bent forward and peered hard at her, and then smiled again before she began telling her fortune. But all she would tell Karenza was that she would lead a long life and a happy life, she would marry a handsome man and have a large family. Though she did say, with a secret smile, that there would be much travelling in her life.

And fancy, almost as soon as she came out of the fortune-teller's booth, Karenza tripped over one of the ropes at the back. Someone cried out, a hand caught her as she fell, and she felt herself lifted light as a feather, and placed straight.

The lifter was a wiry, dark-faced man, long black hair pushed back and a handkerchief round it. When he smiled he had strong white teeth, and it was a sly, sort of humorous smile. His eyes were black, and when Karenza met them she felt her strength and aliveness transfixed and possessed, so that she shuddered. The next moment there was warmness stealing over her, a blush on her cheek.

The dark-eyed man took her arm and they walked down the long avenue between the brightly lit stalls, with the sound of the cranking swings, the strident cries of the stall-keepers, the music and bustle of the gipsy fair; walked forward over the soft green grass, and into the distance, and it was strange, but she felt she had known it all along in her heart and her blood. So were her thoughts, walking with the strong arm around her, down the long avenue of fairy lights and on into the dusk and the evening mystery.

Well, the fair was at Penzance three days, and each day Karenza caught the first bus in the morning and came back on the last bus at night. After the third day she brought back with her a little present from her lover of the dark eyes, a bundle of shining brass and silver, bright ear-rings for a bright-eyed girl. But that night she put them away under her pillow and then lay herself down to weep. For early the next morning there would be a rumbling of cart-wheels through Penzance streets, a clip-clopping of horses, and the gipsies and their circus would be journeying on. Over the hills and far away. Here to-day and gone to-morrow. The wanderers.

And so there was Karenza back at her work, the same to look at as before and yet not the same, like when she was all alone and gave her wild laugh, and brought out her ear-rings, and let them dangle and jingle from her pretty ears ... The sheep growing and the clock ticking, the smoke winding from the village chimneys, the mild cart clattering by; all much the same, indeed. But old Madoc up there, he was not the same. It is very tired you get to be after eight and eighty years on this earth, and most of them spent being a prophet of old. There is an ache in the bones and a heaviness around the eyes, so that all you would really like to do is close those eyes and rest the old bones; fall into a nice gentle sleep and never wake up.

That was in the winter, with the leaves red and the winds blowing up from mountain bellies. You might have thought then that the old man would rightly go out with the end of the year, like a puff of wind, on his peaceful way to heaven. But there was something still fussing Madoc, binding him to the grey old earth and its days and nights, and he lingered on through all the frosts and the rainy months. He didn't go out much now, and you could find him sitting in the old straw-backed chair by the fireplace, staring into the inscrutable flames. That is, when he was alone. When Karenza was in the room as well, the weakening blue eyes fastened upon her and watched and watched, and followed her about; here to the cupboard to get some flour, there to the sink to fill a bowl with fresh cream. There was an urgency about the way the watery eyes focused on Karenza, with her tall thick-limbed body and her soft white skin; as if each time, each moment, they expected to see some revelation, to unveil some secret.

It used to make Karenza blush to herself and feel quite uncomfortable sometimes, so that she would grow irritable, and flounce out of the room; or angry, and wrap up Madoc's shawl around his shoulder and pack him off earlier than usual to bed. Not that eyes eight and eighty years old could be very keen for spotting things, she told herself, especially when they watered and blurred each day. In her own heart she had already decided that as soon as Madoc was gone from her, then she, too, would pack her bags and wander away. For there was all the world calling her to come, that itching in her veins, not to stay and rot away in a tiny grey cottage. But at the sad note of her thoughts she would be flooded over with pity and reproach, she would fall down beside the thin old man and throw her young arms around him, nestling close and weeping for his vanishing life. He who had never spoken a cross word to her, brought her up as his own daughter, guided her life into flower.

And it was when she did this one early spring afternoon, with a warm kiss of love and affection lingering on the old wrinkled forehead, that Madoc's eyes suddenly flashed with fire and his head jerked back, and a thrill of wonder ran through his body so that for one moment it became like it was seventy years ago, when he saw the light and heard the call.

'Why, Mary!' he exclaimed, his old voice faltering, and two crabbed bony arms folded round her and held her nearer to him, so that he could listen again for the faint pulsating sound of the miracle.

Then he gently pushed away his Mary, looked up at her with eyes that shone, and said quietly, 'Take off your dress.'

'But, Madoc ...?'

'Take off your dress!'

So Karenza slowly took off her threaded tweed dress, slipping it down from over her whiteness and standing there by the fire-light ... and there was no mistaking the round firm swelling up of her flesh, like the bud of a rose swelling to unfold. There was Karenza called Mary, the dark little girl with the halo round her shoulders, now growing ready to flower a child, a magic new life.

'Mary, oh, Mary!' said old Madoc and the tears welled up in his eyes like raindrops, and the burning light of his eyes lit them up like rainbows, and they fell soft and happy as dew. For thus was the miracle at last come to pass.

At this unexpected perception of her secret, Karenza was frightened. Seeing his evident happiness she grew curious.

'Madoc, you *are* sure – *you* – you're not angry? Because you see how it was, it was like this ...'

But old eyes and old ears can deal with only one thing at a time, and the eyes and the ears and the whole life of Madoc, were filled to brimming with the one miracle.

'Now they will listen. Now the world will listen to the prophecy of Madoc, for the miracle is coming to pass.'

And when he spoke thus, Madoc's face shone with the strange light of the faithful, so that to Karenza it seemed for a moment that she was looking at the face of a saint. Before it she felt humbled and unworthy, and fell silent, obedient to this old man with the light of God in his face.

After a time Madoc stirred himself, getting up from his chair and reaching for his brown cloth cap and his white scarf and the big warm fleece coat that had shielded him from many mountain winds.

'Where are you going, Madoc?'

'I am going out. I have news to tell the people.'

'But – but Madoc, it's not right you should go out. There's clouds about, it might rain. Don't be foolish. Wait for a warmer day.'

Karenza watched him in alarm, for even as he moved about the old body seemed to crumple and sag, as if there was little strength left in it.

'Do not be foolish, girl,' cried Madoc. 'Let me go, I say.'

And with a bang of his stick to open the door wide, out he went into the garden, sweet-smelling from recent rain, and down to the grey lane wandering across the mountain stream and towards the village roofs.

Ah, there was a fine sight he was, too. The sun seemed to kiss red and gold again into his old white hair and the fresh winds seemed to smarten him up and blow great life into him, and he went stalking down the lane like the prophet of fifty years ago, waving his stick in the air and calling out strange words and warnings. While up at the cottage window Karenza sat and watched, aware that she had no place in the strange pilgrimage, one hand gently rubbing the roundness of her belly with its stirs of new life.

When he was in the village square Madoc took deep breaths and filled his lungs and sang out in his strident old voice, and the people came running to their doors wondering what on earth was happening.

'Listen to me now!' cried Madoc the Prophet. 'That which has been prophesied will shortly come to pass. Take heed, to the words of the prophet. Ye who have not listened before, listen now. There shall come a day not many months now, when there will once more be a Virgin Mother given birth to a Child. Therefore, take ye heed!'

Seeing who it was and knowing the voice of old, the people smiled to themselves and shrugged, and went behind their doors again.

But Madoc went on crying out his message, standing in the

village square, and he was no longer despairing or wearied, for now he knew that he told the truth. And when at last his throat was dried and parched up from hoarseness of his shouting he stamped across to the warm parlour of the Miner's Arms and slaked his thirst. Then he stood up and looked round and cried out again his news and his vindication. He was in great heart that night, they always said. Words flowed out of his mouth like water of a mountain stream, never a hesitation or a damming up, only a pause now and then for the revival of a long cool drink. Half of what he said was nonsense, they said, and the other half was beyond their understanding, but there was no doubt that Madoc had reached some sort of fulfilment in his life; the prophet was come into his own that night.

So in a way it did not seem to matter a great deal that later, walking away in the darkness up the moorland road the old man tumbled into the river and was drowned. There was his stick lying on the bridge, and his brown hat tumbled into the mossy reeds at the side, and the next day they found Madoc washed up into a gentle backwater further down the valley. Perhaps he put one of his old legs in the wrong place and tripped up in the dark, said someone. Or perhaps he saw something to give him a start, said someone else. For there was a glimmer of moon showing, and you know how that can make the night strange and alive, with white things moving, like ghosts. He died quite peaceful like, they said, and he did not look in any way unhappy.

But wasn't it strange how old Madoc used to rave and rant all that stuff about young Karenza being the Virgin Mary? Because, bless me, if not many months afterwards she with her saucy eyes and bold looks that would turn any man's head went and gave birth. Only it wasn't one child, but two; a black-eyed boy and a brown-eyed girl. The Holy Twins they used to call them in the village, joking like. Well, of course, it's too late now to know whether they really were very Holy, for it wasn't long afterwards that Karenza packed up her bags and herself and her babies and left the village for ever. She was never seen in the village since, though there was a farmer who once came across her at a fair up country. She was sitting at the back steps of a gipsy caravan, and the twins were sitting beside her. She had rings in her ears, just like the gipsies, and so did the little boy and girl. There was a little dark-eyed gipsy there whom she said was her husband; and indeed, the boy had much the same dark looks about him ... But, of course, whether the gipsy was the father of the twins or not is entirely a matter for conjecture.

And so, as the years roll on, there are many who gather of an evening in the Miner's Arms up on the Cornish moors and talk about old Madoc and his wild red hair and how he believed he was a prophet of old, and how in a strange way his prophecy came true. Sometimes, when the lights are low and the night is drawing near time for sleeping, there is more than one of us that pauses and thinks, and wonders deep down whether for all we know Madoc's belief was not as good as any other, and the only pity of it was that none of us believed enough with him. For there is no denying, that belief is what makes miracles.

# II

## A Parcel for Rogers

The parcel came by the afternoon post. The School was in session and the Lower Fourth were doing maths. The big, rather bleak classroom, was silent, except for the scratching of chalk on the blackboard as the master wrote up the next complicated problem: 'If an engine is travelling at 60 miles an hour ...'

In one of the furthest corners the boy divided his attention between the words on the blackboard and the shafts of sunlight falling like snow through the high windows. He wished that his desk lay in their path, so that he would become alive and bright; so that he might perhaps feel as he used to sitting on the cliffs at home, watching the seagulls wheeling and hovering above him.

Then he saw the time on the school clock, and turned to look out of the side window, as he had done at that time every afternoon for many weeks, searching the long, straight road for the scarlet flash of the post van. In a few moments it came, streaking along as neat and compact as the tiny clockwork model he had once played with at home. He watched, fascinated, as it pulled up outside the iron gates and the postman got out and carried in a small mailbag. Secretly, as he had done a score of times before, the boy pretended to himself: 'Today the postman has brought my parcel. I'm sure he has. He – he looks like he has a parcel in his sack.'

'Rogers!' said the master, sharply. 'Will you please pay attention?'

But in the mid-afternoon break, wandering aimlessly around the dusty playground, he was surprised to be accosted by one of the boys in his dormitory.

'Rogers! There's a parcel for you. I was there when the matron was sorting.'

It really had come, then. At last! He knew it was no good trying to get it now; he would have to wait until the post was handed out after tea. But the knowledge was within him, and, like a parcel bursting open, he let this knowledge shower all over him its contents of wonder and joy.

'A parcel for Rogers.' That was how the master on duty would make the announcement, and a moment later it would be in his arms, real, secure, a potential marvel. As he contemplated the moment, he could hardly contain himself and his excitement. He would have danced for joy, there in the playground, if he hadn't been afraid of his form-mates and their making fun of him. But, anyway, he had something to tell them all now. How often had he been a jealous watcher, as one of them went round beaming, and whispering: 'I've got a parcel; just you wait and see what's in it!' Well, now it was his turn.

All through the remainder of lessons that afternoon he could hardly concentrate for the excitement of his thoughts. He had waited a long time for this day. And, indeed, he had come a long way for it. The place where the parcel had come from was two hundred miles away, a tiny village, tucked into the folds of Cornish hills and facing the great booming roar of Atlantic waves. He had been born there, he had grown into boyhood there, and he had never wanted to leave there – never, never, never! But his father, a fisherman, had been left some money by an uncle, and that money, he had decided, would be used to give his son a chance to become something better than a fisherman. It had been no use arguing, or pleading; not even tears had availed. One cold January day he had made the long, rather terrifying journey, across the West of England, up to a semi-public school, near the wilderness of Salisbury Plain.

It had been lonely at first. Even now, though more acclimatised, he felt lost. So the idea of a parcel from home had come to mean much, perhaps more than could be fulfilled. Of course, there had been letters, yes – once a week his mother wrote, in her rather stilted handwriting. But her letters were not full of the gossip he would have liked, only of warnings and admonitions: 'Remember to wear your woolly underwear and let me know if you need some more socks.' Letters were not like a parcel. He could not pass his letters around among his dormitory mates, as he might pass a great bulging parcel. A parcel it must be! And every time he wrote home he begged his mother: 'Please will you post me a parcel? All the other boys here get parcels.'

He had not thought he would have to wait so long, know, a nothing of his parents' difficulties – the succession of bad catchesing fall in the market prices of mullet, some unexpected damage to the fishing nets by a floating spar. He had fretted and fumed, and grown more and more unhappy. He had even sometimes cried himself to sleep. But now it was going to be all right.

He was waiting excitedly in the main hall when the master called out his name. In a flash he was up at the top table, receiving into his hands the beloved parcel.

It was a large one, too; there could be no grumbles about that. He felt the weight pulling down his thin arms, and he was glad to rest the parcel on a table. Around him several of his form-mates watched curiously.

'Coo, look! Rogers has got a parcel.'

'Let's have a dekko. Come on, Rogers, open it!'

'Bags me a sweet!'

He smiled benevolently upon their eagerness. Vaguely he *had* thought about delaying the moment, savouring the sweetness of his anticipation still further.

'Oh, come on Rogers. Let's see what you've got.'

'All right,' he promised, suddenly. 'Up in the dormitory.'

They followed him up the stairs, about half-a-dozen boys of his own age. Usually, they were casual towards him – now, for the moment, they were accomplices, his pals.

He put the parcel on his bed and stared down at it. How square and solid and immense it seemed!

'I'll bet,' he said aloud, his mind filling with visions, 'I'll bet there are ever so many things. Soldiers, and cars, and storybooks, and coloured crayons … P'raps a water pistol, something like that. Maybe a cowboy suit!'

He remembered he had several times asked for a cowboy suit, because only recently one of the other boys had been sent a most wonderful suit, with a shaggy waistcoat and silver spurs.

'And sweets?' asked one of the boys.

'Of course,' he said. 'Lots and lots of sweets.'

Then he untied the string and opened the parcel.

There were some sweets; at least there were some sweets! Homemade toffees that his mother had made with treacle and carefully-saved sugar. Home-made treacle toffee! Hurriedly he shared them out among his friends.

But the other things … Unhappily he picked them up. Three pairs of grey socks. A new shirt. Four pairs of underpants. A big navy blue jersey, like a fisherman's jersey. A jacket he had forgotten to bring with him – and two coloured storybooks, which he had also forgotten and left at home. And then, at the bottom, as the *pièce de résistance*, a new pair of shoes. A pair of shiny black shoes, which he had no doubt his mother had travelled into Penzance to get at one of the shops there. Black, shiny, glistening *new* shoes. How new they looked, how expensive they must have been – and how uninterested in them he was!

He looked perfunctorily at his mother's note. '… sending you a few things … don't forget to wear the pants … and there's a nice new pair of shoes … ask the matron to make sure they fit; we can change them if they don't … Daddy sends his love and says he may put something in …'

The last remark registered vaguely, and he searched among the socks and pants and books, without success.

Around him he became aware of his followers disintegrating.

'Well, thanks for the sweets, Rogers.'

'Yes, jolly good.'

'I'll give you some sweets when my next parcel comes.'

They were disappointed, like himself: he could sense that.

In a way their awkward politeness hurt more than if they had spoken outright, if they had pulled faces, and said: 'Coo, what a rotten parcel!' Somehow, he felt he would have minded that less.

Then, just as they were going, one of the boys stopped and bent down.

'Hi, Rogers, what's this! Something must have fallen out of your parcel.'

He took from the boy a small bundle of tissue paper. It felt light, so light, that for one awful moment he thought it was just paper. Then he felt the hardness beneath, and with fumbling fingers he opened out the paper.

'Coo!' exclaimed one of the boys, turning back. '*A boat!*'

A boat it was: a tiny model fishing boat, carved out of a piece of hard mahogany. He held it gently, almost fearfully, between his fingers, marvelling at the sudden wonder of it. He stared round-eyed at the intricate carving, the curved sweep to the bow, the little raised foredeck, the firm little mast, the neat piece of canvas pinned on as a sail – the tiny flag fluttering from the rounded stern. A faint singing of joy flooded over him, like the very ebb and flow of the waves on the shingle at home.

'My dad made that. My dad made that boat. He *carves* them out of old bits of driftwood ...'

And long after, a little humbled, the others had gone away, the boy sat on his bed staring down at the little hand-carved boat. It seemed to him curiously alive there, between his fingers. He could almost *see* his father making it – and, indeed, as he felt the smoothed sides and the gentle curves, he was transported through time and space. He saw himself once again sitting on the little quay, among the painted green and yellow and white boats and the drying fishing nets; and beside him sat his father, a familiar blue-jerseyed figure, brown faced, keen-eyed, a peak cap pulled low over his forehead ... and in his hands a large jack knife, cutting patiently at a piece of sea-washed wood. The sun rode high in a blue sky and the sea lapped gently at the beach below, and all around were the familiar grey cottages and the tall cliffs and the greeny-grey rocks covered with seaweed and lichen. It was home, dear, familiar, faraway home, that he had feared to lose for ever when he set out on that long railway journey. And now, across all the distance, a tiny boat had sailed, launched by that strong brown hand that he knew so well, that had so often crept round his shoulders to comfort him ... a tiny boat had sailed into harbour, here on a grey-blanketed bed in a bare school dormitory.

The boy's eyes filled with tears, but they were tears of happiness. He lifted the little carved boat and held it close to his face, smelling the driftwood's indestructible tang of seaweed and salt.

Then, with a smile, he gathered together the socks and the pants and the shirt and the jersey and the jacket – yes, and the bright new gleaming shoes – and carried them off to the matron for her attention.

'Look, Matron,' he said, importantly, 'I've had a parcel.'

But he didn't show her the boat. That remained in his pocket, clutched tightly in one sticky, warm hand. It was the link he had needed: touching it, he lived and breathed again in his real world.

# III

## So Near – So Far

The roadmen appeared, like the narrow grey ribbon of the
road itself as if by some process of magic, from another world,
another time perhaps; or so it seemed to the woman of the
solitary blue-slate cottage mid-way along the remote valley.
One day she had the whole of the moors to herself, the gorse-
flecked slopes stretching away on either side of the tumbling
waters of the stream; the next there was a subtle change in the
atmosphere, the noise of machinery at work and a spiral of
black smoke – and just visible when she had climbed up to
where the old granite steps began their long climb over the
unfamiliar distant contours of the valley's first road.

For some reason the sense of intrusion disturbed the woman
more than might have been expected. Already in her early
thirties she had the brooding introspective personality of
someone already sheltering from the outside world. She had
once been quite pretty, with a mass of dark, curly hair, but
now the hair had grown long and untidy and her whole
appearance was curiously faded. Usually she would have
taken a lonely afternoon walk up into the marvellously clear
and remote air of the moors, but now she stayed in the cottage
waiting restlessly for her husband's return from teaching at
the village school three miles up the valley.

When he came he was full of the news of the road. It was
being built through to the big dairy farm at the other end so
that the milk vans could get through more easily. According to
the foreman the work should be finished before the end of the
summer – pretty good going, wasn't it? So next term he
needn't walk to school, he'd get a bicycle and ride in style.

While the woman's husband was recounting his news he became quite animated, frequently running a hand through his sandy-coloured hair and now and then cocking his head to one side, like an expectant bird. It was the same when he was at school; instructing his class in the poetry of William Wordsworth, of the facts about the Industrial Revolution he became almost vivacious, full of quick gestures and glances. But the moment the lesson was over or, as now, the story was told, he seemed to withdraw into some private solitude. After his busy day in the outside world he liked nothing better than to come home, eat his evening meal, and then curl up by the fire with a book for hours on end.

The woman did not really mind, for her own tastes were very similar: that, indeed, was what had first drawn them together, a mutual, rather shy interest in the things of the mind – poetry, music, paintings. They both liked solitude, and after their companionship had drifted unhurriedly into marriage and then there had come the chance of the job down here. They had been thrilled to find this cottage going at a very low rent. Its solitariness had not bothered them, indeed they had taken advantage of it to build for themselves a kind of secret world. Things that might have bothered other people – the loneliness, the nearest neighbours were a mile and a half away – were of no importance: they had their books, their radio concerts, their pleasant discussions about the whiffs of gossip brought back from the village school. For the woman it had been enough: she, who was much more alone, had come to enjoy, even to indulge in the solitude – perhaps in a way to look on the whole valley as her own private world.

Now, instinctively, she sensed a threat to that privacy: but when she tried to voice her uneasiness her husband brushed aside her fears.

'Don't worry. It'll be a convenience, that's all.'

That night, while her husband slept peacefully enough, the woman lay wide awake, occasionally moving from side to side of the old-fashioned bed, most of the time staring out of the narrow window at the mysterious starlit sky. Although she felt she was being ridiculous she found herself listening, straining her ears, as if half expecting to hear the alien sounds of the roadmakers reverberating through the night.

In the morning, after her husband had gone off to work, she found that what had been the night's delusion was now a real factor – by listening carefully she could hear the faint hum and buzz of that distant machinery. Once she had caught the sound there was no escaping from it – it went with her about the household tasks and even, later on, it seemed, grew a little louder, a little nearer.

After lunch, drawn by restless curiosity, the woman set off along the bank of the river, heading towards the top end of the valley. She walked thoughtfully with her head down, lost in her brooding thoughts, and coming round a bend in the cart-track was almost on top of the road workers before she realised it.

Startled, the woman stood still for a while, staring at the unfamiliar sight. Across the track straddled two bulldozers with engines humming, their great scoops travelling ahead and levelling out the bumpy ground by gnawing huge slithers of earth and spitting them out to one side. Behind the bulldozers a dozen men with spades and shovels waited to complete the levelling process ... further back the road was already taking shape, and squatting in its centre, like a broody hen, was a smoking belching asphalt machine, laying the surface.

The woman stood staring in amazement at such a vision in the midst of the familiar tranquillity. With the smoke belching, the machine roaring, the great scoops shovelling ferociously, the men's spades and shovels glinting in the sunlight – there was the vivid impression of a miniature inferno on earth. Even the men, sweating and grimy in the hot sunshine, could be likened to slaves at the pit.

The woman broke from her reverie, conscious suddenly that she, too, was the subject of inspection. One or two of the men leaned on their spades and waved to her cheerfully and there was a friendly smile from a blue-dungareed god in charge of one of the bulldozers.

Blushing violently the woman made her way onwards, skirting past the noisy machinery along the edge of the cart track. It seemed to her that there were men everywhere, swarming about like an invading army, and she kept her eyes averted until she felt she had passed the centre of operations. When she looked up at last she found she had reached the finished section of the road, stretching smooth and glistening away down the valley. Here the last of the workmen was methodically hammering down a series of wooden shafts along the edge to hold the paving stones.

Despite herself the woman stopped and watched in fascination. This was not one of the older men but a young man with a mop of curly blond hair – he could not have been more than twenty or so. Like many of the others he had taken off his shirt because of the heat and was working just in a pair of black jeans. Now, as with regular movements he raised up the big iron mallet and hammered it down on the wooden stakes, the powerful muscles of his back rippled under the brown skin and the woman found herself unable to look away from a semblance of such grace and beauty. Indeed she watched almost as if hypnotised, her head unconsciously following the movements of the shoulders, the raising of the arms, the crashing swing of the hammer ... as if in a purely physical way she was joined with the young man in some strange ritual.

When at last the man paused in the middle of a stroke and looked quickly at her the woman was caught off guard. She did not know where to look, what to say, before the sudden penetrating stare of his bright brown eyes. And oh, how bright they were indeed, they seemed to burn as with some secret fire and vitality. In some obscure way the woman was reminded of her husband's erratic vivacity, but she sensed that here there was a different quality, more physically lasting ... as if it was part of the young man's very life force.

'Hullo,' said the young man abruptly.

'Hullo ...' said the woman, a little confused.

'Nice day.'

'Yes ... it's lovely.'

The young man waited a moment, as if half expecting her to say something more: then, with another bright smile, he picked up the big mallet and began swinging it up and down as before, in rhythmical movements.

After a while the woman walked on until she came to the finished part of the road stretching onwards smoothly and in some strange way already blending into the landscape as if it belonged there. When she turned and looked back suddenly it seemed as if the rest of the valley was being obliterated by this sprawling yet purposeful mass of men and machines.

For a moment the woman was overwhelmed by a sense of panic, a fear that perhaps the way back to her home had been obliterated as well, and she began hurrying back the way she had come. As she was passing the young man again he paused and leaned on the top of his mallet and grinned.

'Going home?'

The woman nodded.

The young man lifted his head and looked with idle curiosity along the valley, maybe for the first time – as if it was not normally his custom to wonder about the future, only to exist in the moment.

'That's our cottage further up,' said the woman diffidently.

'Uhuh,' The young man nodded, stretched himself luxuriously in the sun, then picked up his mallet again. 'We're heading that way.'

Before the woman could say anything more he had begun swinging his mallet up and down again, beating the stakes relentlessly into the soft earth with regular inevitable movements. It was a gesture that was almost indifferent, and all at once it struck the woman as a symbol of the whole situation ... Wasn't it like the road itself, appearing from out of the blue, careless of what stood in its way, threading itself across a whole peaceful world without a second thought?

Upset, she lowered her head and hurried away, ignoring the young man's shouted farewell, looking away as she passed the other men, the belching machines, the hammering and pounding and gorging and grinding and devouring of the very earth – hurrying on until at last she had crossed the far field and was out of sight of the invading monsters.

When the woman got back to her cottage she found she was trembling. She was still upset when her husband came home that evening, but somehow she found it difficult to put her feelings into words. The two of them spent the usual quiet evening, reading by the fire until about ten and then putting on the last log and having a desultory chat before going up to bed. The woman longed to brush aside these superficial exchanges, to turn to her husband and suddenly pour out her heartful of vague uneasy intimations; but somehow it was impossible. She was afraid he would scoff at her fears, perhaps even tease or taunt her – already, she thought unhappily, it is as if the road has come between us.

The next day the woman did not go along the road, but instead she climbed up the side of the moors. It was the sort of cool crisp summery day that she loved, when to be high up was to be in heaven itself. But today the crisp sunshine was not enough: in the background, echoing and reverberating, came the snorting of the machines below.

As if mesmerised, the woman abandoned her idea of following the steps to the top, and instead took the path running along the side until it brought her round and above where the men were working. She sat there for an hour or more just watching, and even in that period it seemed to her that the road inched itself forward a little. At the very rear of the patch of activity she fancied she could see the blond figure of the young man, still swinging his hammer ... and at the thought of that hard, sinewy body relentlessly pressing on and on, as inevitably as the snaking road, the woman was filled with a curious apprehension. The road, the young man, life itself – she sensed their implacable intervention into her secret, withdrawn world.

In the afternoon she had to go into the village. She walked along the cart-track with bowed head, past the machines and the asphalt layer, but when she estimated she was safely past and raised her eyes she found the young man still ahead of her, leaning on his spade, as if waiting.

'Hullo.' He grinned. 'Off again?'

'I'm going shopping.'

The young man whistled.

'A long way to go on your own.'

She stiffened. 'I like being on my own.'

He grinned again.

'Yes, I saw you this morning ... saw the colour of your dress.' He paused and looked across the moors quizzically. 'Must be nice up there.'

She swallowed nervously.

'Yes ... Yes, it is.'

He brought his casual gaze back to rest on her again. By now, subtly, she had become more at ease with him, so that she did not resent the directness, even though she had the strange feeling that he saw not just her, but her secret thoughts, and fears as well – as if someone of his intuitiveness could tune in effortlessly to someone like her.

'I must go,' she said hurriedly.

He nodded and watched her hurry along. Just before getting out of earshot she heard him call.

'See you on the way back.'

But by the time she came back he had gone and the road stretched ahead smooth and quiet to its abrupt, ungainly end, looking curiously dead without all that bustling life. She knew he would have gone away because the lorry carrying the gang had passed her just as she was setting off from the village. She had looked up quickly, imagining she had heard a call, and somehow it was as if instead of seeing a dozen faces, she saw only the one face, the now familiar grinning face of the fair young man. Perhaps, she thought confusedly, they were indeed all of them fair young men with brown young bodies and lazy smiles with no thought for the past or fear of the future, just treading their abandoned way across life like the road across the valley.

That night the woman dreamed about the young man, and all the next day she found herself unable to banish him from her thoughts. In some way he had become inextricably mixed up in her mind with the road itself, pushing itself relentlessly forward so that in no time at all, it seemed, the first jagged patchwork approach had arrived within sight of the cottage.

For some days the woman felt unable to go along the track towards the road, but each afternoon she climbed up the pathways and, moving along the boulder-strewn sides, she kept watch. But now that the road was suddenly so disturbingly near, even within sight from one of the bedroom windows, she was overcome by her apprehensions, unwilling even to leave the cottage. It was almost as if she wanted to shut herself up, to hide and pretend there was no road inexorably unwinding past her front door – while yet aware there was no escape.

Somehow there was no surprise in her when one afternoon she heard a tap at the back door and, opening it, found the fair young man standing there, a large billy can in his hand.

She smiled faintly. 'Did you want some water?'

'Please.'

She took the can and filled it under the kitchen tap. When she turned she could not help giving a little gasp, for he had come into the kitchen and suddenly his presence seemed to be everywhere, much more formidable than out in the open.

'What's the matter?' He laughed easily. 'Did I frighten you?'

'No, not really.' She looked suddenly at the kettle boiling on a low flame. 'Would you like a cup of tea? I was just going to make one.'

'I won't say no.'

He settled himself on the window seat, crossing his legs, and she took him a cup of tea.

'Thanks.' He sipped it appreciatively, looking around with the faintest of curiosity. 'Nice place.'

'Yes.' The woman answered automatically, unable to take her attention from the sight of the young man framed by the sunlight in the window, looking like some young god – so alive that she could almost feel it. A vision crossed her mind, bemusingly, of the afternoon she had first seen him, stripped to the waist, working on the road.

'Where – do you come from?' she said abruptly.

'What me?' He pursed his lips and then grinned expansively. 'Oh, I come from the North originally. But I've been all over the place since then.'

He drained his cup and passed it over for her to refill.

'That's what I like about the job, we go everywhere.' He laughed. 'Join the road gang and see the world ... Still I don't mind, it suits me.'

'Yes ... I imagine it does.'

She saw him suddenly, him and all the others who somehow looked like him, travelling heedlessly across the remote faces of the earth, bringing with them the abrasion of fire and noise, the torment of their irrepressible youth. It wasn't fair ...

He got to his feet.

'Well, I'd better be on my way.'

As he spoke he peered through the kitchen door to the hallway and room beyond, shadowy in the fading afternoon light. For a wild moment she imagined taking him through, showing him the cosy fireplace, the rows of books, the secrets of her life unknown to him ... but she kept silent, sensing his almost physical revulsion from the dark, the unfamiliar shadows.

'Well, thanks again,' he said, back at the kitchen door. He took the can of water from her and stood outside looking, as she herself often did, up towards the distant moorlands, still catching the late sunshine.

'You know, I can understand you liking to go up there.' He glanced at her with faint interest awakening in his eyes so that they seemed brighter than ever. 'Yes, it must be all right up there, all alone and free, eh?'

She nodded, standing where she was as if petrified, fixed and immobile, in some way waiting for something important to happen.

'Yes, well ...' He made as if to move off, then turned back and peered round the doorway, his blond presence seeming to glow, to illuminate everything, even the darkest corner. 'Maybe you can show me sometime?'

After that the young man came each day to fill the can of

water for his workmates and each day before he left the woman made him sit down and have a cup of tea, while she stood watching him silently from the far side of the room. Sometimes the young man came early in the afternoon, sometimes much later, but whatever time he called the woman was standing there as if waiting – as if indeed that was the most important thing she had to do, to wait.

Day after day the road crept nearer to the cottage – each time she looked out of the window the shadow of the machines loomed larger, their iron teeth seemed about to devour the earth almost opposite the cottage. Night after night she tossed and turned uneasily on her bed, aware no longer of her sleeping husband but only of this outside threat – the road creeping ever onwards, the fair young man travelling with it, who might never pass again.

At last one morning, looking out of her window early before the road men arrived, she realised that the grey thread of the road had reached as far as the cottage – that when the men began work that day their journey would begin taking them onwards, onwards and away.

That morning the woman moved about the house restlessly, waiting with pent-up apprehension for the coming of the young man. As the usual time went by she began to fret and worry. Perhaps he had stopped coming, now that the road was going further on he would call somewhere else, perhaps the farm at the end ...?

In the midst of her fears she heard the familiar tap at the back door. When she opened it and saw him standing there, flooding her with the sunshine of his youthful presence, the relief that overwhelmed her was so consuming that it swept away all her doubts and hesitations. Just as he was about to go she followed him to the door.

'I was just going for a walk,' she said meaningly.

He was turning to go when she spoke. He paused and looked back with a faint smile.

'See you in my lunch hour, then?'

An hour later, sitting on a grassy mound high up in the

moors, she saw the bright colour of his blue shirt moving among the trees below. Looking up he waved, then came agilely and effortlessly up the steep path; in no time it seemed he was by her side.

'Here I am.'

He looked around, sniffing the clear air gratefully. She pointed.

'These are the old steps. They lead to the top.'

'What are we waiting for then?'

Quite unselfconsciously he took her by the hand and led the way up the steps. She felt the unfamiliar touch of his hand as something almost mysteriously alive and separate.

When they reached the top the steps opened out on to a long soft grassy plateau. There was a flat rock at one point where the woman liked to sit and look out on the world below. Now she went over to this. The fair young man followed, stood casually on the soft grass beside the stone. He stared pensively down upon the valley and its new discolouration, the pitted line of the road he was helping to build.

'So that's what it looks like from up here?' He snorted disdainfully. 'Like a lot of ants, that's what we are ...'

'Oh, no,' said the woman with feeling. 'No, not at all ..."

At the inflexion of her voice the young man propped himself up on one elbow and half turned towards her. At the same moment the sun emerged from temporary eclipse behind a passing cloud, its rays falling with astonishing brilliance all around the fair head of the young man, almost like an aura.

'How do you know?' he said teasingly. 'How do you know what we are?'

Slowly, unwillingly, the woman met his bright eyes. If they had mocked her she could not have borne it, but they were gentle in their irony; the look implied some kind of secret understanding. Encouraged, she began speaking.

'Perhaps I do, a little. Aren't you a bit like the road – at first there's almost nothing, just a speck, and then somehow it gets larger and larger, longer and longer, until it seems that there will be forever the road winding towards you – and then suddenly, hey presto, it's gone, the road has gone away.'

As she spoke the woman caught the vivid image not merely of this golden young man but of all the golden young men in the world, their hair in careless disarray, their handsome faces lifted casually towards the sun, their brown young bodies moving lithely and effortlessly, their smiles reflecting some eternal playful joke ... It was impossible to imagine them pinned to one place, immersed in dark shadows, growing old. But on, she thought, pain clutching at her heart, oh, if only, if only ...

Tentatively, shyly, the woman put out a hand and touched the dishevelled golden crown of the young man's head – a gesture so fleeting that even she could not be certain of its reality.

Feeling the touch of the afternoon breeze in his hair the young man turned quickly, smiled up at the woman, then scrambled to his feet. He reached forward and took her still trembling hand.

'Come on now.' He looked quickly down at the pattern below, broken by the sudden puff of the awakening machines. 'I'll have to be getting back.'

He gave his gay, abandoned grin.

'We'll run down – the whole way.'

Before the woman could protest he had pulled her laughingly to the top of the stone steps. For a moment she was acutely aware of him standing there and surveying the world below as if it were some wonderful personal kingdom of his own – then there was an insistent tug at her arm and he dragged her after him at gathering speed down the winding steps. Down and down they flew, leaping and jumping over the old stones, just as perhaps some young Celtic warrior had done two thousand years ago – down and down and down, the wind blowing in their hair and their eyes, the world below beginning to spin round. Yes, for a few magical moments the woman felt herself at one with the young man, soaring with him into the unknown regions of wonder, floating through the air ...

Then she cried out, tugging heavily on his arm.

'No, please – I can't go on.'

'Yes you can!' He dragged her after him willy-nilly. 'You can if you try. Just forget everything else and hold on to me!'

'No!'

She suddenly screamed out the words and then staggered to a halt.

Ahead of her he barely paused, calling out that he had to get back to work – then he was gone, on and on, down and down, weaving his bright way against the back-cloth of green and grey, scampering through the trees and out at last across the bottom fields. She sat and watched his progress as one might indeed watch a shooting star soaring across the sky and disappearing at last into oblivion.

When at last the woman had recovered her breath she made her way back to the cottage. She felt quite tired, and went upstairs on her bed for a while. About an hour later she awoke to the familiar thudding noise of the machinery. Yet wasn't there something curious about it, as if somehow it had faded slightly?

Crossing to the window she peered out. There could be no doubt about it, the road was already journeying beyond the cottage. The first machines were some way along, devouring new earth, gnawing further into the valley. Everywhere the air was blue with smoke and reverberating from the steady thumping: behind the machines advanced the perpetual invading army of the road men. For a moment her eyes rested sadly on one familiar figure, bending in unending rhythmic movements, but he was quite unaware, it seemed, of her wistful scrutiny: he did not look up once, he was immersed in other thoughts.

Later that evening the woman sat before the fire with her husband. It had grown dark and they had lit the oil lamps. Now she crossed to the window to draw the curtains.

'By the way,' said her husband, looking up from the book he was reading. 'Have you noticed how the road is progressing? It's nearly finished.'

For a moment the woman peered out of the window to where the moonlight fell in lonely splendour on the shining surface of the road, stretching smooth and empty towards unknown horizons; and a single tear rolled slowly down her cheek.

Then she drew the curtains firmly and went back to her chair and picked up her book and began reading.

# IV

## The Anniversary

Like so many strange, indeed, unforgettable evenings, this one began quite casually. I was on a motoring holiday in Cornwall with several friends, and we had spent a pleasant hour or two drinking in a quiet pub outside Penzance. At closing time, as we were unwilling to end such a beautiful summer evening so early, we decided to search for a country club which one of our party had been told of by a friend in London. 'Mind you,' he said, 'it's a long time since he was there – during the last war it was, when he was stationed down here. But he says it's a lovely old place. Somewhere near Land's End ... He told me the way.'

We piled into three cars, two larger ones filled with my friends, and my own two-seater, in which I brought up the rear, driving alone. Just in case we should lose touch, the man who knew about the club had told me: 'You can't go wrong; about eight miles along the road from Penzance, and then there are some big gates, and you'll see a large drive leading to the club. It's called The Silver Wings.'

It was an exhilarating journey along the lonely roads that headed towards Land's End. The air smelled sweet and fragrant, and though dusk had fallen, there was a curious phosphorescent light out of which hedges, walls and occasional buildings loomed in shapes of fantasy. I drove on and on, along interminably winding roads, one eye fixed on the red light of the car ahead, the cool summer night air ruffling my hair, my eyes fixed on that elusive red light.

Suddenly I realised that the red light had disappeared, that I was alone, somehow having lost track of my leader. It didn't seem to matter. It was such a lovely night; I remembered the instructions. And, sure enough, after a while I saw the huge stone gateways to a drive. I swung my car to the right, my headlights picked out the signs: 'The Silver Wings Club'.

I drove my car up a long drive, lined on either side by rhododendron bushes. I felt a strange excitement as the drive curved round, but even so, I was hardly prepared for the grandiose final sweep up to the massive porchway of what seemed to be a manor house in the great tradition: rambling, with big bay windows and ivy-covered walls, and even small turrets, whose outline I could make out against a moonlit sky. Behind the drawn curtains there were lights.

I was puzzled that I could not see my friends' cars, but as there were several rows, disappearing into shadows, I assumed they were somewhere in the darkness. I turned and walked over the gravel and up the steps. Perhaps it was the effect of the night air during the drive, but I felt very gay and carefree. I was reminded, curiously, of those wartime years when everything seemed on razor's edge, and one grabbed at the moment in defiance of whatever grim destiny lay ahead.

I pushed open the door and went into an impressive hallway, with dark panelled walls and a stone floor covered here and there with rugs. One or two oil paintings hung on the walls, portraits of ancient cavaliers and coquettish ladies, perhaps family heirlooms. But now this one-time family house was plainly given over to its new function, for I could hear quite clearly the murmur of voices raised in conversation and laughter. Pleased to have reached the end of my journey, I went through some swinging doors at one end of the hall.

Here, obviously, was the hub of the Silver Wings Club. It was a long, low room, with carpets as well as dark panelling, altogether more cosy than the hall. The air was thick with smoke. I could not see my friends. But this was hardly surprising, as there must have been fifty or sixty people in the room, standing around in groups. Quite a few of them, I noticed, were in RAF uniforms. Everyone seemed young and in high spirits. I felt curiously at home: not exactly that 'I-have-been-here-before' feeling, but, well, something like it.

Above all, I had a curious sensation of being at ease, of people who were making me feel welcome.

Indeed, a man at the bar beckoned to me and said heartily: 'My dear fellow, have a drink on me.'

I smiled. 'But I don't really know you.'

'That doesn't matter, old boy. All friends here. What'll it be?'

I accepted his offer of a whisky and stood leaning against the bar, surveying the scene. Over in one corner a group were playing bar billiards, in another a large circle talked animatedly – at the far end of the room couples were dancing to the tinkling sound of a rather decrepit old piano. I had to admit that the girls seemed all good looking, and yet — and yet there was something about them that slightly bothered me, something a little unfamiliar. I studied one of them closely. Wasn't there something unusual about her hair, her dress, her general style ...? Yes, I decided, in some curious way the girls seemed to be dressed in an old-fashioned way. That was it! But somehow, in such a setting, it did not matter. What mattered was the air of gaiety, of happiness, of everyone having a good time.

Indeed, as the evening grew livelier and livelier, it began to dawn on me that there was about it a sense not so much of abandon, as of – desperation; as if, in some way, these people had an awareness of time and its limitations. A curious thought, I reflected, and I attempted to rid myself of it. Yet it came back to me again and again, as gradually I became enveloped by the celebrations, joining in groups, drinking to people's health, dancing, toasting, laughing. Several times I caught remarks from men in uniform: 'Off duty tonight?' and 'I've a thirty-six-hour pass.' I guessed there must be an Air Force station near.

As it got later, we seemed to gather in a circle around the piano. The young man playing was good looking, with fair hair and a moustache. He held his head up as he played and hummed the tunes, and soon a lot of us were singing. Something about the tunes, like the women's dresses, seemed again a little unfamiliar. And yet there could be no doubt that the men in the club knew every word of the tunes. For that matter, so did I, really – only it was some time since I had heard them.

It was a strange and wonderful experience, standing in close comradeship with the others, while the smoky air got thicker and thicker, singing to the tinkling sound of that old piano as it trundled out all the old sentimental, ephemeral tunes ... 'Smoke Gets in Your Eyes,' 'Cigarette in the Dark,' 'Night and Day' and 'As Time Goes By.' Somehow, whether it was the experience or the smoke, I could not be sure, it almost brought tears to my eyes. I felt conscious of a tremendous wish to stay there forever, never to move from that spot, that moment, that experience.

And yet, of course, in the end I knew that I had to go. Indeed, there was a certain pressure on me in the end, a feeling that I had overstayed my time. By now I had given up trying to find my friends; indeed, they had obviously not come. I stood at the door, taking one last look around, wondering if, perhaps, I might see them.

I shall never forget my last lingering view of the scene, the couples arm-in-arm, singing, the smoky air, the sentimental piano music. How strangely settled they seemed there, as if, indeed, they would never move. For a moment I almost called out to them: 'Is anyone coming? Does anyone want a ride?' But somehow I knew I would call in vain; they would go on and on, singing and laughing, pirouetting in their slow, sad dances. So I shut the doors, went out to my car, and drove off into the now darkened night.

It was around noon the next day before I saw my friends again. I at once accused them of missing a good evening.

They looked at me in amazement. 'Come off it – we couldn't find the place. It's been closed down for years. We asked someone today.'

'Don't be silly,' I said. 'I went there.'

'You're having us on,' one of them laughed.

I don't know why, but I felt quite angry. 'All right, to settle it, I'll drive you there now.'

As it was a fine day, they did not mind. This time we all

went together in a large car. The driver professed to remember
the directions, but it was a good thing I was there to guide
him. Otherwise, I felt sure, we would never have found the
right road. At last we arrived at those massive stone gateways.

'There,' I exclaimed. 'Now you'll see.'

As we turned up the drive, I was puzzled not to see the huge
sign, 'The Silver Wings Club'. But there could be no doubting
the rhododendron bushes lining the drive, nor the wide sweep
up to the huge manor house. As we came round that final
bend, the words were on the tip of my tongue: 'There – now
do you believe me?'

But they were never uttered. For now, as the big car came
gently to a stop, and my friends looked at me in astonishment,
I saw in front of me the stone steps and the massive porchway,
and the beginnings of old ivy-coloured walls – but nothing
else. For the rest of the manor house was a mere shell, a frame
– nothing, in fact, except hollow emptiness, green grass
growing out of old stone floorways, collapsed stairways
leading to nowhere: a gutted memorial.

I don't know how long we sat in the car staring at this – this
apparition. I think my friends must have realised that I was
really shocked, for they were sympathetic in their gentle
questions. 'Is this the place?'

I stared. Yes, this was it, there could be no doubt. But ...?

As if in answer to my unspoken question, we suddenly
caught sight of an old man leading a dog across the nearby
fields, and called him over.

'Excuse me,' I said, 'but I wonder if you can help me – I
thought there was a club here, The Silver Wings Club?'

I felt the old man looking at me curiously.

'The Silver Wings? Ah, yes that's what it used to be – a
good many years ago.'

'But – but –?' I stared at the old man, almost appealing.
'What happened?'

The old man leaned on his bike and surveyed the hulk of
what had once been the Silver Wings Club. 'Twas during the
war – you see, there was a big RAF Station then, just down
the road, and them pilots and the WAAFS, they all used to

come here every evening. It was their club, you see. Lively lot they were, too. Ah yes.'

He paused for a moment, and I could feel him remembering their gaiety – a gaiety which, somehow, I felt I, too, had witnessed.

'Yes?' I said, unable to wait any longer.

'It was the Germans,' he continued, 'the German bombers. They must have been aiming for the aerodrome, of course. They were coming back from a raid on Plymouth one night. They dropped several fire bombs direct on the club.'

'And were there people there?' I said, my voice almost a whisper. 'Dancing and drinking – ?'

'Oh, yes,' said the old man. 'It was very sad, very sad – a whole crowd of them there were. Nearly all killed ...'

The old man went on talking then, about the club, about the gay times there, and about the way things had changed since. But I hardly listened. I was waiting only to ask one more question, and somehow I knew the answer already. 'What was the date when the club was bombed?'

'Why, let me see, it was the first Saturday in July,' said the old man; and then paused, as if surprised. 'Why fancy,' he went on, 'that was last night.'

I felt my friends eyeing me curiously, but suddenly I did not wish to talk about the subject any more. I did not even want to go and walk about the ruins to try and convince myself either that I had been there, as I imagined, or that I had not. Now there was nothing there, just old ruins. And yet, what if sometimes ruins come to life, we touch some chord, or happen to interrupt an anniversary? Who can possibly say, one way or another, in an age when we are just dimly beginning to understand our massive ignorance?

I only know that some other year, on a certain night in July, I think I shall make that drive again in search of an old manor house, where golden haired men and women laugh and sing and dance eternally, and a tinkling piano plays those old sweet songs.

# V

# A Voice from the Past

William Hocking and Samuel Leddra were Cornish born and bred, and as befitting two Celtic patriots they had always taken a devout interest in Cornwall's history and mythology. William was a librarian and Samuel a schoolteacher, both occupations which permitted a reasonable time for reading and studying. When they were not engaged in the pursuit of ideas they often followed more active projects by attending field days and digs held by local archaeological societies. In this way they had visited the Lanyon Quoit near Madron, the ancient village at Chysauster, the Porthmeor settlement near Zennor and a number of other such monuments scattered about West Cornwall.

For some reason, however, they had never managed before to visit Castle Pednolva, reputed to be one of the very earliest settlements of its kind. Several times, in fact, they had planned such a visit, but always something had arisen to prevent the journey – one or other of them taken ill, an unexpected visit from relatives, some other call on their services.

'You know,' said Samuel one day. 'It's almost as if we're not *meant* to go to Pednolva.'

Whereupon William, who was the more determined of the two, declared forcibly:

'Tommyrot! It's high time we went then, don't you think?'

Which was how, one lovely spring day, William and Samuel at long last found themselves climbing the steep moorland path, strewn on either side by granite boulders over-grown with moss, which led to the craggy hilltop where the ancient British had built Pednolva. For some years now the Ministry of Works had been in charge of the site so that everything was pleasantly laid out, smooth lawns running between the fortifications, protective fencing guarding the deeper caverns, and unobtrusive plaques placed here and there to inform the curious holiday-makers who came in their swarms during the summer months.

But at this time of the year there were no holiday-makers, and indeed William and Samuel were the only visitors. The hut which at the height of the season contained a guide and display of appropriate literature was locked up. Over the whole site there was an air of loneliness, even of desolation. Even the slanting sunshine, silhouetting the outline of the ruined walls, seemed to strike a false note.

'Brrh!' said Samuel, shivering for no apparent reason. 'It's – it's peculiar, isn't it?'

William nodded grudgingly.

'I'll admit there's quite an atmosphere.' He pulled out the guide-book he had brought from his library shelves and began studying the plans.

'You know, it's in a marvellous state of preservation, really. I mean, just look over there. That would have been the central courtyard. And see the way each habitation was arranged to link up. Why, you can still follow the walls. And there, part of the drainage system. Marvellous, really.'

They spent an hour wandering about the marvels of Castle Pednolva before at last climbing to the top section, with its thick granite look-out from which sentries of olden times could keep watch over the wide terrain running from Land's End to St Michael's Mount. Here William and Samuel ate the sandwiches and fruit which, as usual, they had brought with them ... and afterwards, suitably replete, sat themselves down on the smooth grass, leaning against the high granite slabs which had once formed the wall.

It was hot, very hot, and where they sat the crumbling granite kept away any vagrant breezes. As they leaned back they could feel the burning sun beating upon their faces – were aware, too, of it burning into the granite all around, as it must have done down all the long, long years. They closed their eyes and gave themselves up, as they imagined, to the sunshine of this twentieth century day.

At first they dozed fitfully, half asleep, half awake. Then William – it was at first – started into wakefulness, almost as if impelled to open his heavy lids. Blinking in the brightness he had the strangest of sensations: as if nothing in that bright scene was quite the same as before. Yet when he looked more closely there seemed no pronounced change … Only perhaps – yes, it was curious, but he could have sworn to this – only that perhaps the crumbling walls were larger, larger and higher. Yes, they really looked almost as if … but of course, that was nonsense. He shook his head deprecatingly, and dozed off again.

It was Samuel's turn next. He had his head inclined to one side so that his eyes, when they opened, gazed out upon the long green sward. When he had first dozed off he had felt sure it had been bathed in sunshine. Now – now it was curiously darkened, as if under a shadow. For a long time Samuel stared at this darkness in growing perturbation. Then, quickly looking around, he had the same immediate sensation as William, of walls growing higher.

But of course, it couldn't be – it must be his imagination. Afraid to voice his fears to William for fear of being ridiculed, Samuel closed his eyes. But he found it impossible to doze off again.

William found it difficult, too. In fact the two of them lay there in a sort of suspended trance, neither asleep nor fully awake; both filled with growing fears and forebodings, of which they yet dared not speak. Once William opened the corner of one eye and it seemed, horrifyingly, that where there had been bright sunshine and the scent of heather, now there was only semi-darkness – and a kind of musty smell. And once Samuel half peeped and found the same enveloping shadowiness, and was too frightened to do anything but lie there with his eyes closed, trying to persuade himself it was all part of a bad dream.

But it was no dream. And when, feeling their bodies growing quite chilly, William and Samuel at last opened their heavy-lidded eyes, the sight that met their eyes was one they might well have preferred never to see. Gone was the view of crumbling ruins of ancient times. Gone was the air of genteel guardianship, the rows of fences, neat lawns, the box office. Gone in fact was every vestige of Castle Pednolva, the carefully preserved ancient monument, as they had seen it. And in its place ...

'My God!' exclaimed William, seeing the white bareness of his legs.

'Heavens!' observed Samuel, discovering his own semi-nudity.

They looked at one another. William saw a slim, rather under-nourished looking Celtic warrior with a tunic made of animal skin, and sandalled bare feet. Samuel saw a similar apparition, except that William also wore a crude kind of helmet.

They stared at one another in petrified astonishment, as if at ghosts.

'It can't be – ?'

'It's not possible – ?'

But it was: it was. From outside what they now saw to be a full-size building, built in huge blocks of granite, they heard sound and movement. Nervously they crept to the door and looked out upon a large circular courtyard, across which bustled other human beings – men dressed like themselves, and women, too, tall graceful women with flowing hair ... One of them, carrying a pitcher of water, suddenly came over towards them, before they could hide. She showed no surprise, but smiled, handing them the pitcher, and then going on her way.

William and Samuel retreated into the shadowiness of their fortress lookout. At first they were too shocked to speak. Then, pathetically, they turned to one another, as if seeking comfort in mutual recognition.

'Samuel,' said William, hoarsely, stretching out a hand and clutching at the other's arm as if for reassurance. 'You do – *remember*?'

Samuel nodded miserably. That was partly the trouble,

indeed. They found they could remember only too well. They sat there in their tunics and sandals and they remembered ... I am really a schoolteacher, I am a librarian, we both live in Penzance and have an interest in archaeology ... and the unspoken, fearful question remained: how can we get back into our own time?

For there could be no doubt about what had happened. Twentieth century men they might be, a schoolmaster and a librarian indeed, with pressing demands on their services – but somehow they had slipped back into time. And time now was nearly two thousand years ago, when Castle Pednolva had been a large encampment of the local Celts among whom now, obviously, they lived as members.

And were well known, indeed. That was the curious and most worrying aspect. They were obviously two of the guards who took turns in keeping a watch from the fortress lookout: they even had nicknames which were meaningless to them – but then so was the stream of words which emerged from their mouths when they spoke.

'Obviously,' whispered William, 'We have inherited the bodies and characters of two Celts of this age ... so we can speak their language.'

At the same time they remembered their English – just as they remembered many other aspects of their twentieth century knowledge. How to drive a motor car ... how to use electricity ... how to print a book ... how to operate a washing machine ...

But unfortunately most of this knowledge was useless indeed, even dangerous. Once or twice when William and Samuel forgot themselves and tried to demonstrate a simpler way of achieving some end, based on their superior knowledge, they were viewed with sudden suspicion.

'For goodness sake be careful,' hissed William. 'They'll think we are sorcerers or something.'

Gradually, over a period which might have been weeks or months – for without clocks and calendars they were lost – it became evident that such a suspicion was, indeed, being created. The men and women with whom they mixed daily in the village square could hardly be called over friendly. After a while it began to seem they were watching William and Samuel wherever they went – even following them into their dwelling place.

'I can't stand it,' whispered Samuel. 'Oh, if only we could go back!'

'Forward, you mean,' said William with a certain dry humour.

They sighed. They had done everything they could think of, sitting down in the same spot at the same time each day, closing their eyes, hoping for a miracle. But there had been no miracle, and somehow they knew there wasn't going to be one.

'Perhaps,' said William thoughtfully, 'it would help if we could write a message and bury it.'

Samuel nodded eagerly. 'Excellent, excellent.'

They looked at one another in sudden desolation.

'No pens ... no paper ... nothing.'

But twentieth century ingenuity came to their rescue. William found a sharp-edged flint and a long slate and they sat down and laboriously began compounding their message to posterity, scratching the words out as neatly and compactly as possible.

'Our names are William Hocking and Samuel Leddra, and we are prisoners in time. Please rescue us if you can ...'

When the message was written they dug a deep hole in the earth and buried it, marking the spot with a round blue slab.

It was the summer dig of the Penwith Archaeological Society, this year being held at Castle Pednolva. A team of enthusiastic young students were led by an even more enthusiastic geology master from the local grammar school. They dug, they explored, they excavated. At last one of them gave an exultant cry, having turned back a round blue slab and picked up from underneath it a long slate, with words scratched on the surface.

Excitedly he took it over to his leader.

'Look, there's some sort of message. Fancy, after nearly two thousand years!'

The geology expert held up the slate, and sniffed.

'Use your intelligence boy. Why this is written in English! As if anyone two thousand years ago could speak English, let alone write it!'

With an expressive gesture he threw the slate away.

'Rubbish! Someone trying to play a practical joke I expect. Come along now, back to work – you never know, you might find something really important.'

And somewhere in the ghostly shades two weary Celtic warriors heaved a despairing sigh at man's inhumanity to man.

# VI

## Aunt May

I first met my Aunt May on a hot summer afternoon a few years after the war ended. It was at Pentire, a small seaside resort on the coast of North Cornwall, where for years it had been our custom to spend the summer holiday with my grandparents, on mother's side. Their eldest son, Jack, had married a year or so before the outbreak of war, when I was too young to remember much about it, and then taken up a job in the Colonial service out in India where he and his bride had spent all the war years.

From time to time, as I grew older and more aware, I had picked up scraps of information about Uncle Jack and his wife: they had moved from Bombay to Delhi where my uncle had an important post in the Education Office – Aunt May had had a baby girl which only lived a few days, sad to say – now they were on the move, Uncle Jack had been transferred to Malay where they lived in a magnificent white house in Singapore overlooking the bay – but after a year or two, movement again, this time to Borneo, north or south I really could not recall ... Always, it seemed to me, they were moving from one place to another: the picture I had built up was a restless, constantly disturbed one, albeit one coloured with tantalising overtones, of life being one long round of cocktail parties, official dinners and the ultimate, the Governor's annual ball.

I don't suppose it was quite like that really, but that was the overall impression I had gained, as I changed from a seven year old child into a rapidly maturing boy of fifteen and then sixteen, about my distant, practically unknown Uncle and Aunt.

And then on the second day of the holiday, just as I was off to join my friends for a game of tennis on the beach courts my mother called out to me warningly:

'Now don't be back too late – I meant to tell you, your Aunt May has flown home for a holiday – she's arriving today. You can meet her at St Erth if you like, she'll be on the London train.'

My father was still away working in his London office and my mother wanted to make sure to have a nice hot meal ready for her long-absent sister-in-law, so I suppose it was a natural enough thing for me to go along as the official family representative. All the same I often wondered afterwards what might have been the chain of events if I had gone along to the station merely as one of a group of relatives.

But there, I didn't. I went alone, a young schoolboy not all that long out of short trousers, yet inordinately proud of his smart new grey flannels and bright red school blazer. I remember I had carefully combed back my rather long dark hair, with the neat parting in the middle that was then apparently fashionable, and I have no doubt my face was still pink from an unfamiliar washing. I was very self-conscious about my youth and awkwardness and added to that I had the extra worry that despite my mother's detailed description I might not recognise my unknown Aunt.

I need not have worried. When the train hissed to a halt, blowing out clouds of white steam, no more than a handful of passengers emerged, and only one of them could remotely have been my Aunt May. I don't know what I had expected, but I found myself staring at what seemed to me the most beautiful woman I had ever seen in my whole life.

Of course, looking back in wisdom, I don't suppose my Aunt May was really beautiful, not by the text-book: she had, for instance, rather uneven features, a retroussé nose and a pouting underlip, all technical flaws. But then as the saying goes, it's what's in the eye of the beholder that matters ... and to me this unexpected, radiant, vital being who now stood on the platform in front of me, smartly, indeed by local standards, chicly dressed in a sheer white two-piece suit and wearing not one of those ugly flower hats favoured by my mother, but an entirely appropriate saucy little green beret, perched back on a bubble of flaxen hair – this was a beautiful woman, indeed.

'Well,' said my Aunt May, extending her hand, 'you must be Stephen?'

I took her hand: it was soft and cool, yet brown from unknown suns of other lands.

'How do you do,' I said very stiffly. She laughed, gave my hand a friendly squeeze, and said as naturally as if she had known me all her life.

'Well, lead the way then, Stephen.'

We took a taxi back to Pentire. When we had reached the gable house on the crescent corner it was only natural that my aunt should be temporarily enveloped in the reunion with my mother and grandparents: there was much embracing and kissing, laughter and tears, too, but of happiness. My granny wiped her nose violently and went to put a kettle on, and my mother and Aunt May sat side by side on the sofa exchanging one reminiscence after another – and I sat a little shyly by the window, pretending to be looking out, but every now and then shooting a tremulous glance at the two women and marvelling that my mother's sister-in-law should really be so much, much younger and, I reflected a little guiltily, prettier.

But in general after that first upside down day of comings and goings and neighbourly reunions, it became quite a recognised pattern of life for Aunt May and I to spend a good deal of time together. I am sure that it was an exciting occasion for her, revisiting after all these years the scene of her romantic youth, and it was only natural that she should be eager to wander about, re-discovering so many remembered treasure troves. My grandparents were really too old to walk very far, and my mother was adamant that she should handle all domestic problems, so that Aunt May should have a real holiday. And so ...

'Do you know the way to the falls, Stephen?'

'Of course. I've been there often.'

'Come on then.'

And Aunt May would run upstairs and put on some of those casual clothes she had brought with her in which she still managed, somehow, to my eyes, to look quite ravishing; and she would come down into the hall and call me, a strange smile playing at her lips:

'I'll bet I've been to the falls, more times than you, young man.'

Torn between challenging her claim and being flattered at the epithet I could not find words easily: and anyway in the meantime Aunt May would laugh and take my hand and start hurrying away down the road and out across the fields that led, in the end up through the woods to the falls. I remembered afterwards, rather curiously though it was I who was supposed to be leading the way it was always she who went first, walking gracefully and gaily along the steepening path, looking this way and that, her face bright with enthusiasm not only for the immediate prospect but, I fancied, for life itself. And when we at last reached the bubbling, magical cascading falls and stood on a narrow wooden bridge, she turned to me with eyes that positively sparkled, green and glittering with excitement.

'Oh, Stephen, Stephen – isn't it marvellous? Isn't it wonderful? Isn't it – ?'

My Aunt May stopped then, as if at a loss for the right words. I think it may have been then that some part of me comprehended that what she was seeing was not merely the immediate view, but something more – scenes and times that belonged a long way away, to those golden years when she had stayed at Pentire, and when she had first met my Uncle Jack. He would have been about thirty, then, Uncle Jack, I supposed; from the photographs I had seen, a fine figure of a man as the saying went, tall and dark and good looking in a rather solid sort of way. And Aunt May, well I knew she was a good deal younger, my mother had told me – how old would she have been?

I looked at my Aunt May, at first shyly then more boldly as I realised she was still engrossed in staring out over the lovely vista. There was a cool breeze blowing up from the sea, tongues of wind forking this way and that, catching up her blonde hair and blowing it backwards so that her face was curiously cleansed and exposed like the rocks washed by the waterfall ... The same wind tugged at her clothes, pulling back the usually loose and frothy material so that in a way not only her face, but the whole of her unknown being was quite strikingly outlined – a soft, unmistakably womanly outline, vibrant with movement, with life. I suppose, though I might have cast curious eyes on some of the village girls of my own callow age, it was the first time in my life I had ever looked at a full grown woman in such a manner. She was for me in that awe-inspiring moment even something more than a mere woman – yes, a goddess of old, some mythical beauty standing, like the provocative figurehead of some ancient ship, defying all that might come, wind and rain and storm, and perhaps man, too.

I was still staring, my eyes round and open with wonder and I suppose all unbeknown to myself, a kind of innocent desire, when my Aunt May suddenly turned her head. It was a slow rather than a hasty movement, as if some foreknowledge impelled it, and yet there was a reluctance on her part to confirm what she expected. I felt her green eyes rest on me a little sadly, and yet, curiously, in some way shadowy with another, less explicit sentiment. Then, with that impulsiveness which I came to recognise and love she put out one hand, ruffled my hair and, bending towards me, brushed the side of my cheek with her parted lips.

'Silly boy,' she said, and at first I was afraid she meant it mockingly. 'Silly boy,' she repeated, a little huskily, and then I knew in some secret part of me that it was not mockery but affection that coloured her voice, and I felt ridiculously, wildly happy.

'Come on now,' said Aunt May, turning abruptly so that she became sufficiently part of the everyday world again. 'Time we were getting back.'

That night I lay tossing and turning in my bed, haunted by shadowy shapes and figures ... in the end my mother, hearing

my movements, came in to see if I was all right. I shook my
head wearily from side to side.

'I just can't seem to get to sleep.'

'Never mind.' I felt a cool, familiar hand on my head. 'Just
try and relax.'

I lay there for a while, and somehow the shadows receded.

'Mother,' I said suddenly, almost without thinking. 'Why
didn't Uncle Jack come with Aunt May?'

My mother hesitated.

'Well, he's a very busy man you know. He can't just come
away for a holiday when he feels like it.'

'Couldn't he have made an effort?' I could not comprehend
how this unknown Uncle could bear to be apart from such a
woman even for a day, let alone three months.

'Well, yes, I suppose so. Why do you ask?'

'Oh, I just wondered.' It was my turn to hesitate and then
awkwardly I said: 'Do you think they're happy?'

My mother rose to her feet.

'Goodness me – it's three o'clock in the morning nearly and
you start asking questions like that. I'm sure I don't know,
darling, really.' My mother paused, unexpectedly, as if
contemplating the question for the first time, and then went
on hurriedly, 'Jack's a reliable sort of man, he's got an
excellent job ... they live very comfortably, you've seen how
well May dresses ... yes of course they're happy, I'm sure.'

But somehow she didn't sound very convinced.

The next week slipped by in a golden haze. Each morning I
would wake up and wonder why I felt such a sense of
happiness and exhilaration – and then I would remember:
Aunt May. Only by now she had forbidden me to use such a
formidable prefix, on threat of addressing me as Nephew
Stephen.

'And that would be silly, wouldn't it? Because we're not
nephew and aunt at all – we're not even really related.'

My aunt made the remark lightly enough, but its
significance seared into my mind. It was true enough, we were
not blood relations, simply two strangers who happened to

have met ... and now? I did not know what was happening to me, I only knew that everything else in my life seemed to have faded into an insignificant background. All that mattered that each day, *all* of each day, should be spent with my Aunt May.

This was simple, indeed natural enough. We played tennis together, we larked on the putting green together, we had chattering, argumentative cups of coffee down in the little beach cafe together. And when it was a really fine hot day we chivvied my mother and grandparents out of their habitual reveries and all of us went down to have a picnic lunch down on the flat sandy beach that looked out on the restless sea.

Afterwards, while the others slept in the sun, my Aunt May and I liked to go for a swim. Though I had beaten her at tennis and golf I had to admit that she was a far better swimmer, taking to the water as naturally as any fish, weaving and bobbing about.

'You're a real mermaid,' I called out once, after we had swum quite a way out to where a sand-bank protruded just above the waves.

My Aunt laughed and turned her head, so that I caught the gleam of white teeth, the glisten of green eyes ... the unfamiliar luminosity of her limbs, dark brown from years under tropical suns.

'Am I, Stephen? *Really* a mermaid?'

Looking deep into her glowing eyes that in that sea setting seemed deeper and more mesmerising than ever I was suddenly amazed at the welter of feelings that swept over me, like great waves of that very ocean – a tumult which was unfamiliar, and yet delicious. I began splashing and flailing the water around me, and shouting wildly as I did so.

'Yes, a mermaid – and I'm going to catch you in my net!'

Entering into the spirit of our strange mood my Aunt May gave a shriek, and dived into the water, swimming away from me with powerful strokes. Elated by the challenge I swam after her, more furiously and energetically than I had ever swum before. Every now and then, looking back, Aunt May would give a mock shriek and change course as if desperately trying to elude capture.

I never knew really whether she was really trying as hard as she could have done, but just as we reached the shallow water I caught up with her and grabbed her by the shoulder, so that suddenly the two of us tumbled on to the sands, half in the water, half out.

As we did so it seemed to me that in some mysterious way our two bodies became inexplicably mixed up, limb against limb, and a sense of a strange awakening quivered through me like some electric current. My Aunt must have been aware of it too, for with an abrupt, almost rough movement she seemed to throw herself to one side. Then, without looking at me, she jumped to her feet and walked away across the sands towards the distant shadowy figures of my mother and grandparents.

I squatted where I was, bewildered, for a few moments, and then, scrambling to my feet, ran after my aunt, catching her up half way up the beach. I was too bemused, and anyway too young, to understand what had happened; but I knew something was wrong.

'I'm sorry ... have I annoyed you?'

My Aunt walked on, her head averted. Shyly I put out my hand and took hold of hers.

'Please don't be cross ... I can't bear you to be cross.'

My Aunt did not pause in her quick walk, but suddenly squeezed my hand hard, until it almost hurt.

'It's all right, Stephen, I'm not cross with you,' she seemed to sigh, on the passing wind. 'Only with myself ...'

For a day or two after that my Aunt seemed curiously subdued, and even went off for one or two long walks on her own. But somehow whether it was my persistence or her own loneliness, I never knew – in the end whatever her resolve might have been, it weakened. And soon we were inseparable again; but somehow, I sensed, more truly so than before.

One day my mother and Aunt May and I decided to have an outing to St Ives. Just as we were getting ready to catch the local bus to St Erth station my mother appeared looking rather pale and confessed sadly that she was beginning one of her migraine attacks.

'I'd only be a misery if I came – you two go along and enjoy yourselves. Oh, and here's a small shopping list, May, if you can remember.'

It was a curious sensation walking along at the side of my Aunt May on the platform of the little yellow and brown station, with its pretty flower borders giving a cheerful welcome – this was somehow different to the local walks we had gone together, it was our first proper outing together. I felt proud and possessive and insisted on buying the cheap day excursion tickets out of the pound my mother had given me, and then, when the little local train puffed in, I rushed forward to open the carriage door and usher my companion into the corner seat, and sat myself opposite her. I had picked seats facing the sea side of course, all the way from St Erth round the curving coast to St Ives we both of us stared with our noses to the window panes watching the sea views.

'Do you often go to St Ives, Stephen?' said my Aunt May, looking back with her tongue to the tip of her lips.

I had to admit, rather ashamed, that I seldom made the trip.

'You must, more often. It's so beautiful.'

'Did you used to go with Uncle Jack?'

My Aunt May gave me a curious look, and then laughed – suddenly she looked very young and – yes, there could be no doubt – rather mischievous. Her eyes sparkled with some lively memory.

'Oh, no that was before I met Jack.' She seemed suddenly in gay spirits. 'When I was still young and gay and fancy free.'

I felt an unexpected stab of jealousy.

'I suppose you had lots of boy friends?'

'Yes, I suppose, I did really.'

'But – you married Uncle Jack.'

She looked away, out upon the great empty bay.

'Yes ... I married Jack.'

The train came to a halt against the buffers at St Ives. We emerged into brilliant afternoon sunshine and in a few moments were walking down the long High Street, alive with colourful shop windows. All at once, for no reason we were caught up in an absurd mood of gaiety. We peered into every shop window as if we intended to buy a hundred and one marvellous and exotic objects, though in fact all we bought in the end were a couple of large ice cream cornets.

'I love creamy ice cream,' said Aunt May gaily licking at her own. 'We can't get it like this out East.'

We walked from the shops and down to the rough granite harbour. I was conscious that Aunt May made a striking companion: she wore some kind of rather flimsy summer dress that fluttered gaily in the breeze, and carried a yellow cardigan on her arm – her hair, gloriously free, blew about in gay dishevelment. More than once I caught an envious glance from some lonely passerby and I filled with a wild warmth and pride, especially when, after a while Aunt May held my arm. I felt, ridiculously and yet startlingly, like a boy out with a girl: and I wondered, but did not dare ask, if she felt just a little bit the same way.

'What's it like? Where you live?'

'It's a pleasant life I suppose.' She paused, and then looked at me with a smile. 'You mean, *how* do Jack and I live out there? One long round of pleasure and that sort of thing? Well, it's not quite like that. Jack works very hard, actually. In fact, he over-works. I don't see all that much of him. He often has to make trips up country for a week or two at a time.'

'Oh,' I said. And then, haltingly, 'You must miss him.'

'I suppose so. But of course, you know, we've been married a long time. It's not quite like – ' She stopped herself abruptly, and then went on with what, if I had been older, I might have recognised as a wry note to her voice. 'You know the old saying, familiarity breeds – well, familiarity. Jack and I, well we're so used to each other – a few days apart doesn't really notice.'

But all the time she was speaking I could not help feeling she might be trying to persuade herself, as well as me.

Soon after we went to have lunch in the Harbour Cafe. Although the room was crowded we seemed to form a curiously self-contained oasis. At first Aunt May seemed a little quiet, depressed even, after our last conversation; but when, a little awkwardly, I tried to cheer her up she seemed suddenly to respond.

'Would you like a glass of wine, Stephen? Does your mother allow you?'

I had never tasted wine before, to tell the truth, but I would not have admitted this for the world. Aunt May called the waitress and ordered a glass of white wine each. When the glasses were filled before us she raised hers and said, laughingly:

'Here's to you, Stephen.'

I held my glass forward and clinked it against hers, as I had seen done in a film once.

'Here's to you – May.'

I put the glass to my lips and swallowed the cool white liquid, at first uncertainly, and then, as I felt its warmth sliding down my throat, more eagerly. It was my first experience of one of life's greatest pleasures, and perhaps my lifelong love of wine was burned more deeply in me because, on that very first occasion, as the wine coursed through my body and suffused me with an unfamiliar but rather exhilarating glow, I was sitting opposite the cool, rather wistful beauty of Aunt May, whose eyes seemed to glitter and glow greener and brighter with each sip.

'Do you like the wine, Stephen?'

'Yes,' I said earnestly. 'Yes, it's lovely. I do like it ... *lots* and *lots* ...' I took some more sips and stared boldly across the table. 'I – like being out with you, too.'

I saw that she was looking thoughtfully into the depths of her wine glass. For a moment I wondered if she might take offence; but when she looked up her eyes were moist and luminous.

'*Lots* and *lots*, Stephen?' she said softly.

'Yes,' I said hastily. 'Oh, yes.'

After lunch we decided to climb up to the cliff at Clodgy Point. On the way Aunt May turned to me authoritatively.

'We've talked enough about me, Stephen. Now tell me all about you.'

I felt a little awkward to begin with, but once I got going I spoke with increasing confidence, until at last the words came fairly tumbling out. I told her about our home outside London, about the grammar school I attended and the sort of work I was doing – next year I hoped to take my higher school certificate and then pass on to university.

I was in full spate of talking when suddenly I checked myself angrily.

'You're laughing at me!'

'No I'm not Stephen, really I'm not.' Aunt May smiled. 'As a matter of fact I was envying you, with all the world before you ...'

I couldn't see it from her point of view then, it seemed to me quite natural that the world should be at my feet.

'When I'm at university I'll probably specialise in English literature because you see I really want to be a writer. But if I can't, well I suppose there are all sorts of other things. Politics, the law, teaching. Or maybe research, that would be interesting.'

'Yes,' said Aunt May, rather sadly. 'I was going to do research once.'

'Couldn't you still do it – I mean, even now?'

It was the first time I had seen her look as she did; older, somehow more tired. She shook her head.

'I don't think so, Stephen. Not now.''

The unfamiliar mood of sadness, now that it had returned, seemed to hang about her pervadingly. To me it was a kind of challenge, I felt determined to break its shadowy spell, to bring the smile back to her lips, the glisten to her eyes. As we neared the top of the cliff I took her hand.

'Come on, I'll race you!'

'No, Stephen, really ...' she protested, but in vain – I only pulled her hand harder, until she was forced to run with me. Still holding her hand I sped across the long grassy slopes, upwards and upwards.

'Let's pretend we're birds, flying through the air – come on, hold out your hands and fly – look I'll show you!'

She tried to stop but I wouldn't let her. All at once something of my impulsive mood reached through to her, and she began laughing out aloud.

'Oh, Stephen, you are a funny boy!'

'Come on, we're nearly there!'

We ran on up the long green sward until at last we breasted the top and there was the great vista of the rich sea ahead of us, stretching for infinity in the afternoon sunshine.

'Oh,' cried out Aunt May. 'Oh, I'm out of breath!'

She sank into a sitting position on the grass, propping herself up on one elbow, and looked up at me. Her eyes were sparkling, her cheeks flushed, her whole being suddenly animated. She looked ageless, eternal – the eternal Eve.

I sank on to the ground beside her and leaned over and, clumsily but urgently, took her in my arms and began kissing her: her hair, her throat, her cheeks, her forehead, and at last, drowning among the magic of her soft reality, her lips.

Perhaps I ought to say that my Aunt May was shocked at my movement, that she tried to repel me, fought against my embrace ... But then it would not be the truth, not the whole truth. For a moment or moments that seemed to last an eternity the body that was in my arms became vibrant with passion and life, like a river suddenly pouring through some new tributary, turning to meet with equal passion my sudden embrace: for that same magic period the lips upon which I pressed my own with clumsy almost painful passion were soft and parted to meet me in a kiss which, perhaps for both of us, was like no other kiss we had ever quite known, we might ever know again.

And then, then only, did my Aunt break away, her chest heaving with emotion, tears springing to her eyes. I sat staring at her in astonishment at what had happened ... until, as if somehow she could not bear to contemplate the moment any more, she scrambled to her feet and, with a cry, began running away down the grassy slopes.

'Aunt May!' I called, falling back into the ridiculous epithet in my upset. 'Aunt May, wait!'

I began running after her, but she seemed impelled by some new force, so that she fairly sped away. Faster and faster I ran, but faster and faster she went ahead of me, down and down and down ... only when she had reached the very bottom where the land levelled out on to a wide beach and she was running more heavily in the soft white sands – only then did I manage to catch up with her.

'Please don't run away from me ...'

Gently, but compellingly I put my arms around her. She leaned back fearfully, but managed to smile through her tear-stained face. We stood like that for a while and then, as if relieved at the dying down of passion, she put up one hand and gently wiped a curl of hair off my forehead.

'Dear Stephen,' she said. 'Dear Stephen ...'

As I made to speak, she put a finger lightly to my lips.

'No, don't, don't say anything. It's better that you don't. It's – all my fault really, I should have realised.'

I pushed her finger aside roughly.

'I love you! I love you!'

For a moment my Aunt May seemed to close her eyes and a look that was curious, something of pain, something of pleasure, illuminated her features, so that they were all soft and tender. When at last she opened her eyes there were tears in them again.

'Perhaps you do, Stephen, perhaps you do. And perhaps ...' She checked herself, and stroked my cheek gently.

'But you must understand, my sweet boy, that this is all wrong, all terribly wrong.'

I stared at her angrily, perhaps arrogantly.

'How can it be wrong to love someone?'

Slowly she hung her head: when she spoke it was almost a whisper.

'Stephen, do you know how *old* I am? I'm *thirty-eight*. More than twice your age.'

'I don't care. What does age matter? People – '

My Aunt May looked up again, and I was discomforted by a new almost look of determination in her eyes. Slowly she raised her hands and pulled at the skin on her forehead.

'Look, Stephen. See the lines? They're there all right, even I can see them in a mirror. In a year's time there'll be more lines, and in another year, more lines – in five years' time, Stephen, I'll be a middle-aged woman. And how old will you be? Twenty-two – the prime of your life.'

'No,' I said in anguish. 'No, I don't want to hear. I won't listen!'

But somehow, steelily, she made me listen – that long interminable afternoon as, after a while, we began walking up and down the white sands facing across the estuary to Gwithian, and the high white cliffs beyond. Against the hot passionate romanticism of my youth she matched the remorseless logic of what she called her old age, wearing it down with the inevitability of water dripping into stone – until in the end, emotionally exhausted, I could only crave sleep and oblivion, and we caught one of the last trains home.

For years afterwards I would always remember the moment of our return; how we came out of the dark into the sitting room and my Aunt said to my mother in a strange, flat voice: 'I'm terribly sorry dear – we forgot all about your shopping.' For in the harsh stark brightness of the electric light I perceived for the first time that my Aunt May was beginning to look quite old.

A day or two later, much earlier I am sure than she intended, my Aunt May went away. I did not see her again for some years until, quite by chance, I called in at Pentire to find that she and Uncle Jack were staying there. My Uncle Jack was a plump, solid man in his fifties who sat most of the time in an armchair smoking a well worn pipe and doing the *Times* crossword: I had no time really to get to know him, though he seemed a nice enough man.

My Aunt May sat in the chair opposite, bent low over some sewing: her hair had turned grey and she wore glasses, but otherwise she had not changed a lot, there was about her trim and attractive personality the same perennial grace. When she looked up and took off her glasses to smile a welcome her eyes were as green and bold and bright as ever: for one bewildering moment time vanished and we stood together on a distant cliff top and we both, perhaps, wondered what had been lost ...

And then, wryly putting things into perspective once and for all, my Aunt May got to her feet.

'I'll just go and make a cup of tea – Nephew Stephen.'

# VII

## Tommo by Moonlight

When Loveday was thirteen her father took her to live in the old cottage above the Penpaul reservoir. In fact the two events coincided: one day her father, pushing aside his early white hair and looking quite animated, said to her: 'I've got a surprise birthday present – do you want to come and see it?' They drove from their home in Bristol, heading westwards, westwards all the time – on and on through the lush red fields of Devon, encircling Exeter, then crossing Dartmoor – on and on into the deepest heart of Cornwall and all its magic moorlands where the undulating land became suddenly remote and very wild … and then, as they climbed over the brow of a hill and saw the familiar huddled shape ahead, her father said quietly.

'That's the cottage I've bought – we're moving in next week.'

It wasn't the first time they had seen the cottage – they had come across it by chance one Sunday when the two of them had gone away for a weekend soon after Loveday's mother had died. It was now a year or two since that terrible period, and meantime she and her father had grown very close. Fortunately as he was able to earn a reasonable living as a free-lance writer he had been able to combine the practical duties of both father and mother. In this way they had been drawn together constantly, not least by their frequent expeditions like this one. For Loveday it seemed their comradeship always found its happiest expression on those weekend wanderings in the country.

Loveday had never forgotten that memorable occasion

when they had caught their first glimpse of the blue slate rooftop tucked in a fold on the side of the hill – and beyond it, dominating the view and enhancing a huge sense of solitude, the vast sheet of green-grey waters of the reservoir. She had stood transfixed, her mouth pursing in wonderment.

'Wouldn't it be marvellous to live there!'

At the time her father had not said much but he had been as excited as she when he discovered the cottage was empty. They had scrambled about the garden like a couple of children peering in at the bare windows to see the shape of the rooms. It had been a heavy disappointment to find the front and back doors securely bolted and locked.

'Never mind,' Loveday remembered her father saying. 'Never mind.'

And, of course, what he had done had been to find out the name of the local estate agents and start making enquiries ...

A week later they moved in, taking with them the familiar furniture from the flat and a few not so familiar pieces installed by the local furniture shop the day before their arrival. Loveday had the smaller of the two upstairs rooms for her bedroom, the small old fashioned window peeping out over the silent reservoir. The other larger bedroom was converted by her father into a cosy study where he could work undisturbed on his new novel.

It was holidaytime so there was no need yet for Loveday to start the daily journey to school at the nearest market town. Instead she gave herself up to the novelty of a new way of life, a solitude enhanced by the self-imposed withdrawal of her father, who worked for long hours in his room. For a time she would play the role of the busy little housewife, washing up and tidying the downstairs room, but before long she would be restless and get away down to the strange new world of the reservoir below.

She felt she would never tire of that daily pilgrimage. In many ways it was rather like walking beside the sea, for the waters of the reservoir were just as moody – one day all calm and innocent, but another suddenly alive and angry, frothy wavelets breaking on the green banks. Now that it was no longer in use the reservoir had acquired a strange air of desolation, the borders overgrown with weeds, here and there a crumbling of the old walled banks. It was like some weird country of its own, and indeed often after she had walked to the furthest extremity she would feel quite nervous, glad to turn and catch a glimpse of blue smoke curling up from the chimney of the distant cottage. Perhaps she would turn and hurry back, relieved to return to the warmth and familiarity … and yet before long, paradoxically, she would be leaning out of her small bedroom window staring in fascination at the mysterious scene as it became gradually swallowed by the evening shadows – as if somehow it had for her a special meaning.

One day when Loveday came down to the reservoir she found the water level lower than usual, exposing a stretch of white-grey mud that had now dried in the early sun so that it looked rather like a seaside beach. She climbed down the wall and began playing among the reeds, imagining herself beside some distant sun-warmed sea.

After a while she paused, aware of a curious feeling of disturbance, of being watched. Looking round suddenly she saw that the flat top of the reservoir wall above her was broken by a small squatting figure – a boy, clad in blue jeans and a bright red sweater, and wearing a little dark beret on the back of his curly head.

Loveday was so startled that she continued to stare upwards for several moments, noting the boy's unfamiliar, almost alien look, the rather sallow complexion of his skin. At last, bothered by the fixed gaze of the boy's bright brown eyes, she stirred uneasily.

'What do you want?'

As if he had been awaiting some such signal the boy scrambled to his feet and took a quick jump downwards, landing on the mud quite close to Loveday and sitting beside her, cross-legged.

Now that he was closer and more visible Loveday felt less

nervous. The boy, who must have been about her own age, seemed harmless enough. She supposed he was one of the neighbours.

'Do you live here?' she said, curiosity overcoming reticence.

The boy shook his head, but as he did so a slow grin spread over his face, giving him a vaguely impish look.

'Well, where do you live then?'

The boy shrugged.

'All over the place ... Dad works the fairs, you see. We've been down at Penzance and Redruth – now we're heading north.' He grinned again. 'Always on the move, that's us.'

Her attention suddenly gripped, Loveday looked at the boy more closely. She had always wondered what a gypsy boy was like and now she realised she was seeing one. That explained the sallow complexion, the faint and unfamiliar air of foreignness. And perhaps, too, it explained the curious, wise, almost old look – as if in some way the experience of centuries was passed on more directly than in the less nomadic races.

She was about to make some comment when suddenly the boy put a finger on his lips and pointed silently over to the bank. Following his gaze she was just in time to see an enormous water-rat sliding into the muddy water.

'Ugh!' Loveday jumped to her feet.

'It's all right,' said the boy soothingly. 'They won't harm you. There'll be dozens of them along here, if you know where to look. And stoats, too, and probably badgers ... Oh, yes.'

As he made the last exclamation the boy stood up, hands on hips, looking about him, and Loveday felt abashed, as if aware of his superior knowledge. Catching her glance, perhaps reading it, the boy laughed.

'Don't worry, I'll look after you ... Here, what's your name?'

'Loveday.' She paused. 'What's yours?'

'Thomas.' He grinned widely. 'But everyone calls me Tommo.'

That was how her new life began. After they had duly inspected the water rat's hole they wandered further along the bank. At one end they sat on a protruding point with a pile of shingle stones and began throwing them out into the water. Loveday couldn't throw nearly as far as Tommo, who had a dramatic style of doubling up and sending the stone zooming high up into the sky.

'Goodness,' exclaimed Loveday. 'I'll never throw that far.'

Tommo gave his broad, already familiar grin.

'Yes you will. It's like this, see.' He leaned over and bent her arm almost double. 'There now, have a try.'

She threw as hard as she could, but still the stone fell short.

'Never mind, just keep trying – you'll manage in the end.'

As if suddenly losing interest in the game Tommo got to his feet and peered around. For a moment, fleetingly, Loveday remembered girlhood adventure tales she had read, the pirate on the deck staring out to sea ... A pirate – was that what Tommo was, perhaps, really?

Turning he caught her expression, and not for the first time she had a curious sensation of her thoughts being read.

'You haven't been around much, have you. What do your folks do?'

'My mother's dead. My father's a writer – you know, he writes stories.'

Tommo nodded, as if this was quite normal.

'My Aunty Gracie is always making up stories. She lives in the New Forest, there's a big camp there, you know. If we call on her she always makes us sit round the fire and then she tells us them – real stories they are, mind.'

'Oh,' said Loveday lamely. 'Well, my father only makes them up. At least, I think so.'

'Mmmmh,' said Tommo, as if the whims of grown ups were not of much importance. He looked over to the blue-tipped top of the cottage.

'That where you live?'

'Yes.'

'I've never lived in a house. Must be queer. We've always been in caravans, see? Me dad and mum, and me.'

'What, with a horse?'

'Oh, we don't bother with horses now. Dad's got a jeep,

that pulls the caravan along fine.' Tommo eyed her almost arrogantly. 'Like to come along and see?'

Loveday followed him along the edge of the reservoir until they came in sight of the fields to the west. In a distant corner a curling column of smoke emerged from a corner where she could vaguely make out the shapes of a caravan and jeep. Suddenly her courage deserted her.

'I forgot, I've got to get back. I'm late.'

Tommo made no protest. He walked some of the way back with her. When they came to the edge of the reservoir he stopped.

'Well, so long then.'

'Goodbye,' Loveday hesitated, feeling a strange sense of letdown. 'Will you be moving on tomorrow?'

'Don't expect so. We'll be here a few days – the old man's doing some trading over at the market, see? He and mum go in every day, but they don't need me.' He shrugged. 'Expect I'll be around tomorrow.'

'You will?' Loveday felt a curious lightening of spirits.

'Then I'll – ' She stopped herself from seeming too eager, and added more casually, 'Well, perhaps we'll meet then.'

The next afternoon Tommo was waiting on the bank when Loveday came down the path. He waved to her cheerily.

'Here you are.' He pointed to a large mound of stones. 'I got these ready for you.'

It seemed to Loveday that she threw the stones much further than the previous day, but somehow her own efforts were quite eclipsed by Tommo's. When he threw he bent his whole young body back, like a bow itself, and there was inherent grace in the movement. Watching she suddenly realised that in a way he was almost beautiful.

'It's no good,' she said at last, shaking her head glumly. 'I shall never be able to throw like you.' She pouted. 'Let's do something else.'

'Righto. What would you like to do?'

Loveday looked about her restlessly. She caught sight of the strange little island in the middle of the reservoir, whose existence had often puzzled her.

'What's out there do you think?'

Tommo shaded his eyes.

'Dunno ...' He paused and looked quickly at her, in his eyes a light of excitement. 'Shall we find out?'

'But how – ?'

Tommo pointed to a heap of old logs washed up on the bank.

'We can float on these all right – come on, we'll have a race.'

Loveday had to admit it was an exciting idea, but when she sat astride a log like Tommo she felt so unsafe she hardly dared concentrate on racing. In the end Tommo came alongside and paddled them both along. She felt safer then.

When they reached the 'island' it turned out to be little more than a wooden platform built on stilts. Tommo, who seemed varied in his knowledge explained that it would have been erected by the local squire in the old days as a convenience for guests who wanted to do some duck hunting.

'Maybe geese, too.' Tommo shaded his eyes and looked expertly along the horizon. 'Wouldn't surprise me if there were some wild geese about.'

Loveday soon tired of the bare platform, but she was beginning to feel she would never tire of Tommo's surprising company. It seemed that the life he had led, wandering the face of the land in the back of his father's caravan, had taught him much more than mere geography. She couldn't help feeling, sometimes, that Tommo – who probably seldom read a book – knew a great deal more about life than her father, for all his book learning.

She wondered, on her return that day, whether to tell her father about Tommo; but some instinct made her keep quiet. It wasn't so much fear of what her father might say as fear that, even by referring to it, she might unwittingly dispel her new secret world, like a pricked balloon.

On their third afternoon together she and Tommo went looking for bird's nests, mostly in the copse beyond the reservoir. Tommo taught her how to move silently among the foliage, so that not even a broken twig disturbed the air. Under his guidance she was able to discover wonders she had never known before – a robin's nest, a blackbird's nest, and wonder of wonder, a plover's nest.

Tommo bent down and gently removed one of the blue-tinted eggs, holding it up for Loveday to admire.

'Isn't it a beauty? A real beauty?'

She looked in wonder ... but as much at 'Tommo, as gently and almost reverently he placed the egg back in its nest, as at the egg.

That afternoon when they came out of the copse Tommo pointed across the fields and said:

'Would you like to see my home?'

She would like to have gone, but still felt too shy to meet his parents. But when he said they would be away the following afternoon, at the market, she agreed to come then.

She was surprised when they came up to the caravan how clean and tidy everything was. Somehow in her mind she had had a vague idea about gypsies being rather dirty, but there was no sign of that here. Inside the long caravan was spotless, and quite gay, with bright embroideries and painted cupboards.

Towards the rear of the caravan was a small area curtained off by red and blue woven curtains. Tommo pulled these back and revealed a bunk bed and an old armchair in one corner. Coloured pin-ups of film stars were strewn around the walls.

He grinned. 'My room.'

From the way he spoke Loveday sensed that he was fiercely proud of this tiny space that was all his own, and the knowledge touched her. She looked round in wonderment, trying to encompass this image of Tommo and his tiny shell travelling up and down the country, always voyaging on.

'Here,' said Tommo with sudden excitement. 'Let me show you my eggs.' And delving under the bunk he produced a large cardboard box full of dozens of birds eggs of all shapes and sizes, handing them up one by one for Loveday's inspection.

It was quite late when Loveday got back to the cottage and her father looked at her curiously. But somehow she could not bring herself to begin to explain – it was too complicated, really. A grown-up would not really understand, anyway. And besides it was not a time for explanation – it was a time simply for being: for greeting each new day with a sudden catch of excitement as one remembered, today's Tuesday and Tommo's coming early and we're going to try and build a little house up in the trees in the copse ... Every day, it seemed, was a sunny one, the sky a careless blue, summer drowsy in the air, birds cawing and winging low above the still waters of the reservoir. Up at the cottage Loveday's father sat tapping away at his typewriter busily engrossed in his new book, and Tommo's parents went each day into market to dispose of their wares – and Tommo and Loveday, like little fawns, played at the water's edge.

And then one night, one memorable night when Loveday was lying in bed watching the moonlight slanting through the top panes of the window and magically touching the edge of the counterpane, she was startled by a rattling sound of something being thrown against the window-pane. The noise was repeated, followed by a low and unmistakably human whistle.

Quickly, afraid of her father waking, she ran to the window, opened it and peered out. She could just make out a familiar figure below.

'Tommo! What is it?'

'Can you come down?'

'What now? It's the middle of the night.'

'No, it isn't. It's just about midnight.' There was a pause and then, unhappily, Tommo went on: 'We're going off early in the morning ... I've come to say goodbye.'

Loveday shut the window and hastily dressed by the light of the moon, trying to pretend that she hadn't heard the words right. When she got down, she told herself, it would all turn out to be a joke – Tommo would laugh and grin and tease her that he had only been pretending.

But when she got down Tommo wasn't laughing at all. She could not see his face very clearly but she sensed that it was unaccustomedly grave, clouded with unhappiness at the thought of their parting. The knowledge, even as it upset her, gave her a strange almost sensual pleasure which she did not really understand.

'Sshh!' she whispered. 'My father ...'

Tommo took her by the hand.

'Let's go down to the reservoir.'

He didn't add the words 'for the last time', but the shattering awareness fell upon Loveday.

'Oh, Tommo, is it true – are you really going away?'

He walked ahead, pulling her after him almost roughly. It seemed a long time before he spoke.

'My Dad's got a date at a big fair up country. It's a hundred and fifty miles, he wants to get off early.'

'Oh, Tommo ...'

Ahead of her he shrugged, as if for the moment consigning the unhelpful whims of grown-ups to perdition: and they walked on down the field paths to the reservoir, awaiting them like some mysterious shining lake.

Down by the water all was still and quiet except for the occasional hooting of an owl. Loveday followed Tommo to the white edge of the mudbanks and they sat down. After a while Tommo picked up a stone and flung it out across the gleaming surface, but they listened to the distant splash with no pleasure.

For a moment the moon passed behind a large cloud and everything became shadowy and fearful: then the shadows went and moonlight poured down again, lighting up the scene in an almost magical way.

'I know,' said Tommo suddenly, as if somehow it was a solution not merely to their unhappiness but to all unhappiness, all problems. 'Let's do something we've never done before, something we'll always remember ...' He paused, and then went on excitedly:

'Let's go for a swim!'

Loveday stared at the glittering sheet of water.

'Here?'

'Yes,' Tommo took her by the arm insistently. 'It's a lovely night, and the water's almost warm ... Look, I tell you what,

we can swim to the other side and back again.' He broke off
and looked at Loveday critically. 'You can swim, can't you?'

'Yes, quite well.' As she spoke Loveday felt Tommo's sense
of excitement communicating itself. Suddenly it seemed part
of that strange night that they should do something
remarkable.

'Oh, Tommo,' she said wistfully, 'I wish – I wish – '

But somehow she couldn't finish the sentence – and in any
case the time for words was past. Tommo had moved away
from her and she heard the rustle of clothes being taken off.
Swiftly she undressed and followed Tommo's vague white
shape as he glided ahead of her towards the water.

'It's all right,' he called. 'Don't be afraid.'

She wasn't afraid, that she knew. She would never feel
afraid, not so long as Tommo was there. She could just
glimpse his whiteness ahead, and then there was a loud
splashing as he reached the water.

'It's lovely – lovely and warm!'

Once they were in the water the faint shock seemed to
invigorate and exhilarate them and they began splashing
about and playing as if they were a couple of mischievous
dolphins in the sea. Indeed, the more they gambolled about in
the shallow warm water the more Loveday indulged in the
fancy that this really was the sea, washing some distant
foreign shore.

'I'm a mermaid!' she called out. 'I'm a mermaid out of the
ocean.'

'Ho-ho!' called back Tommo across the darkness. 'If you're
a mermaid then what am I? – a merman, eh?'

At last they tired of their play and Loveday became aware
of Tommo looming nearer, his voice hissing strangely on the
night air.

'Ready then? Come on, we'll swim over.'

They swam steadily, quite easily really, to the distant bank,
taking less time and effort than she had expected. After resting
a while, they slid into the water again for the return swim.
Tommo set off as strongly as ever, but Loveday began to feel
unfamiliar weariness in her arms and legs, unaccustomed to

such sustained exercise. Gradually Tommo's fleeting white shape began to forge ahead into the darkness, and as it did so Loveday began to be assailed by an unreasonable sense of panic. She kept gritting her teeth and telling herself that she was a good swimmer, that she had often swum much longer distances, that there was nothing to worry about – yet with every stroke it seemed more of an effort and her pace slackened, while all around the water loomed threateningly.

She could see the moonlit line of the shore some way ahead, and Tommo's whiteness almost there – but suddenly she knew she had not the strength to make the journey. Latent fears swept over her, she began floundering and splashing, with only enough strength left to give the feeblest of cries.

'Tommo … oh, Tommo …'

Miraculously, somehow, he was there beside her again, one wiry arm around her trembling shoulders, edging her forward.

'It's all right, don't worry … It's not far now. Look, you'll touch bottom in a minute. Just hold on to me.'

She clung fearfully to him, her arm clasped around his narrow boy's shoulders, as with fierce concentration he brought them both to the shallow water. But even then she felt too frightened to let go, she still clung to him with blind determination so that, after stumbling once or twice, he bent low and picked her up bodily and carried her towards the bank. As he did so she was aware of a curious all-pervading feeling of contentment, and she nestled her head against his narrow boyish chest and smelt the water on his skin and heard his tremulous breathing. It was a moment of awakening and awareness that transcended any other she had ever known, even though it was as brief as the journey to the bank, where, rather shyly, he put her down on the grass.

'Are you all right?' he said anxiously.

'Yes.' She swallowed uncomfortably, and shivered. 'Can you pass my clothes.'

Quickly he got the clothes, and then both of them dressed, a little self-consciously.

'I'm sorry, Tommo,' she began. 'I got frightened.'

'That's all right …'

She was aware of a curious pause; and then, there in the silvery half light, of Tommo coming closer and squatting down beside her. One hand reached out and gently touched her under the chin.

'Now then,' he said reprovingly. 'You weren't really scared, were you? Not with old Tommo ready to come to the rescue?'

Suddenly it seemed to Loveday that she was no longer herself, that indeed the old self had vanished forever, and some new, much more tremulous and uncertain self, an older self, had arrived.

'Tommo,' she said. 'Tommo ...'

And as she spoke she reached up with both hands to take hold of his and to press it fiercely against the wet softness of her cheek, rubbing it gently up and down ... at last by some ageless instinct turning the hand over and kissing it gently, once, twice, and a third time. The kiss said what she was too young and inexperienced to put into words: I love you, Tommo, my gypsy boy – I love you.

They squatted in that rather uncomfortable position for what seemed an eternity until at last, because his arm was aching intolerably, Tommo sat himself down and Loveday leaned back against his chest, looking out over the lake. The silvery moon danced and glittered on the water as it had done perhaps a million times before, as it would no doubt a million times again. But there would never, she knew sadly, be another time like this.

'Listen,' said Tommo. 'Can you hear the old owl hooting?'

They listened to the lonely echo.

'Why must you go away?' said Loveday fiercely.

Beside her Tommo sighed.

'It's my dad, you see, got to be at the fair ...' And then, aware of the inadequacy, he went on earnestly. 'But you mustn't worry, you know, as I shall be back again soon. I tell you what,' he went on, seeming as he talked to regain a restless confidence, 'Next time I'm down let's do lots of things like this, eh? Lots of things we've never done before – we'll do them together, the two of us.'

And as his voice went on and on, racing towards each new

adventure, somehow Loveday felt caught up by its gay unquenchable spirit; she could almost see the events as he described them, could imagine the whole exciting future to which there would miraculously never be an end.

When at last they felt it was time to go Tommo walked with her to the top of the towpath but she said he had better not come any further in case of waking her father. For a moment they stood irresolute, holding hands tightly as if they would never let them go: then awkwardly, indeed clumsily, Tommo bent forward and pressed his warm lips on her forehead. A moment later he was gone into the darkness.

She crept back in the moonlight and managed to clamber unseen into her silent bedroom. She had expected to feel miserable and unhappy, even heartbroken, but somehow she didn't. It was as if the experience of a first independent relationship with another human being had touched the keystone to some endless font of knowledge, and now suddenly she felt strangely buoyant. Of course, there would be a sad tomorrow, but there would be days after that, and one day Tommo would come back. She would see him again, the wonder would continue and widen, and perhaps explode into even greater wonder ...

She fell asleep, her head deep in the pillow, the moonlight touching her copper coloured hair and changing it into silver – just as the gypsy boy called Tommo had begun the long and mysterious process of changing her from child into woman.

# VIII

## Cat Without a Name

Once upon a time there was a cat: a large, grey, inscrutable cat, that awaited us when we moved into a furnished cottage in St Ives, in Cornwall. Yes, I know that cats are almost synonymous with the town of St Ives, and, indeed, wherever you walk about the narrow cobbled streets, you will come upon them – cats in doorways, cats in windows, cats on rooftops – large, sleek, smug fat cats, considerably over-fed out of the daily hauls of fish brought in by the fishermen of St Ives.

And yet this cat was different. In the first place, it wasn't our cat – and yet it seemed to be there waiting for us, when we moved in one cold and blustery autumn afternoon.

'Well,' said my wife, 'how on earth did it get in?'

The cat didn't enlighten us. It stretched out on the hearth rug, and watched us with eyes that were large, limpid pools of grey-green, unblinking and entirely without emotion.

It was the eyes that worried me from the start. There was something almost human about them. It was as if, when I looked into them, I saw something familiar … That was it. I recognised the familiarity at once. But I wasn't going to say anything, if it hadn't been for my wife. When we had put our son Stephen to sleep and were downstairs unpacking, she said uneasily:

'Did you notice that cat?'

'Yes?'

'Well, I mean, didn't you notice? How much it looked like Len?' We looked at each other uncertainly. It was a name neither of us had mentioned for several months. Len had been our closest friend, a man younger than myself, gay, good-looking, charming, almost fatally attractive to women. It had hardly been surprising that my wife had been drawn to him. I would not go so far as to say that she fell in love with him, but let us say there was a strong mutual attraction. Let us say, since we are being honest, that there was the beginning of one of those tricky situations that might have ended who knows how? Might have – because one night our friend, Len, was killed in a car smash. Fate, it seemed, had written finis to that episode.

But now, as we both looked at this strange grey cat, which had so obviously been awaiting our arrival, I think we both began to wonder just how finished it all was. I say 'I think', because after that moment of recognition, my wife and I attempted to stifle our natural reactions to the cat. We didn't want to upset each other, so we kept our thoughts to ourselves as much as we could. At least, we tried. From the moment that it occurred to us both that there was something about the grey cat which strangely, indeed, sinisterly, reminded us of Len – we tried to avoid the subject. But – the subject did not want to be avoided.

Later that night we went up to our bedroom. Some while previously I had put the grey cat outside. My wife went in first and put on the bedroom light. She gave a little shriek. Coming in hastily after her, I saw her staring at the bed. Reclining in the centre of the counterpane, curled up and already asleep, was the grey cat.

'But this is nonsense,' I declared. Angrily, I bent over and picked up the cat. How warm and throbbing; how alive it was. I remembered Len, and a strange, haunting feeling of regret came over me. And then I thought: did my wife remember, too? Did the same thoughts occur to her?

By silent consent, I did not put the cat out of the window, but took it downstairs and poured out a bowl of milk – which it sniffed at and, almost haughtily, refused.

I went upstairs again, careful to shut the door after me.

'Well?' said my wife, avoiding my eyes.

I shrugged.

'Don't let our imaginations run away with us.'

We lay in bed and tried to go to sleep. It was our first night in a strange house, so I suppose we were bound to find sleep difficult. All the same, we did seem strangely disturbed, floating about on the borders between reality and fantasy. Suddenly, I heard a scamble and a mysterious thud.

'What is it?' My wife sat up beside me, clutching my arm.

I peered across towards the window, faintly lightened by the night sky beyond. There was a mysterious darkening in one corner, which I recognised intuitively.

I flicked on the light. Across the room, perched on the dressing table under the window, was the grey cat. It sat calmly, almost benevolently, staring at us. And the eyes – the eyes were surely – ?

'Put out the light,' said my wife, unsteadily.

I did so, and we lay down again, aware unmistakably of our companion. How it had got there, *why* it should want to do so – what further action it might take. Suddenly we felt too weary to be able to grapple with this weird, indeed, supernatural problem.

I imagined we would never get off to sleep, knowing the cat was there. But somehow its presence was almost a relief; it was certainly not an antagonistic presence ...

Before long, I dropped off into a long sleep.

The next morning the cat was gone from our bedroom. But when we went down, there it was, asleep in the armchair. 'Look, there's pussy,' cried Stephen, and he made a great fuss, stroking the smooth, grey fur, until the cat purred with pleasure. But my wife and I – we were less enthusiastic in our approach. We kept eyeing the cat curiously, wondering, suspicious ... and then each other, worried and puzzled.

That was how it began. We didn't look for the grey cat – the grey cat found us. It simply came into our lives, and stayed there. Of course, I made inquiries locally. I knocked at doors and asked if anyone was missing a grey cat. But nobody seemed to know anything about it. It was no one's cat; a cat without a name. 'It's not surprising,' said one neighbour. 'Cats are always wandering off in St Ives; there's too much for them to eat, they're not dependent on anyone.'

But this one was, very dependent. So much so, that it would hardly ever leave the house, as if afraid of losing us. At least, when I say us, I suppose I really mean my wife. Len had been fond of me, in a way, but he had, I now realised (somehow this seemed suddenly much clearer) – he had been in love with my wife.

'In love ... and now this cat ... how ridiculous.' Yes, I used to tell myself exactly that, looking down at the bundle of grey. It was only a stray, grey cat. And then the cat would arch its back and turn its head and look at me: and before those eyes, those unmistakably familiar eyes from the past, I could only turn away, fearfully. For I think even then, in my heart, I knew, well, let me say, I *suspected*, that in some supernatural way (there's no other word for it, I'm afraid) that cat was ... Len.

You see, there were so many signs. The way it stayed at home all the time. The way it persisted in being with us. Even in little things – the way it never ate the food placed out – the cat reminded me of Len, his touchiness, and stubborn pride, his – but no matter, I don't want to discuss Len. I want to talk about the cat. But then, perhaps, at the same time – who knows? – I am talking about – Len.

From the beginning, I suppose, my wife and I thought of the cat by the obvious name, though we never used it openly. But perhaps one of us might have done: because, coming home one day, we were startled to hear Stephen calling out: 'Lenny ... come on, Lenny.' It was yet another turn of the screw. We came in and looked at him inquiringly. 'But hadn't you noticed?' he said. 'How like Lenny the cat is?'

After that there was a certain outlet in laughter, in near-hysteria. As one is wont to do in such situations, we joked about the very thing that ran so close to tragedy itself. We talked about letting Len in from the rain; we teased one another for spoiling poor old Len. Underneath every phrase lurked a sort of time-bomb of remembrance.

At first I was relieved. I almost managed to convince myself that we had been imagining things, that it was all a sort of lark. I even used to persuade myself that it was all pure coincidence, that next time I returned home there would be no cat, and we would never see it again.

But what happened the next time I returned home was quite different. There was a soft glow from the fire, and my wife was sitting in the armchair with the cat asleep on her lap, and a strange, faraway look in her face.

Don't misunderstand me. I don't mean that in this affair my wife and I were divided. She was really as much upset as I was, if only because of the macabre implications.

If there *was* some shred of truth in what we suspected, if, in some way, the spirit of Len – the ghost of Len, if you like – had come back to us in the person of a grey cat ... Well, I mean to say!

Yes, it would be upsetting, indeed, to say the least. And upset is the only word I can think of to describe our life at that cottage. From the time we entered we never felt at ease, never at peace. I don't suppose a child like Stephen noticed much; and anyway, he was out playing on the beaches half the time. But I'm a writer, working at home, and my wife is home a good deal, too; so, in the way of things, we say a lot of the grey cat ... and the grey cat saw a lot of us.

That was what used to disturb me most – to look up from my work and find that familiar, arched grey shape sitting on a chair, staring across at me. What was it thinking? What was behind that mysterious, bland gaze? Was it, could it really be Len watching me?

Well, I expect you think I was getting pretty hysterical by this time. Maybe you'll nod knowingly when I tell you what happened next – fancy, he really let it bowl him over. But I must add that my wife was quite in agreement. 'You're right,' she said. 'We'll never get peace in this place.'

So we gave up the cottage and took the lease of another house, right over on the other side of St Ives. I suppose it must have been nearly a mile from the first cottage. In fact, we deliberately selected it because it was in a different part of the town altogether, a quiet, residential area, where we could get away from the atmosphere of the fishing quarter.

We moved on a Saturday, hiring a taxi to take our things

and Stephen all in one journey. I can remember looking at my wife as the taxi started off. She looked at me, too; but we didn't say anything. We didn't say anything, even when we were in the other house settling in. We didn't like to admit how much supernatural ideas had got hold of us. We didn't like to confess our secret fears.

At last that first evening drew on. After putting Stephen to bed, we sat by the fire, reading. It was quiet, peaceful. In the end, I stoked up the fire and we went to bed for an early night's rest. I don't suppose either of us expected to sleep much; but in the end we did, quite heavily.

In the morning we awoke to find sunshine streaming in the windows. Below, we could hear the sound of Stephen running around exploring his new home. I looked at my wife, hesitated, and decided to say nothing for the moment. But as I went downstairs, I felt a new buoyancy in my step; I was aware of a sensation – what was it? Yes, a kind of freedom. Ah, I said to myself, it's going to be all right. I decided that after breakfast, when we were alone, I would confess my fears to my wife, and no doubt she would do the same, and we could then have a good laugh.

Soon it was time for Stephen to go to school. I bent down to fasten his mackintosh.

'Thanks, dad,' he said, cheerfully, turning to the door. Then he paused, as if remembering something.

'Oh, dad,' he said casually. 'You won't forget to look after Lenny, will you?'

I stared at him.

'But Stephen, we left the cat at the cottage. I don't think …'

He looked at me with wide-eyed innocence, impossible to doubt.

'Don't be *silly*. When I came down this morning, Lenny was curled up there by the fire. I just put him out for a while.'

Stephen began to move towards the door.

'But I expect he'll be back soon.'

# IX

## Embers

The old man was glad when he came to live by the harbour.
Some distant relatives arranged it, twinged by a sudden sense
of responsibility. They moved him there one blustering April
day, summoning taxis and porters, finding him a corner seat
on the train, showering him with magazines that he didn't
want but not with sweets which he would very much have
welcomed, impressing upon him their genial good wishes and
waving from the platform as his white old face slid away,
behind its glass frame – then forgetting it all as they plunged
back into the bustle of their everyday lives.

There was not much of him to move, anyway, a couple of
trunks, and the small figure curling up into its thick overcoat,
silk scarf and tweed suit, woollen underwear, tired dry flesh
and hollowing bones. It wasn't much bother getting him
installed in the big bed sitting-room on the first floor with the
bay window that looked right out upon the harbour. Breakfast
was brought to him every morning, tea and toast and a hard-
boiled egg. And the other meals were served in the cool, blue-
carpeted dining-room, with the glossy sideboard and the
grandfather clock (sometimes a passing commercial traveller
or a family on early holiday) for company. The landlady was
efficient and considerate, the maid a blousy, red-cheeked Irish
girl with a kind heart who slipped him extra sugar for his cups
of tea. In no time he was settled into the sort of comfortable
routine which rather suited an old man on his own.

But he was very glad there was the harbour and that he
could sit in an armchair looking at it out of the bay window.
Without it things might have been different: a certain

deadness, like a blank wall, his moustache drooping and his eyes dull; an uncomfortable disinclination towards the effort of going on living.

It was a delusion, he sometimes admitted, but the fact was that he could sit there at the wide window – open if it were sunny, but firmly latched if the eastwind had whisked up – and imagine himself participating in an entire world of vivid and ceaseless activity. He sat there for hours, sunk deep into the high-backed leather arm-chair so that anyone opening the door it might seem there was no one there except perhaps a ghost. He folded his long bony finger tips against his dry old mouth, and he stared with his watery grey old man's eyes upon the great smooth circle of blue, at the painted dinghies and the sleek red and white yachts bobbing up and down like corks, behind them the gaunt hulks of unloading cargo boats rising up as an immense horizon. There was enough there, more than enough, to fill not one but many worlds, and it would give him a slow satisfaction to meditate upon this thought, sipping his occasional extra sweet cup of tea or coffee, nibbling at his afternoon cake, while his eyes flickered from here to there, noting the fresh smoke belching out from a ship getting under way, the white flash of a yacht setting sail for the headland, or the fussy manoeuvres of the tugboats which guided in the larger ocean liners, like worrying sheep-dogs.

He shared with increasing avidity each of their worlds, speeding to meet them from his dreamy chair, out across the wide open ageless water ... He wondered who was the owner of the fat white motor yacht that set out to see every morning but always came back at night, as if engaged on some endless quest that would never be satisfied. He grew familiar, almost as a friend, with the crew of the paddle-steamer that plied regularly from the harbour across the bay to the opposite ports, savouring their nimble movements as they moored up, their ribald comments shouted across the water at other boats.

He became excited when a strange ship hove to, some bright and unfamiliar flag fluttering from its pennant. It was a challenge, like a crossword; his eyes darted about seeking

clues, his satisfaction was immense when by a combination of
factors he was able to identify it as a Norwegian boat, or a
Swedish tramper. And then he began wondering about the
sailors moving about her decks, what their names were, and
from which strange-spelt part of Scandinavian geography did
they come? He visualised their homes, their families and
wives, he saw into their cabins, the faded sentimental pictures,
the packets of letters, the gaudy ornaments, or the pin-up girls
cut from film magazines. He saw their lives as adventure,
adventure, adventure; the endless changing seas, the exciting
new ports, the world your country; and he envied them with a
peculiar intensity out of the finality of his own agedness.

He supposed that as one grew old one lost the desire for
mobility. He began to lose the wish to get downstairs. He
preferred his room, the glass screen upon all these other
worlds. It was like attending a perpetual cinema show. You
were caught up into someone else's life, and you escaped from
your own. Or most of the time.

At night, perhaps, you did not always escape. At night there
were the bobbing paraffin lamps on the mastheads and the
occasional chugging of a fishing trawler, but activity slackened
and eventually there was stillness, only the glitter of reflected
lights across the smooth, dark water, transforming it into a
vast mirror reflecting a hundred eyes and memories. Then he
would find himself remembering and wondering, and feeling
sad. It was an awful thing to have a life behind you instead of
before. He could still remember when he was seventeen and
how he never believed he would grow any older, and how the
years slipped by treacherously like friends that failed you,
tumbling faster and faster, like a mountain river – restless and
frustrated, not still and at peace like the water outside. Now,
at night, with the Northern star bright and the cleft moon
hanging at a corner of the window, his mind darted about into
the past, ferreting out delicious long buried, avoiding the less
attractive episodes. But all that he recovered, caught in the
fishing-net, eventually he threw back into .the bottomless
water, aware of an ultimate inadequacy.

Gradually his sense of dissatisfaction began to carry over,

out of the dark lonely nights into his golden days. He began to view the harbour and the little boats and the smoke-steamers, the water lapping around the pier heads and the seagulls perched on the rusting oil drums, as a canvas of his life. He felt the need to grasp from the picture some meaning and purpose to compensate for this threat, this shadowy suggestion of a lifetime of emptiness. But no, something in him protested: I have not been born and lived and grown old, I have not acquired the wrinkles and the hardening arteries, the silver hair, the money in the bank and the pages of memories – all to no purpose. No, he would say, his cracked old lips pulled hard against the false teeth, and he would stare fiercely upon the harbour and the gentle rippes of the water, each ripple a year of his life, hiding in its gentle folds – what?

And because of the intensity and the desperation of his search he found, one day, the little girl in the blue sweater and the short red frock, climbing down the harbour steps when the tide was out, and the bottom lay exposed. He saw her suddenly like that, one morning, the red and blue catching his eyes almost with familiarity, as if striking some dim chord from the past. He felt that indeed there must have been some long-forgotten incident connecting in his mind, and sometimes he struggled to recapture it, punting on the river at Oxford, or running across the hot beach at Majorca, or a girl he saw across the tables at a seaside cafe ... it was all blurred and unreachable, it didn't matter anyway now.

But here there was the little girl in the coloured dress with the untidy auburn hair who might have been there many years longer than he had, but whom he noticed for the first time one morning, and after that every morning, as she came down to the harbour to play among the sand and the seaweed and the dead fish and the stranded boats. The little girl who, he knew somehow, held the secret of life and of his problem.

And where he had sought in the harbour a hundred different worlds, a hundred lights and shades and horizons beyond which he could travel with his armchair imagination, now he focused his bushy, white eyebrows, screwed up with the effort of staring, upon the simple world of the little girl.

Every morning he waited anxiously until she was in the range of his window vision, sitting back with a sense of relief as the red and blue caught his eye. He watched benevolently as she danced about the quayside, as she shouted a greeting to some fishermen's boys. He craned his neck forward to follow the direction when she raised a thin arm and pointed to some object of interest: a fishing boat heaving to, a commotion on one of the cargo-boats, a star-fish cast up by the tide. He became excited at her excitement; he lost interest when she lost interest; he grew morose when she grew morose, stubbing her foot idly against the harbour rail and staring glumly at the muddy bottom. He basked in a gentle, untroubled happiness when she was happy playing among the sands clambering into one of the dinghies, pretending she was a mate or a skipper, pretending she was now a mermaid, now some monster of the deep – pretending the pretending that was the secret of childhood.

For a long time there was a curious peace about the old man's life, almost as if in the little girl he had captured a focus and a meaning. For a long time he was happier than he had been for many years and it was all to be obtained sitting in an armchair in the sunny morning and watching a little girl playing in a harbour.

But slowly there grew upon him a terrible conflict. For it seemed to him a terrible thing that he was an old man with seventy odd years of his life ticked away and accumulated in all their miseries and their blessings and their learnings, and there was a little girl of no more than seven years who knew nothing of all this, before whom lay the whole time and trouble, like an unmapped country.

He wanted to cry out to her: wait a minute, let me pass on to you all my life experience and the wisdom I have accumulated. Don't you see? Be forewarned: then you will be spared so much needless pain and worry and suffering. Oh, you must listen to me. I'm an old man and I've seen a great deal of the world, I've made a lot of mistakes and I've had to pay for them – and he remembered them, the long, wondering list, the business partner whom he ought never to have trusted, the mother whose domination he should have resisted, the lover he never took and the wife that he did, the son he spoiled and the daughter he forgot to give love, the old friend he hurt for the sake of cheap vanity.

He saw them all now in the neat perspective of time, like the boats in the harbour anchored around him. Familiarity and experience had engraved an understanding into him – but there is no need for you to suffer all this foolishness, little girl, he thought, gazing from his bay window. Why should you?

And so it was with an intensified, almost unbearable senility that he began to watch the little girl. He no longer thought of himself as separate, but as a part of her existence. When she clambered carelessly down the harbour wall his old body shrank in sudden fear and he whispered: be careful, little girl, careful. If she played with the little urchin boys he pursed his lips, disapprovingly – they will lead you into mischief, little girl, and get you nowhere, they will always be urchins. And now all the time the little girl was playing in the harbour the old man lived in a state of nervous tension instead of at peace, for it is difficult enough to lead somebody else's life from an old leather cushion.

And at last, as the summer streamed on – the blue skies and the blue waters, the tall masts and the painted funnels and sometimes the rainbow coloured flags of a regatta and crowds dancing along the cobbled streets of an evening – and always the stolid laconic fishermen in their plump dark-blue jerseys and their bell-bottom trousers leaning on the harbour wall and staring with great weighty thoughtfulness at an inch or two of frothy water – at last it grew upon the old man, older with each deceitful day, that he and the little girl were two islands in the sea of time and space, and somehow he must build the bridge that would link them. And if he could only do that then nothing in his life would have been wasted.

And so one day the old man bade his kind Irish maid call him an hour earlier than usual, and his breakfast served very promptly so that he had plenty of time to get himself dressed, for he was going to take a walk that morning. He put on his best serge suit with the double-breasted waistcoat, and a high white collar and a cravat and he took a stout walking-stick to help him down the stairs and out into the day's sunshine.

Ah, it was a fine day, and the breath of it stirred things deep down in the old man that had slumbered almost into death. He remembered a good many other fine mornings in a good many other places of this world, but he didn't suppose, really, there had been any finer. He walked slowly and carefully along the cobbled roadway down to the harbour head, tapping with his stick on the stones as he went and nodding to the people as they passed. And somehow that morning there was something stately and of dignity about the old man, his body held nearly straight and his white hair ruffling in the breeze, such an air of purpose and assurance about him that there were many who automatically touched their caps or foreheads.

It was whispered round among the gossiping housewives leaning on their dusters, the old gentlemen from the hotel was taking his first walk out this morning since a long time ago, as if somehow it marked the beginning of a new life for the old man, as if by some miracle his life would now start rolling backwards and he would grow younger and younger until he was a little boy in a sand-suit again.

The old man sat down on the parapet when he reached the shallow end of the harbour, and he took out a large white handkerchief and mopped the sweat off his head and looked round at all the familiar objects that now seemed ever so much closer and more real. And patiently, happily, he waited.

And before long there was a clatter of clogs on the cobblestones and he looked up and blinked his half-closed eyes against the sun and saw the little girl descending from the mystery of the world that was her home and life. Today she had on a plain white dress and a green bow in her hair, but it was exactly the same little girl that he had sat and watched for so many days and so many weeks, and she ran past him as swiftly and effortlessly as the wind and almost before he could turn his head.

The old man watched while the little girl swung on a fishing-rope and then climbed up to look at the top of a buoy, and while she scrambled about among the sand and the rocks, and while she climbed aboard one of the dinghies, crouched down and pretended she was rowing.

Then, a little venturesome, he raised himself to his feet and ambled along to the top of the sloping causeway leading down to the sand. He stood for a moment leaning on his stick and staring out at the sea and the sky, very much like an old sea captain or an explorer, or perhaps a prophet of old. Then he called out softly:

'Little girl, little girl.'

At the sound of the voice and its unfamiliar urgency the little girl swung round from peering into a lobster-pot and leaned back against the blue and white side of the boat, looking up at the old man, though she could hardly see him because of the bright sun shimmering around him, turning him into an ethereal figure – like a ghost a'most, she thought.

And, seeing the little girl like that, with her thin brown arms resting lazily along the rim of the boat and her legs stuck into the sand like two sapling trees, and her brown face turned laughing up to the sun, the old man remembered with curious vividness a painting he had once seen, a famous painting he seemed to remember, that had shown just such a little girl of the sea. He could not be sure quite how much he was remembering the picture and how much he was seeing the real little girl on the sand below him, but when he met her eyes it did not seem to matter.

For when the old man met the little girl's eyes he saw the eyes of a hundred and a thousand and a million children, the children of all time that had been and all time come. The eyes were coloured only by the day's sun and the sky's blue, the idle thoughts and the beauty of fresh carelessness. And in them the old man saw the enormous unmapped, beautiful innocence of children – a world once his own and yet now so remote that perhaps it revolved on a separate axis, moved in a different cosmos.

When the old man did not speak the little girl stared puzzledly for a few moments, then smiled and turned away. A few moments later she was scampering across the sands to another boat. A few hours later, when the evening lights were hanging out, she lay fast asleep, dreaming of the day's happenings.

But the old man was not asleep. He was sitting at the big bay window staring out upon the moongleamed harbour, the sleeping boats and the silent quays, aware vividly of the steady swish of the waves lapping upon the shore, each wave seeping a little further forward and obliterating another ridge, another line of footprints and memories, another day of life. And yet somehow, remember the little girl and the golden day, the old man was not as sad as he might have been. All at once he had forgotten about his secret dread of being like a leaf blown into a corner in the glory and wonder of remembering the little girl ... and life and how sweet it was to be at the beginning, like a fruit swelling out to meet the ripening and the harvest. And how lucky simply he was to be alive, oh alive. ...

# X

## Summer with Miss Owens

I heard of Miss Owens long before I ever met her. Every summer we went down to spend our holidays at one of those rather domestic little fishing ports on the South Cornish coast, nestling under the shadow of rambling moors and, in the distance, white tipped china clay tips. We used to stay with my Aunty Lil in a quiet house off a cobbled terrace near the harbour. At the end of the terrace, much higher up, there was a huge white gate labelled: PRIVATE : NO ADMITTANCE. Behind that gate, in a huge granite house that was all corners and gables and drooping ivy, lived old Miss Owens. Alone.

I suppose it was this quality of aloneness that always caught my imagination about Miss Owens. At first, as I say, I learned of it by hearsay. We would be sitting out in our porch late of an evening and perhaps a single light would flash out high up in the old gabled house. My Aunty Lil would shiver slightly and pull her shawl round her shoulders, and then, as if reminded of something, she would pat me on the shoulder.

'Now, then, come along, time for your lovely hot chocolate.'

But as we turned and went in, invariably she would glance over her shoulders at that lonely light and I can always remember the meaning way she would murmur to herself, 'Tut-tut, the poor soul ...'

I was about thirteen at the time, that curious half-way stage between childhood and teenage wisdom: an introspective time, when one's imagination grasps hungrily at half hints of worlds and ideas beyond immediate comprehension.

'Why is she a poor soul, Aunty Lil?' I said.

But of course I had no satisfactory answer, was merely

shushed off with my hot chocolate. That night I lay in bed and thought about Miss Owens, all alone in her big house with the forbidding gate. Why did she live there all alone? How did she spend her time? Why did she behave in such odd ways?

As time went on I became more familiar by personal experience with Miss Owen's oddities. Her manner of dress, for instance, was often peculiar. Some times I would catch a glimpse of her pottering about in her overgrown garden, wearing a dressing gown of bright yellow and black stripes and a large white panama hat ... while her feet, I noticed, were bare. On another occasion I saw her mowing the lawn with great ferocity clad in a voluminous garment which my aunt later told me was a pre-First World War bathing dress.

But perhaps Miss Owens' greatest oddity was her habit of appearing on a noisy auto-cycle, clad in a black leather coat and gaiters, and a fearful conglomeration of goggles and leather helmet. It was not often she emerged in this way (it seemed to me about the only occasion she ever left the seclusion of her own home) but there was naturally great competition among the local children to witness the event. At the sound of the angry phut phut of Miss Owens' ricketty machine they would stop playing games and even leave meals and dash out to lean over garden walls and stare, open-mouthed, at the fearsome apparition. And of course, as the bike and Miss Owens disappeared down the road they would break into shrieks of laughter.

But somehow I never felt like laughing. I suppose Miss Owens' loneliness must have touched a chord deep in me, without my knowing. I could not help thinking about the *person* behind the mask of goggles. What was she really like?

Then one day, quite accidentally, I found out. Not in the familiar environment of the village, but way up the moorland road, up by the side of the carn with its rambling boulder strewn flanks spotted with green and yellow clumps of gorse. I had wandered up there one hot and sunny afternoon and was about to turn off the road which led over the moors to St Austell when I caught a glimpse of a familiar leather-coated figure bent over a prostrate auto-cycle.

Going nearer I found Miss Owens tinkering with a spanner at the engine. 'Er – can I help you?' I said awkwardly.

Filled with the children's lurid tales I half expected her to turn round in a fury – or perhaps to scuttle away, like a witch disturbed. I was surprised when, instead, she looked up quite placidly.

'Aren't you the little boy at the cottage down the road?'

'Yes,' I said. As I spoke I was secretly staring into Miss Owens' face, maybe half expecting to find reflected in it some ogre-like sort of characteristics – but seeing, instead, what must once have been a rather lovely face, now lined with time and worry, yet still bearing a certain nobility and delicacy, and enhanced by two strong, almost jet black eyes that peered at me fiercely.

'I don't suppose you know anything about auto-cycles that won't go?'

'No,' I had to admit.

'That makes two of us. Well …'

It seemed that with the unexpected advent of company Miss Owens was glad of an excuse to forget about her troublesome bike. Indeed, she turned her back on it completely and strode to the edge of the road, looking over the panorama of fields and distant sandy shores.

'It's lovely, isn't it?' I ventured. And then, after a pause. 'Have you ever been to the Giant's Chair? You get a better view there.'

Miss Owens sniffed and seemed about to say something, but in my eagerness I interrupted.

'Yes, really. It's over there – come with me and I'll show you.'

Looking back I can only suppose that my childish impudence captivated Miss Owens, so that almost meekly she followed in my wake. If anyone had seen the curious procession, a young boy leading a large goggled leather coated figure up a lonely track, they would have assumed it was another of Miss Owens' eccentricities. But the fact was it was I who took Miss Owens to the Giant's Chair, she who obediently followed and finally sat by me on the wide slab of granite which someone, giant or otherwise, had set up in such a magnificent position.

As if pleased by my fulfilment of my promise Miss Owens looked about her quite jubilantly and, misled, I began pointing out spots.

'That's Porthnoon over there ... and see, there's the old mine shaft, and over there you can just see the tip of the lighthouse, and the bay – look, the sea's quite rough ...'

'Child, child,' said Miss Owens, but not unkindly, 'I was born and bred here – I know all these places like the back of my hand.'

'But you didn't know the Giant's Chair?'

A curious smile softened Miss Owens' parchment face.

'Well, it *is* a long time since I came up here, I must admit ... a long time. Maybe I had forgotten ... a little.'

I didn't know to what she was referring, but obviously it must have been something terribly important, for the recollection seemed suddenly to loosen Miss Owens' tongue. Now she began talking about those distant past days, not altogether, I felt, directly to me, yet needing me as an audience. I have often tried to remember more exactly the things she talked about, but somehow their detail is lost in a haze. But I do remember the strong feeling underneath, the curious sense of tender regret, almost of painful memory, of something precious that had been lost. I had some sort of picture of a young Miss Owens with long black hair and beautiful white skin and a slender gracious figure, the world at her feet, the horizon full of rosy promise ... and of someone she had loved, romantically, tenderly, who had perhaps loved her, too ... and then of something happening, something going wrong ... and suddenly there was Miss Owens, old and tired, withdrawn into her shell, living alone and shut away in her secret unhappiness.

I suppose I must have felt this almost in a physical way, for I remember putting out a hand and taking Miss Owens' gnarled fingers and pressing them gently. And then I said, regretfully, I had better be getting home or my parents would be worried.

So we went back to the road and Miss Owens picked up her bike and began wheeling it back alongside me. We must have looked an odd couple, and yet somehow we were in harmony. When, just before she left me, Miss Owens asked me to call in for tea the next afternoon, I was delighted.

All the same I didn't say anything to my parents about the visit, nor the others that were to follow. From the beginning I sensed, or perhaps I decided, that my experience with Miss Owens was something quite private, and perhaps, I now think, unique.

She wasn't at all the cross, wizened old witch one might have supposed from the local tittle-tattle. She was a tall, wiry old lady with a wry and humorous nature, full of secret laughter, and gifted with an imagination that seemed to bubble with all kinds of bizarre ideas. I suppose I was the spark that set her off, I with my thirteen innocent years reaching out to her across all the decades. She must have been nearly seventy, yet in a way in my company she became young again, perhaps the young Miss Owens who had once stood on the threshold of all sorts of wonderful and glorious things. I even thought sometimes, looking at her shyly as she sat by her sitting room window looking out at her favourite marigolds, that she looked young and pretty again.

Perhaps I was imagining things? It is difficult to say, for it was such a strange summer, what I now think of as the summer of Miss Owens. We used to meet, rather like conspirators, two or three times a week, and once together the outside world seemed to recede and become unreal. *This* was the real world, this strange old house, most of whose rooms were dusty and empty, this house given up to Miss Owens and her memories. Photographs, trinkets, heirlooms, pictures – they were all constant reminders of experiences I could never know.

And which, bless her heart, Miss Owens never wanted me to know. That was the only time I ever knew her to be cross, the time when once I began to say, excitedly, 'Oh, when I grow up I do hope I live in a big house on my own like you and – and – '

That was the time Miss Owens' face went almost dark with anger, and she stamped her foot several times, and her black eyes glowered.

'Child, you must never, *never* talk like that again. Because when you grow up – ' and her voice softened suddenly, ' – when you grow up, my dear, I want you to fall in love, to marry, to know what it is to have a *real* home, children of your own, a whole fulfilled life ...'

She paused before the picture she had painted, and then said, almost in a whisper, 'Yes, I want that for you so very much, my dear.' And perhaps only many years later was I old enough to really hear and comprehend the undertones of yearning for what might have been, beyond that wish for my own fulfilment.

I suppose that summer came to an official end, as all summers do, and I went home with my parents. The funny thing is, in some ways I often think it never ended. Some years later Miss Owens died, and her big old granite house was taken over by a family from up country and turned into the inevitable guest house ... yet somehow it didn't seem to matter. For what I have realised as the years go by is that for me, in some way, it will always be the summer of Miss Owens.

And so I like to think that even now, though I am long ago married and there are children's voices to echo around the walls of our home, yet in a strange way Miss Owens shares a part of the joy it has all brought me. Because, you see, in that distant summer I learned from Miss Owens, who never found it, that there is nothing so precious in the whole wide world as love.

# XI

## Miss Vivienne Potts

Valentine Mercer took his only voluntary action in the whole affair when he wrote the letter. It was a silly idea, perhaps, but it came spontaneously, and he liked to regard himself as the sort who acted on impulse.

He was a tall, stooping, quite handsome man in his late thirties, the streaks of grey in his hair belying a certain youthful charm in his manner. For some years, he had occupied a comfortable niche in the literary world as a short-story writer and critic, but more especially as the editor of a magazine devoted to the work of new and promising writers. When, after the fashion of such magazines, this one came to a sad but timely end, almost in a fit of pique he gave up the lease of his London flat and went to live in a remote Cornish cottage, nestling on the cliffs not far from Land's End. Here for a while he was able to feel a sense of escape from the over familiarity of the rather bitchy literary world.

All the same he still regretted the loss of his magazine, could not help feeling curiously cheated, as of a whole, secret world of his own. Sitting in his study and conducting a wistful postmortem, he would glance idly through the bulging file of contributors' correspondence. Some of them had seemed to regard him as a mystic father to whose anonymous being they could entrust all their most intimate feelings. Others remained at the opposite extreme, typing cold, professional letters that might as well have been addressed to a commercial periodical as to the editor of a magazine which, with all its faults, had been concerned with human principles.

It was by chance, he supposed, that he came across her

letters – perhaps half a dozen in all. There was nothing at once remarkable about them. They were written on a pleasant, but quite ordinary, blue note-paper; their phraseology was almost formal; and they were all – even the one thanking him for accepting her short story – comparatively brief. Yet he remembered about them, as about her fragmentary, tenuous sketch, an extraordinary, even breathless quality of urgency. In a few words she had made the ordinary, the expected, spring into a vivid sphere of excitement: there were tantalising, exquisitely intangible hints of drama, the promise of revelations.

He flicked through the letters, frowning. He was thinking about the story, a quick, subtle cameo of a woman enslaved to a man whom she expects constantly to leave her; and the unreality of the final moment when he proposes to her. It was a little masterpiece of exploration of human psychology, sophisticated and perhaps cynical. It had always worried him to think that it had been written by a young woman who signed herself 'Miss Vivienne Potts'. Surely, he had thought, surely she had experienced more of life than was implied by such a maidenly epithet?

Now the conjecture returned. He turned the letters over, like cards in a pack. They were all the evidence he had to go upon, and they remained baffling and irritating. The address was a flat in Pimlico, near Victoria Station. The writing was feminine, rather careful. There was nothing else, not even a faint scent about the paper. And yet he remained intrigued. Why?

He sighed, and pushed away the papers.

But later that same evening he stood by his desk again, looking down, fingering the already familiar bundle of letters. What sort of person was she? What did she think about, how did she feel about things? Why had she sent her story to him in the first place? Had she known in some curious, intuitive way that it would appeal to him? And why, really, had he accepted it?

At length, apparently to solve these and other problems, he sat down and wrote her a short letter. He had always been most impressed by her writing, he explained, and if the magazine had not ceased publication, he felt sure he could have used more of her work. Even so, it had occurred to him that he might be able to offer some helpful advice as to the future trend and development of her writing. Perhaps next time he was up in London they could meet for a chat?

He signed the letter with something of a flourish 'Valentine Mercer'; and all the way to the village post box he walked rather airily, as a monarch about to dispense some favour. But once he had dropped in the letter, he felt curiously nervous and uncertain, as if he was aware, indeed, of the small stone in the pond sending ripples on some endless journey.

In her reply she invited him round for coffee one evening.

A few days later he made it his business to come up to London, booking in at a cheap quiet Hotel near Paddington, and took her up on the invitation.

He took the tube to Victoria, and, following her instructions, soon found the road, one of those rather sad, half hidden streets in Pimlico where, he reflected, thousands of women just like her sat in their little bed-sitting rooms, waiting and hoping.

She, at least, had a little more to offer: a small, neat flat on a floor of its own, including bedroom, sitting-room, kitchenette, even its own little bathroom. It was all on the top floor and relatively beyond intrusion. All this he was shown, almost without pausing, on his way from the front door to a seat on the comfortable divan before a cheerful gas fire. Only then could he really pause, sit back, and take in the surroundings, above all, his hostess.

At the doorway, in a hall only dimly lit, he had gained a confused impression of someone slim and perhaps rather smart, closing the door and guiding him upwards with a sophisticated assurance. Now, in the soft, friendly light of the sitting-room he decided at once that the assurance was misleading: behind it hid a rather naive, charming girl who would need all the encouragement he could give her.

'Well ...' He settled himself on the divan. 'This is very comfortable.'

'I'm glad you like it.' She stood before the fire, a slender, boyish figure, delicately outlined in a dress that should, indeed, have been smart, but somehow wasn't quite. She was not unattractive though, he reflected. Her features were strong, her brown eyes deep set, her hair a mass of almost golden curls. And now, of course, she was probably nervous, and it was up to him to ease things.

'It was kind of you to ask me. I hope you didn't mind my writing? But the fact is, well, I do think that you show great promise, great promise indeed ...'

As he spoke the words, her story flashed into his mind again, and he thought, but surely this slip of a girl cannot have written that? A slip of a girl ... He eyed her more closely. Well, perhaps she was more than that. He could see she was a little older than he had imagined; and perhaps she was after all a little wiser? She didn't seem quite as shy as he had assumed ... For the first time he felt a stir of interest.

'How long have you been writing?' he said.

'Oh, I don't know. Since I was tiny, I suppose. At school. Wet Sundays at home. In the evenings sometimes, up in my bedroom. Can you remember? Was it the same with you?'

'I can't really remember – after all, I'm much older than you, you know.'

She leaned on the mantelpiece, and cocked her curly head to one side, almost like a sparrow. For a fleeting moment he had an illusion that she had the wild, untamed look of a gypsy.

'I'm thirty-one. You can't be very much older?'

'Well,' he said, ignoring the compliment, 'I must say you look much younger.'

'Writing's the only thing I care about.' She spoke now with quiet conviction. 'You know how it is, one builds up a secret world, you get lost in situations, people become real. I mean the people you create, your characters.'

'More real than real people?'

She looked at him blankly.

'How can I say? Can you? Sometimes I feel as if someone I'm writing about is more real than I myself, and certainly more real than any Tom, Dick, or Harry in the street outside.

I mean, I *know* this character of mine. I don't know the people outside.'

'But don't you sometimes feel you want to – perhaps you should? I mean have experiences and so on?'

'Oh, but I have had all sorts of experiences. You'd be surprised, really. You wouldn't believe ... The things that have happened to me!'

Dimly he became aware that in her conversation she was, just as in her stories, somehow imparting an undertone of drama to whatever she said.

'But come,' he said, almost irritably. 'We all have experiences and they are always apparently extraordinary.'

'Do you think so?' He felt her looking at him, and knew her doubt. Before it, he could not but feel the uneventfulness of his own life.

'When I was ten years old my mother tried to drown herself. I can remember it clear as daylight. She was very unhappy. She put on a mac'intosh and went down to the river. I followed her all the way – I was only ten, you know. It was like a nightmare. When I saw what she was going to do, I took hold of her mac'intosh and pulled and pulled, and screamed at the top of my voice. I shall never forget that moment – the rain in my face, the river swirling by, my mother tugging one way, me pulling the other, and the sound of my screams echoing in the night ...'

'You make it sound like a scene from a novel. What happened then?'

'Oh,' she shrugged, seeming to lose interest. 'After a while my mother went back. It was cold, and wet ...'

'And your father?'

'I had no father.'

'You mean you don't ever remember him?'

'No. He died soon after I was born.' She paused, and then her face suddenly lit up. 'So you know what? I used to make up fathers, different ones to suit my mood. Sometimes my father was grave and pompous with a pot belly, a business man going to the city every day. Another time, he was a bearded sea captain, back from Constantinople with an armful of presents. And then there was another kind of father I liked to have who was very young, hardly any older than I, it seemed, who would take me out to restaurants and dances, and buy me fancy clothes.'

'But your mother – did she never marry again?'

'No. Why should she? She would only have been more unhappy.'

'I see. And where is she now?'

The girl shrugged. 'In the country. She lives alone.'

'Do you go and see her?'

'Sometimes. It's difficult. She is old now, rather peculiar.'

'Peculiar?' He felt rude in asking, but could not stop himself. 'How do you mean?'

'Oh ... living on her own so much. Brooding all the time ... like an old witch, really. Yes, I often think that. She is an old witch, brooding over her cauldrons, brewing strange concoctions.' She laughed and then looked at him in that shrewd, sparrow-like way. 'Perhaps I'm a witch, too. What do you think?'

He was startled out of him. 'You? What nonsense!'

She hesitated, then shrugged.

'Well, don't say I didn't warn you. Now, how about some coffee? Yes? I've got a kettle boiling. I'll make some at once.'

Before he could speak, she had gone into the kitchen. He ran a hand over his forehead, feeling suddenly tired. Feeling, too, the irresistible urge to continue to question, question.

He stood over by the kitchen door, watching her make the coffee.

'Do you live here all alone?'

'Yes.'

'Isn't it rather lonely for you?'

'Not really. I'm out all day at work – shorthand and typing for a firm of solicitors in Holborn. In the evenings I write, mostly. So there's not much time to be lonely.'

'But I mean people – friends – well, you know.'

She shrugged. 'One has interruptions.'

She picked up the tray and carried it into the sitting room. He followed her and returned to the divan.

'Interruptions?'

She looked at him, hesitated, and then began pouring out the coffee.

It was then that the telephone rang. It seemed to him that in a curious way she had almost expected it to ring. And he noticed that she went visibly paler, as she put down the coffee pot and crossed to the receiver.

'Hullo? Yes ... Yes, it's me.'

The rest of the conversation seemed to resolve into a monologue from the other end, and some low monosyllables from Vivienne. Sipping his coffee, he felt more lost than ever; more curious than ever.

At last she replaced the receiver.

'Now then,' he said heartily, rising, 'drink your coffee before it gets cold.'

She came and stood by the fire.

'I'm terribly sorry ... You'll have to go now. That was my husband. He'll be here in fifteen minutes.'

Vaguely he felt he ought to protest.

'You never said ...'

'I forgot. I was married a long time ago. We're separated now.'

'Oh. I see.' For a moment he felt absurdly relieved. Then reflection set in.

'Then why's he coming here? I mean, if you're separated?'

'He does that sometimes. He's – he's rather violent. I have to humour him.'

'But do you have to? I mean ...' He clung anxiously to the phrase. 'If you're separated?'

She looked at him gravely.

'*Separated* is a big word, isn't it? Who can say what's joined and what's separated? How do we know ourselves? Don't you find life is like that, all sorts of lines crossed and recrossing?'

'And you think one can't escape?'

He watched irritably as she fetched his coat.

'Not really.' She crossed to the window and peeped out. 'You must hurry. If he came and found you here ...'

Something of her tension communicated itself. After all, he

was lost in a maze, he really wasn't ready to be involved with a violent husband. All the same ...

'Well, I don't like to leave you. If he's violent, I mean. Might he attack you?'

'I don't think so. I can handle him, usually.' She paused. 'He has sometimes hurt me, yes. Once he got a knife and slashed me. Right down my arm. Here, would you like to see?'

Abruptly, she came close to him and bared her arm to the shoulder. He was horrified to see the faded, writhing scar.

'But – but the fellow should be locked up or something.'

'Yes, I suppose so.'

'I mean, doing a thing like that.'

Without thinking, he traced the journey of the scar with one finger. Even at the light touch he felt her tremble, but she did not take away her arm. For the first time that evening, he became aware of her as a woman.

They were standing very close, by the window. He expected her to move away, but she didn't. He forced himself to look at her, into her eyes. They were large, brown, luminous eyes, that seemed as full of mystery as the rest of her. But somehow he felt that for the first time he had made contact with her.

'You have lovely eyes,' he murmured. 'Beautiful eyes ...'

Suddenly he kissed her. He had not meant to, he was sure he had not meant to; and yet there it was. And once the act had been committed, it possessed him utterly – until she pushed him away.

'Really – you *must* go.'

For a moment he looked at her, confused. Then a warm feeling of well-being swept over him. Something at least had been achieved.

'I'll see you again? I'm up in London – for a while.'

'All right.'

'Tomorrow?'

'Yes. Ring me.'

She opened the door, and he went quickly down the stairs and let himself out of the house. On the pavement, he paused a moment wondering whether she would open her window and wave. But there was no movement, no sound.

He turned and began walking back to the station. Now and then, as he passed a hurrying figure, he would look furtively over his shoulder. Perhaps that was he? Or that one across the road? Who knew? And how symbolic that somewhere in the dark night he and the discarded husband should pass without recognition. He went on his way, convinced now that he had been right in his hunch. There obviously was something most unusual about Miss Vivienne Potts.

And it was hardly surprising, he thought with an indulgent smile, as he settled himself in the train, that her mother was a witch.

The next day when he rang she agreed to see him in the lunch hour. They met in Trafalgar Square, and went strolling through St James's Park. It was a fine day, with lots of people strolling about, all appearing animated by the sunshine.

'This is fun, isn't it,' she said. 'Let's sit on the grass and talk.'

He would have preferred, perhaps, just to have sat and dreamed. But he was to learn that she liked to talk, indeed *had* to talk: it was as if there existed within her a torrential reservoir of words that could never be stemmed.

And the exasperating thing was that he began to want to hear her talk. Despite himself he became fascinated with the things she said, so unexpected, so bizarre, so curiously truthful. After a while, he knew what he would never doubt anything she said, no matter how extraordinary. There existed in her, tenuously, a hard innocent core of truth. Perhaps unconsciously she elaborated and fantasied – but always underneath there was truth.

So, almost without knowing it, he became a part of her world, spun round with her spider's webs.

'Did your husband come?' he asked.

'Oh, yes. He was in an awful mood. I suppose he suspected someone had been there. He's like that, very intuitive. Like an animal, really.'

Not liking the earthy comparison, Mercer changed the subject.

'What does he do, your husband?'

'He's a teacher – art master at a grammar school. Just now he's on holiday, worse luck.'

'I see …' Mercer forced a bright smile. 'Well, and what's been happening to you?'

She looked up at the sky, chewing a grass stalk.

'Not much. At the office it's been interesting. There are some very queer fish there. One of the men is in love with the boss's wife. They meet sometimes for lunch in a cafe on the other side of the West End. I saw them one day … It's a proper clandestine, furtive affair. He's quite young; she must be nearly fifty. I wonder what draws them together? I suppose she's not happy. And yet her husband's quite an interesting character himself. A big, fat man, always laughing. You'd think he hadn't a care in the world.'

Suddenly she swung around, leaning on one elbow.

'But really he's a melancholy. I see it in his eyes sometimes. A real, heavy melancholy. One day he'll commit suicide, I expect.'

Mesmerised, he listened to the flow. She analysed other members of the staff, one by one. As she did so, they became real for him, *dramatis personae* in whom he could believe, human beings whom he could almost see strolling about the park now.

'You really are a writer, aren't you?'

'Do you think so? I'm glad … but of course it's different trying to get it down on paper.'

'Ah, yes, but …'

They were off then on a technical discussion. It was one thing that interested him, the technical side. And as if sensing the moment for silence, she let him talk.

The lunch hour fled. Already he had decided to stay up another week – longer perhaps. They arranged to meet the next day. After that he fixed to take her to the ballet. At Covent Garden they sat perched high up, close together. Fleetingly, again, in the dark silence, he was aware of her physical being, slumbering, for all he knew unawakened. He had a terrible desire to touch her. When he brushed his fingers gently against her cheek, she raised her hand without turning from the stage, and gently touched his wrist.

When they came out of the theatre he hailed a taxi.

'What's that for?'

'I'm taking you home.' He paused. 'You can make me some coffee.'

He ignored her protests and bundled her in, giving the correct address. All the way back she protested, found excuses.

'I shan't listen to you,' he said.

'But ...'

Abruptly she fell silent, as if she had given up the struggle. When they reached the house, she led the way quite meekly up to the top floor.

But when he threw off his coat, and then advanced and took her in his arms, she seemed to strain away.

He looked at her indulgently.

'Worried about your husband?'

'Yes. He knows things by instinct. He might come.'

'Well – let him come! What business is it of his?'

But somehow the words echoed emptily; and after a few more moments he let her go without protest. She went to make the coffee. When it was ready and served, they sat by the gas fire, with the lights out, drinking in comparative silence.

After a polite half-hour, he exploded. 'But this is ridiculous!'

Angrily, he got up and came to sit beside her.

'Sitting in the theatre tonight, I felt a terrible urge to be close to you, closer and closer ...'

She smiled.

'Did you?'

'And you?'

She said nothing. But he thought her eyes were rather bright, and not unfriendly.

Perversely, knowing it was the wrong moment, the wrong mood, he began making love to her. She did not resist, though he could not pretend she responded as ardently as he might have wished. When he kissed her, he felt her eyes upon him, round and grave, almost as if she were studying him, like yet another character. The thought made him angry, even aggressive, and he became quite passionate in his advances.

It was more than possible that he would have accomplished his purpose, with or without her co-operation, had not the signal come that he subsequently realised she – and he – had secretly been awaiting. The front door bell rang, three times, the signal for the top flat.

He sat up, disgruntled.

'What's that?'

She lay passive, looking up at him thoughtfully.

'That's my husband. I told you he would know, somehow.'

Now that a crisis had arisen, she seemed less put out than he had expected. She did not even stir.

'But since the light's out, I think he'll go away after a while.'

'You mean, he's done this sort of thing before?'

She nodded.

'Well, then ...'

But suddenly he felt drained of emotion and feeling. It was then that she smiled at him, rather sweetly.

'You'll have to stay the night now. You can sleep on this divan, it's quite comfortable.'

'And you?'

She eyed him coolly, though not, he guessed, with disfavour.

'I'll sleep in the bedroom.' She paused, and then went on, gently, 'You see, I don't really know you yet, do I? I can't open and shut myself like an oyster. Do you see?'

He saw all right. He cursed himself for his clumsiness, his insensitivity. He became gently attentive, anxious to express as tenderly and non-sexually as possible the reality of his feeling for her. To such terms she responded equally, and they spent a pleasant hour talking in intense whispers. When finally she squeezed his hand affectionately, and tiptoed off to bed, he turned over and went to sleep, feeling almost like a bemused schoolboy.

In the morning, a bizarre incident brought him back to

reality. When she went off to work, she made him promise not to leave the flat for half an hour. He watched out of the window as she stepped out of the front door and set off along the pavement. Thus he saw, unmistakably, the raincoated figure of a man detach himself from the next porchway and begin to follow the girl. It was obviously her husband. He must have sat there all night just to make sure that he saw her. Even as he watched the man caught her up; he saw the two of them talking, arguing, as they disappeared around the bend.

'But if you're separated, why don't you get a divorce and put an end to things?'

'It's not as simple as that.' She looked at him severely. 'You expect things always to be tidy. They're not.'

'But I mean, you don't care about the fellow.'

'I didn't say that.'

He looked at her in astonishment. 'But you're separated!'

She shrugged.

'Of course. He's quite impossible. He's really rather unbalanced. Sometimes he walks down the road talking to himself, saying the most weird things. I think he has strange dreams, too. He would never tell me about them.' She paused, and then again gave him that curiously reproving look. 'We've been married nine years, you know.'

He groaned.

'All right, nine years. And now you're separated. It happens to lots of people. It's happened to you. Now it's time you faced up to it. Make a clean break. That's my advice.'

She looked at him, rather amused.

'Of course.'

There was a pause.

'But, as I was saying, it's not as simple as that.'

The next day the husband began following them. It happened when they met for lunch, outside a bookshop in Charing Cross Road. Mercer was there already idly glancing into the window. When he turned and saw Vivienne approaching, he became aware that something was wrong.

'Oh, dear!' she was breathless. 'Today he was waiting outside the office. I just couldn't get rid of him. He's followed me here.'

'Oh.' For a moment he was nonplussed. Then he swept into action. 'Well, let's get a taxi or something ...?'

'No. He'll follow us anyway. He's like that – persistent, determined.' For a moment her eyes gleamed with an unfamiliar glint. Then she smiled and took Mercer's arm. 'Let's go and eat as we planned.'

So they went into Old Compton Street, to a small Chinese restaurant where they often dined. The place was divided into small cubicles. They settled in a booth in a remote corner. But even as they did so, Mercer was vaguely aware of someone arriving in the next cubicle.

'Is that him?'

'I expect so.'

He looked at her, perplexed.

'Why on earth do you put up with it?'

For the first time since they met, he saw in her a helplessness quite foreign, he would have supposed, to her nature.

'He's so determined ... you don't understand.'

The lunch was ruined. They hardly talked. And just after the waiter presented the bill, Mercer became aware of another figure standing by the table.

'Er, this is my husband,' said Vivienne quickly. 'Danny, this is Valentine Mercer.'

Feeling that he was suddenly taking part in a scene from a play, Mercer climbed to his feet awkwardly.

'Hullo ...'

There was no answering greeting, only what, he supposed, would be described as a glowering look. For the first time it occurred to him that perhaps she was in danger of being attacked. At the thought, weeks of impotent fury kindled in him, and he spoke angrily, 'Look here, you really can't follow people about like this!'

As he spoke, he somehow managed to take in the man opposite, a real Danny Boy, dark, tousled hair, rather wild eyes, a pale face, clothes all dishevelled. He saw, and pitied, the slumbering look of unhappiness. But after all, it wasn't any of his affair.

'I'm not following you.' Danny's voice was deep, and also disdainful. 'This is my wife. She should be with me.'

Something in the tone made Mercer look more closely. He saw a curious film over the other's eyes. Good God, he thought, perhaps he really is unbalanced? Shocked, he looked to Vivienne for guidance.

'All right Danny.' Her voice was weary. Mercer didn't like the inflection of defeat. 'Now you're with me. You'd better walk along with us.' She looked at Mercer. 'Do you mind?'

It seemed to him that it would make very little difference if he did. He fell into step on the other side of Vivienne, and the three of them walked, incongruously, along the streets of Soho in the general direction of Vivienne's offices at Holborn.

For the whole of the journey, not one of them spoke. Each seemed wrapped, rather miserably, in a world of his own. Mercer thought he could guess vaguely at Vivienne's thoughts. His own were pretty chaotic. But what of the other man's? What went on under the tousled, untidy head? What sort of labyrinth of mind existed, that brought him like a ferret, trailing the unfortunate girl as if she were a belonging of his?

By the time they had reached the offices, he was angry again. Ignoring the other, he went and stood close to Vivienne. She avoided meeting his eyes.

'I'll ring you.'

'Yes. Yes, do.'

He hesitated. 'You'll be all right?'

'Of course.' She smiled, and it seemed to him that just for a moment the smile was for him alone. Then she looked across him to where her husband stood, hunched up, leaning against a wall.

'Goodbye, Danny ... be a good boy, now and go away ... you'll only get me in trouble, you know.'

Mercer decided he didn't like either the look or the words. There was an implication of familiarity. He had the muddled idea that this might happen regularly, perhaps every day. If so, how could they really be said to be separated?

Abruptly, Vivienne was gone. Irresolute, Mercer stood with one foot on the steps. In a curious way, he felt connected with the man opposite. What now? Did they catch the same bus or what? It was so incongruous, so fantastic, that he half believed he was dreaming it all.

But the other one did not move at all. He just stood, leaning, his face a mask, his whole being curiously withdrawn.

Mercer hesitated, wondering whether to attack, to plead, to argue. Nothing seemed likely to have any effect. In the end, unhappily, he turned and walked away down the street. He wondered how long Danny would stay there. Probably until five o'clock when Vivienne came out again.

But vaguely conscious of some false move on his part, Mercer disappeared into the early afternoon crowds.

They did not meet again for several days. When they did it was at Waterloo Station, one Sunday morning. She had promised to spend a day with him in the country, without Danny.

By the time she arrived, the train was almost due to depart. He took her arm and hustled her along, glancing now and then over his shoulder.

'It's all right, darling. I managed to give him the slip. I took a taxi.'

He opened a carriage door and pushed her in. As he clambered after, the train began to move.

'That was a near thing.' He gasped for air, meantime looking around with approval at the empty carriage.

'This is cosy. All to ourselves.' He stood looking down at her, curled into the corner seat. Somehow she looked delightful and coquettish today.

'You called me – *darling*.'

'Naturally ... I'm fond of you.'

He sat down opposite her, and took her delicate hands in his own, turning them over, looking at the palms.

'How fond?'

She smiled, and he saw lights dancing in her eyes.

'You seem so different today. In that little flat you always seem a bit subdued, worried or something. I suppose it's because ...' He hesitated, and went on, 'But today you seem free. I feel as if I've got you all to myself.'

She leaned forward and touched him gently on the cheek.

'That's right. Today is our own.'

The train rattled through suburban stations and out into the countryside of Surrey. At Oxshott they got out, and tramped off across the heath, out among the purple bracken and thin pine trees. They walked until midday, and then sat down in a small clearing, to eat their sandwiches under a burning sun. Afterwards he made a pillow of his coat, and they lay back staring up at the infinitely blue sky.

'Like the sea, isn't it?' he said drowsily. 'Not as nice as Cornwall, of course. I mean down there it's wild, elemental.'

'And there's real sea – and ships.'

She wrinkled her eyes. 'Oh, I love ships – I always wonder where they're sailing? Round the world and back again, perhaps. Have you ever been round the world?'

He laughed.

'No.'

'I have. It was before I met Danny. I was seventeen. I got a job as a stewardess on one of those cruise liners. In those days people had more money, or so it seemed. They were nearly five-hundred people on that boat. Think of it, five-hundred different lives, five-hundred separate beings, all cooped up on a boat for months on end. Can you imagine the little intrigues and tête-à-têtes, the involvements, the rows, the scenes, the dramas, and comedies? I saw them all. Every night I used to sit on my bunk and make notes before going to bed. I've still got them. Pages and pages. Raw material, I suppose ...'

He looked at her, propping himself on one elbow.

'You're quite incredible. I don't really know you at all. What else have you done?'

'Well, another time I worked at an agricultural camp. Helping with the harvest. God, it was hot. We used to work in our bathing costumes. There were some Italian prisoners there. One of them said he was a count. He wanted me to marry him and go to live in Venice. Fancy, I'd have been a countess ...'

She went on telling him of yet more adventures, but he only half listened. A part of him believed; another part didn't want to. After all, how did he know it was true? How did he know she wasn't just making it all up, one fairy tale after another? Perhaps she lived in a dream world, as a desperate antidote to that flat in Pimlico, the daily routine of typing? Then he remembered Danny: that had been true enough.

'... I ran away once. From Danny, I mean. I went down to Cornwall. St Ives. I had no money, I didn't quite know what to do. Then someone told me there was a job open at a big hotel. They wanted someone to run the cocktail bar. I'd never done anything like it before, but I pretended I had. So they took me on. Every night, there I was serving the drinks ... But you've no idea. The amounts they used to drink, the people staying there. They were rich people, mostly middle-aged or old. Old men with nasty looks! I ought to have despised them I suppose. But I didn't. They fascinated me. What made them tick, I used to wonder? Why did they want money so much? What good was it? Did it give them happiness? Pleasure? Security? I used to ask them. They were tickled pink. We used to talk and argue for hours, long after the bar was closed ... And then there was the staff. You've no idea what queer people there are in the world. Don't you ever believe – here's an ordinary person. There's not one! Every one is a curiosity. There was a chef there, queer as a coot. Believed he was the Duke of Piccadilly. But he was a good cook, so they kept him on. He used to have note paper printed with his crest of arms, and write around to all sorts of people. In the end, the police came for him. Then there was the manageress. She had a passion for young boys. She was always chasing after the waiters. It would have been ludicrous, funny, if it hadn't been tragic. They were terrified, but they didn't dare complain. There was one, though, George ...'

He listened, bemused, to the stream of recollections. It seemed to him that she had led not one, but a dozen lives; that she had packed into her few years a hundred times more than he would ever experience. In the end, desperately, he cut across her talk.

'Stop, stop. My head's going round. Is it all true, really?'

'But of course. All of it. I remember it all. One day it's all going into books and stories. One day.'

He gave her a hard look.

'Sometimes I get a frightful feeling that you're not really human.'

She looked at him, sadly he thought. Then she smiled, as if to break the sad cloud.

'Oh, but I am. Terribly human ...'

He took her in his arms then. She seemed suddenly to discard the worlds she had been talking about, to come alive for him alone. Again, he had the strange feeling that she had left behind in London, perhaps at the most lost luggage office, all her other complicated selves, all the fantastic entanglements. Here she was, as simple and clean as the wind-swept heath. The sun alone on her golden hair. Her eyes were clear as pools of water. Her mouth opened, and sought his own in oblivion. Wisely, he accepted the day's gift.

They slept most of the afternoon. When he awoke, his mouth felt dry, his stomach empty.

'I'm famished. Let's walk somewhere and get some tea.'

'All right.' She seemed to hesitate for a moment. 'As a matter of fact, my mother lives not very far from here. Shall we go there? She'd be pleased to see us.'

He stood irresolute, suddenly remembering that it had been her idea to come to Oxshott.

'Did you mean to go to your mother's all the time?'

She laughed.

'Don't be so suspicious. I think you ought to meet her, anyway. It might give you some new ideas about me.'

It did, too. But he was not happy about them. When they reached the small cottage, near Esher, he found the mother to be almost a miniature reproduction of her daughter. Her hair, too, was curly, but now streaked with white. She had the same eyes, and the same elf-like look. But of course, she was much older. Sitting hunched up in a high-backed chair, with a red shawl round her shoulders, she seemed all dried up and withered. He could understand the comparison to a witch. He felt immediately uneasy in her presence, and was glad to sink into an armchair and let mother and daughter chatter. When tea was served, he decided it was time for him to be polite.

'I've been telling Vivienne, I think she has a great future as a writer.'

'Oh, yes. So she tells me.' A smile flickered over the wrinkled face; for a moment Mercer wondered if it was a sardonic one. 'She was always writing, even as a tiny mite. Words, words, there are so many of them don't you think, Mr Mercer?'

'I suppose so. They have their uses. Sometimes they create beauty.'

'I distrust them myself. I prefer signs, indications. Symbols are really much more exact, don't you think?'

'Symbols?'

Vivienne intervened.

'Mother is interested in astrology, things like that.'

Witchcraft, too, he wondered ironically.

'She believes that certain things are preordained, and that ...'

'Quiet, Vivienne. How do you know what I believe? A mere child ... Wait until you are a respectable age, like your mother, then you will understand.'

For a moment Mercer thought he saw fear in Vivienne's face, but she only smiled. He realised that there must be a strong bond between the two.

And yet ... there was no doubt that the mother was very eccentric. Sometimes her talk passed over the border from reality into fantasy, or even lunacy. She talked of trees and stones as living things, of dreams and even nightmares as being more real than reality. She seemed to see people merely as pawns in some cosmic game. After a while, he began to feel quite frightened, as much at what he suspected about her, as what he saw and felt.

Several times he looked across despairingly at Vivienne. At last she caught his glance.

'Do you want to go, darling? Very well. Will you excuse us, mother? Don't bother to see us out.'

'Very well, dear. I expect I'll see you again soon.'

Mercer noticed that the mother gave no indication of expecting to see him again. Indeed when he took his leave, she said an almost pointed, 'Good bye.'

It was then, feeling rather put out, that his eye caught sight of the painting in the hallway. At once he went up to it to look closer. It was a portrait of Vivienne, done in oils, possibly some years back, when the face was still soft with youth. It was, in its way, an exquisite and beautiful portrait. And yet it was terrifying, for the artist had conveyed something beyond what was seen, some hint of elemental forces and emotions, strange passions, even weird ones, hidden behind the smiling face.

'Do you like it?'

He became conscious of Vivienne standing behind him. But already, before he turned, he knew that she had become for ever in his mind the girl of the picture.

'I don't know that I *like* it. It's very clever.'

She gave a little sigh.

'Yes. It's by Danny. My mother's very fond of it.'

I'll bet she is, he thought savagely. The old witch would like to see a vision of the young one.

Suddenly, he took her by the arm and almost dragged her out of the house.

'Come on. I've got the willies suddenly. I do not like it here. Let's get out into the fresh air.'

She followed him, not protesting, seeming a little amused. But Mercer was not amused.

'I don't know what it is, but suddenly I feel appalled by it all.'

'What?'

'Your life, your background. The people you surround yourself with. A witch for a mother, a madman for a husband! Doesn't it ever strike you? How can you go on like this?'

He went on arguing, expostulating, all the way to the station. And it was only when their train rattled into Waterloo Station, that the sadness of the day's end seemed to calm him down. He put his arm around her shoulder as they walked down the platform.

'I'm sorry to have gone on like that. Something came over me. I want to change things, that's all.'

'But why? Why not accept life as it is?'

He shrugged, following her morosely to the top of the escalator where she got her tube.

'If I had my way I'd take you away, right away from everything.' He spoke savagely. 'It's the only way. Carry you off, like some pirate of old. Take you down to Cornwall with me.'

'Would you, darling?'

Suddenly he was exasperated by her, by everything, the mockery of it all. When she turned to go, he caught her by the arm.

'No! You can't go like that. Come and sit down a minute ...'

He pulled her across to the buffet, hurriedly ordering two cups of lukewarm tea. They sat at a table in the corner, lost among a confusion of voices, stale tobacco, old cakes, children's whines.

'Look, Vivienne, I feel awful. Sometimes I feel I know you, sometimes you're like a stranger. More of a stranger than when you used to write to me ...' He paused, struggling for words. Then he leaned forward and looked at her appealingly.

'Vivienne ... will you marry me? I mean, get a divorce, and then marry me? We could start a new life – away from all this – far away, in Cornwall. You'd love it there. It's so – so peaceful. Please say you will marry me? Soon.'

Perhaps, in all his life, he had never spoken more earnestly. He could see the urgency of his words register, he could see that he reached through to her, deep down. She looked infinitely, unbearably sad, as she stretched froward a hand and placed it warmly over his.

'That's a big question, isn't it?'

'Naturally. What do you say?'

'Let me think it over.'

'For how long?' He bent forward. 'Let me know tomorrow?'

She seemed to hesitate, and then to make up her mind.

'Very well, tomorrow.'

He saw her to the escalator. He kissed her good bye, on the cheek, like some elder brother. And as she disappeared mysteriously into the depths, he felt a pang at her helplessness in such a wicked world.

The next morning when he rang up, there was no answer. He rang again in the early evening, and then later, but there was no reply. There was only the maddening buzz-buzz of the phone ringing.

Worried he put on his coat and took the train down to Victoria. Walking up the familiar street, he kept telling himself he was being foolish, that in a moment he would see a light at her window. But there was no light: and when he rang the bell there was no response.

After a while he looked at the other bells. One was labelled HOUSEKEEPER. He rang it, peremptorily. After a while, a middle-aged woman came to the door, looking rather cross.

'I'm sorry to bother you. I wanted to get in touch with Miss Potts ...'

'She's gone.'

'I – beg your pardon?'

'Miss Potts has gone from here. Went this morning. Left no address, either. Sorry ... goodnight.'

He found himself staring at a shut door. Somehow it hadn't quite registered. Not until he had walked back to the train, and was sitting in the garish light staring at his vague image in the window opposite, did he really comprehend.

In the morning there was a letter from her:

Darling, when I got home last night Danny was waiting. He was very upset. When he's like that it makes me want to cry. Really, he needs looking after. I'm all he's got. He hasn't even got a mother. And we've been married a long time, you know. Nine years ... I don't think you quite understand what that means. All sorts of webs are woven. We can escape from some, but there's always the odd one we forget about – and we trip over it at the last moment. Perhaps that's what's happened to me? Thank you for a lovely day. You're a sweet person, and I'm very fond of you. If it wasn't for Danny ... Love, Vivienne

P.S. Danny and I are going away to make a fresh start somewhere else.

He read the letter over and over again. His feelings were a mixture of pain and anger, suffering and longing. In the end they crystallised into exasperation. She was so helpless, so much the prey of a determined man. He had bullied her, just carried her off. Perhaps even attacked her – was it another slash of the knife?

Just then a significant fact struck him. At the top of the letter she had printed, quite clearly, an address. Why should she do that – unless, secretly, she needed him?

It was a great relief, like a silver lining to some terrible storm. He looked at the address again. BATH. He rang up the railway station. Half an hour later he was in a taxi on his way to Paddington.

In Bath, he wandered about a maze of long Regency streets, for what seemed miles, before he came upon the right one. By now it was nearly dark. He allowed himself a quick walk down the street, noting the number of her address as he went by. It was a small rather suburban house. He could not imagine her inside it, yet it would appear that she must be. That was it, No 122, West Avenue.

He thought of striding up, pounding on the door, breaking in – all of these things. But he felt tired and rather cold, and it seemed that he had better first go and book a room at some hotel. So, memorising the place, he went away. Later, after finding a room, he went into one of the Bath pubs, a small, cosy place near the Pump Room, and sat drinking whisky. By the time the pub closed, he felt elated, superior, equal to any occasion. There was a warmth, a glow about him such as he had hardly ever experienced before. But this was not surprising, as he had never drunk eight whiskies before either.

The thought of going to his lonely hotel room did not ever occur to him. There was obviously only one place to aim for, and so he did. After all, he told himself, she must *need* him or she would not have given her address. No 122 West Avenue, Bath – he rolled the words unsteadily around his tongue.

When he reached the house, he stood irresolute on the porch. There was a light in the upstairs room. But even as he watched, it was suddenly extinguished. Left in darkness, he felt anger swelling up. This had obviously been done on purpose. An insult, a scornful gesture. Go away, said the extinguished light. But he would not go away. He would never go away. No, he would sit down right here on the porch of 122 West Avenue, and wait.

It was cold, and increasingly uncomfortable humped on the floor of the tiny porch. As his ears grew accustomed to the night's silence, he kept imagining he heard all sorts of noises. Outside there were birds, distant cars, occasional padding footsteps. And inside? What was going on inside? Vivienne ... and that man, Danny. Husband and wife? It was unthinkable! She was altogether too precious a jewel, too fragrant a rose, too extraordinary a person ...

Anger rose again. Something seemed to beat inside him, wanting to burst out. He climbed, perhaps staggered, to his feet, holding on to the side of the porch. He was rather hazy, but he had made up his mind, nevertheless, that this was the moment of decision. No, *le moment de verité*. Firmly he took hold of the door knocker and began rapping it against the oak door.

The noise, even to his bemused ear, seemed rather like thunder rolling across the night sky. Fortunately, it was not necessary to knock for long. In a moment there was a light in the hall, and abruptly the door opened.

Half-blinded, he staggered in. He blinked helplessly.

'Vivienne? I want to see *Vivienne*.'

He became conscious of some alien form standing in his path. Well, he was having none of that. With a sweeping gesture, he pushed the obstacle to one side.

'Vivienne! Where are you?'

Clumsily he crossed the small hallway, opening the first door he saw, switching on the light. It seemed to be empty, a sort of drawing room. Swinging round he lumbered to the stairs, and then up them. As he went something clutched at him, and with a great shove of his arm he sent someone sprawling.

'Vivienne! I'm coming …!'

He reached the landing, flinging open door after door. There was a scream, and another. At the same time he became conscious of movements below, agitated voices; unfamiliar voices.

'Vivienne, where are you?'

He flung open a large door, switched on the light. There was a bed; and sitting up in it, terror on her face, was a strange woman. At the sight of him she screamed, a long, piercing scream that rang through his bones.

He was still trying to cover up his ears when footsteps sounded up the stairs, and to his astonishment, he found himself thrown in a rugby tackle to the floor. It seemed that about eight men had suddenly appeared from nowhere. One of them, unkindly, hit him on the head with a rolling pin, and with a groan he passed out.

In court the next morning, his head still ringing with painful echoes, he could find nothing satisfactory to say to the magistrate. By now he had gathered that No 122, West Avenue, Bath, was the home of a middle-aged couple called Lumsley and their two children. It appeared that he had committed several serious offences by breaking in, by assaulting Mr Lumsley, and terrorising Mrs Lumsley. The fact that he was looking for a person called Vivienne, as the magistrate icily pointed out, was no justification for committing assault and battery on perfectly innocent citizens. The public must be protected from such acts of hooliganism. He would go to prison for three months.

It was perhaps a week later when she came to visit him. Apparently she had only just read the case in the papers.

At first he would not speak to her. Then, peevishly, he demanded:

'Why did you give me a false address?'

'But darling, I'd no idea you'd do such an extraordinary thing. I just put it almost as an afterthought – any old address, I thought. Just to throw you off the scent, so to speak. I never dreamed you'd actually *go* all that way.'

He groaned.

'Well, I did.'

A thought struck him. 'You're – you're not still at that flat at Victoria?'

'Well, ye – es.'

'But the landlady, she told me ...'

'Yes, well, you see, I asked her to pretend. It was for your own good, really.'

He fell into a heavy, despairing silence. Vaguely he tried to put the pieces together; but they would not fit.

When he looked up again, he saw her bright eyes darting about, taking in the atmosphere of cells, bars, prison. She looked at him quite cheerfully.

'You know, it must be *very* interesting. I'll bet you've got a lot of material already?'

He collected himself for one last, tremendous effort.

'Vivienne, will you *please* pay attention? Are you all right? I mean that man, is he bothering you now?'

She looked at him innocently.

'Danny, you mean? Oh, no he's being a good boy. We've agreed to forget the past. We're really very happy now.' She smiled sweetly. 'Thanks, in a way, to you.'

She looked at him anxiously.

'And you – are you all right?'

'Oh yes. Fine. In the best of health. They look after me well.'

She looked at her watch.

'Well ... I'll have to be going now. But I'll come and see you again, don't worry. Would you like me to bring something? Paper, for example? I mean, I expect you feel like writing, with all this time on your hands.'

'No,' he said patiently. 'No paper, thanks. Keep it for yourself. I expect you'll make good use of it.'

'Well, if you're sure there's nothing ...' She gathered together her gloves and bag, and rose. 'In that case, I'll say good-bye for now.'

'Good-bye.'

He watched as she turned and walked away, a slim, confident woman, her mass of golden curls glinting brightly in the sunshine coming through the skylight.

When she had gone he beckoned to the warder.

'That lady who was here just now ...'

'Yes?'

'I don't want to see her again, *ever*. Do you understand?'

'OK. Your privilege.'

He went back to his cell and the door clanged behind him. He lay on the narrow bed with his hands behind his head, staring up at the small window high in the opposite wall.

He tried to think about books, outside people, his writings, Cornwall ... But all he could see was the figure walking away, the mass of blonde curls, the innocent eyes, the incredible yet rarely untrue stories, the whole fantastic episode. Was it real or had it all been his imagination? Had he ever had a letter from Miss Vivienne Potts? Did she really exist? And her life, her perfidious, unbelievable, entangled life? Was it fact or fiction? Or perhaps – was she really a witch after all?

He sighed.

'What on earth made me write to her in the first place?'

But he was glad, for the rest of his rather reclusive life in remote Cornwall, that he had done.

# XII

## The Baroness

'I used to wonder who they were talking about. Bobby would do a fancy walk down the stairs and Max would bow and say "How do you do, your Baroness" – and then Bobby would collapse with laughter and I'd think, what on earth are they making up now?'

Caroline looked at me with her brown eyes wide open in that semblance of innocence she would carry with her all her life.

'Then suddenly I realised it was *me* they were imitating.'

I always loved her for that unexpected side, the way she could turn round and laugh at herself. Sometimes she was so earnest and single-minded, so fanatical in her clinging to some dogmatic proposition, that I could have taken her by the shoulders and shaken her. Why on earth can't she be human and relax, you'd think – and then all of a sudden you'd realise that she did see the funny side, after all.

Like this Baroness business. It was all to do with the fact that Caroline had announced her intention of taking up a teaching post with a language school in Germany. Well, we all knew it wasn't just for the teaching opportunities that Caroline was going. She was a woman, and an unmarried one, too – wasn't it possible she might land herself a husband? And why not a baron, indeed?

Bobby and Max could be a bit cruel about it, of course. They were a couple of queers who lived in a big house up the hill from Pengelly harbour. It was the only big house in the village and then it wasn't theirs – it had been bought for Bobby by a boy friend of his who spent most of the year abroad and liked to think of Bobby safely tucked away. If only Richard had known what went on!

Still, the boys were careful. That was why they had Caroline living there. If there was any gossip it reflected on Caroline more than them. Local interest was automatically focused on her, obviously a fallen woman. Who did she live with, Bobby or Max? – or dare it be whispered, with *both*? Actually the odd thing was none of the three lived with either of the others, they were just two queers and an odd girl out, living fairly soberly in the big manor house. Sometimes Bobby had a boy friend to stay and sometimes Max might do the same, but Bobby and Max were just good friends, and Caroline was just friends with both of them ... only rather more friendly with Bobby. And that, really, is the story.

Bobby and Caroline both grew up in the smoky suburbs of Birmingham. They came from working-class families, really earthy poverty-stricken working-class families, and both had escaped. Bobby had escaped because of a flair for painting which gained him the benevolent patronage of Richard and an open sesame to all manner of things with no need to bother any more about painting. Caroline had done it the hard way, goaded by a dogged determination to escape a drunken father and a despairing mother. She had worked hard, taken her teacher's scholarship, and finally found herself a job in a secondary school down in West Cornwall.

But it wasn't just teaching that had brought her to Pengelly. It was Bobby. For ten years, the most formative years of their lives, Bobby and Caroline had grown up together. They had been at school together, at art classes together, they had gone to parties and pub crawls together, they had shared flats together, and through all this time they had remained very close. Something like brother and sister, yet more so: something like lovers, yet never quite.

Because – well, there was no doubt about it. Bobby was queer. It was something you noted mentally the moment you met. I must say the occasion when I first met Bobby was ideally suited for emphasizing the fact. I had not been living long in the area, and there was some talk of a crowd of painters and friends going over to an arts ball at St Ives, and beforehand Bobby had issued a general invitation for a pre-dance drink at his house. It was certainly everything I had been led to imagine – there was a big sweeping drive leading up to the porchway, and when the front door opened a vision of a crackling fire and a majestic hallway with a grandiose staircase sweeping upwards, illuminated by a chandelier.

And there to complete the illusion of past grandeur there was Bobby himself at the door, wearing a satin blouse and tailored breeches and garters, like some Beau Brummel of old. In fact Bobby was so attired because of the fancy dress theme of the ball, but somehow it suited him perfectly. He was indeed a Beau Brummel, exquisitely dressed and perfumed, excessively courteous to the ladies – yet himself even more feminine than they.

'Hullo,' he said. 'Do come in. So glad to meet you.' And, looking at me with a quick, intimate flash of light in his dark eyes. 'I've heard *lots* about you, of course.'

There was no reason why Bobby should have heard anything about me, but for a moment his manner was so intense that I could not help but be flattered. He put an arm round my shoulder and guided me into the huge lounge for a drink.

'Sherry? Martini? Gin? Dry – sweet – ?'

But I hadn't a glass in my grasp long before the guiding hand dropped into place again and, rather like an excited child Bobby insisted on showing me round his domain. He took me up the magnificent stairway and we paused a moment at the top, looking down on the glistening oak floor.

'Twice a day I have to polish that,' said Bobby, almost petulantly. He gave me a quick look as if to assess my attitude to these things. 'The whole bloody house is a nightmare – clean, clean, clean – you'd be surprised, I never come to the end of it.'

'Don't you have any help?' I said vaguely, for it was obviously quite a task to keep such a huge house in order.

'Help? Goodness, Richard is far too mean,' said Bobby bitterly. 'He couldn't bear to spend fifty pence an hour when he knows I do it for nothing.'

I was amused at Bobby's illogical attitude, as he grandly showed off the house that must have cost his patron some ten or twelve thousand pounds. At the same time there was something very engaging about his boyish ways, his rather beautiful appearance – and I was drawn to him, too, by his natural frankness, the way he did not pretend there was no Richard at the back of him.

As we went round the house Bobby eagerly showed of his treasures, the valuable Welsh dresser, the contemporary Swedish glass, the chandelier he had picked up at a local sale – he had an eye for things of beauty even though, as I reflected they were all sadly inanimate.

'It's a lovely place,' I said, as we stood again at the top of the stairs.

Bobby removed his hand from my shoulders and stood back, his small, rather bird-like head cocked to one side as if he was anxious to study my expression and make sure I wasn't pretending.

'You *really* think so?'

I looked down the stairs and at that moment Caroline, whom I had never seen before, began coming up, a slight but bewitching figure in her Elizabethan dress. She had red-tinted hair and a way of holding her head proudly, and as she looked up I saw that she had the sort of eyes that could dance with laughter – or drown with tears.

'Yes, really,' I said: but in a moment for me the house was an empty shell of bricks and mortar, beside the living beauty of a woman.

'So there you are,' said Caroline, and I couldn't help being a little disappointed that at first she completely ignored my presence, addressing herself quite aggressively to Bobby.

'Oh, hullo,' said Bobby in a curiously unnatural way. I couldn't help noticing that he seemed a trifle cross at this new appearance. But, recovering his customary good manners, he introduced us, and the three of us went down and had some drinks. Soon afterwards we piled into three cars and drove over to St Ives and went to the arts ball. It was quite a lively affair that went on until the early hours of the morning, by which time Bobby and I had sworn undenying friendship, painters A and B had had one of their usual quarrels – and I had two dances with Caroline. When eventually I got back to my little attic room I remembered nothing at all except those two dances: and I knew I had fallen in love again.

But that has very little to do with this particular story, because Caroline was not in love with me. She was in love with Bobby.

For a long time I did not want to believe it. Caroline herself would angrily pooh-pooh the idea. Bobby would laugh outright, saying, 'But dear boy, I can't bear women, don't you know. Now if it was you ...'

Yet five minutes later I would come across Bobby and Caroline nagging and bickering at one another like an old married couple, with all the intimate overtones of two people who had lived together for most of their lives. And I would know in my heart that there existed between them a tenuous and steely bond, too mysterious to define.

Bobby, it was true, never gave the impression of being in love with Caroline. But he was very fond of her, and unfortunately that fondness often seemed like love, and was enough to encourage Caroline.

She loved Bobby. Of that I became convinced. He was like flame that burned through life, gay and charming and very endearing, and she could not stop herself drawing ever nearer to the flame, hopeless as her quest must be. When Bobby got too drunk at a party, it was Caroline who took him in charge, who half carried him home, undressed him and put him to bed. Sometimes, though I tried not to, I could not help imagining that scene, the sleeping young god and Caroline tenderly stripping him, perhaps gazing meditatively at the sun-tanned body, perhaps half caressing him in a yearning, helpless way, before covering him with the sheets and leaving him to his dreams.

I knew that nothing more happened, because Bobby made it quite clear where his interests lay. He liked sailors from the nearby camp, and every now and then he would start an affair with one of them. I would see the two of them gaily romping round the district in a smart sports car which Richard allowed Bobby to run – and then on my next visit to the house I would find the latest boy friend installed in style.

Caroline never interfered, never said anything. She was always quite friendly to these acquisitions of Bobby's; in a way she even seemed to encourage these liaisons. That was another reason why I knew she really loved Bobby. Because I always think it's a sign of true love to want the other person's happiness at all costs.

But of course if one even breathed a mention of this idea to Caroline, that she loved Bobby, she would almost fly at you. By now I had penetrated a little into Caroline's life. I had become a confidante, someone she could turn to. I suppose, come to think of it, Caroline looked on me in the same brotherly fashion that, had she but known it, Bobby looked on her.

Nevertheless at any reference to her passion for Bobby she would become unreasonably angry – and this alone made her seem more desirable than ever, with her eyes flashing and her cheeks pink, what I called her Irish look.

'Bobby's a – a – he's just like an eel. You never know where you are with him. I despise the way he lives on Richard. I despise the way he sits on the fence ...'

And so on and so on. Every angry sentence a mark of her love, her secret regard.

Yet even Caroline made her efforts to break the spell. Usually after she and Bobby had a row. Then, suddenly, Caroline would have her affairs. When I first met her, it was a man called Michael, whom I never met, for it was all coming to an end. But I heard all about it, and remembered reflecting that she seemed singularly unaffected by such emotional upsets.

After Harry and Tom and then Keith I began to realise that it was all meaningless to Caroline, so that it was unreasonable to expect her to be upset. Indeed, it was the men I came to feel sorry for. How could I feel for them – I loved Caroline myself, though from a distance, and I could just imagine their agony.

In particular I remember the case of Keith, for in a way it illustrated my theories – and led to Caroline going away.

It began in the pub one night, when we all sat having a drink and became conscious of a tall, debonair, good-looking man in the corner, obviously a stranger. When we came out Bobby was preening himself and boasting that he had made a conquest. Caroline gave a sardonic laugh.

'Why you are conceited, Bobby. He was making eyes at *me*.'

They had quite an argument about this. To settle it I went back and invited the stranger to come and join us for a drink at home. Naturally enough, for Keith was as normal as I was, it was Caroline who caught his eye.

But Bobby seemed to feel piqued by this, and set out to make himself very charming to Keith, who was a good-natured and worldly sort and didn't take offence at Bobby's overtures. The truth was that obviously Keith fell for Caroline quite strongly but at the same time out of politeness he played along with Bobby's antics, so that Bobby seriously believed that he was attracting him – and Caroline equally became annoyed because she began to believe that Bobby was right after all.

It was all complicated and confused for days until at last, when Caroline was drunk and a little fed up generally, Keith managed to take her quietly to bed with him.

I thought Bobby was rather nice then. He swallowed his pride and seemed genuinely pleased for Caroline's sake. Indeed he made quite a joke of it all, teasing her about the wedding day and so on. He was very fond of Caroline, as I say, and I knew that in a way he would like to have seen her find happiness with someone decent like Keith.

He was overlooking one thing, though. Caroline was in love with him, not Keith. And as soon as she realised that Bobby was being so nice and understanding about it all she dropped Keith like a ton of bricks. Poor Keith, she treated him shamefully.

This was one instance where Bobby actually did not sit on the fence, but came off it with a bump, attacking Caroline for her behaviour and becoming quite honestly angry (partly, I couldn't help suspecting, as he realised that he might have had Keith after all).

Caroline was furious at his attitude. And that was the day she wrote off about the job in Hamburg.

'I can't stand this place any longer. I'm sick of this life ... Bobby and his pranks ...'

She told me all this outside the post office, just before she posted the letter. She sighed, after dropping it into the box.

'Well, that's that.'

I looked at her curiously. Each new development in her life seemed to devour all her attention, to become an obsession with her. It was almost as if she forced herself into this position, as if she was trying to lose herself in some preoccupation. But why?

Just at that moment we saw Bobby passing on the far side of the street, a book under his arm, bound for the library. He was hurrying along, moving with his light, lithe step, looking sleek and attractive. I watched Caroline out of the corner of my eye. For a moment I caught her off guard – a moment in which her face was illuminated by a strange, sad kind of yearning. Bobby walked on up the street, like a brightness passing, and I saw that he took with him the whole of Caroline that mattered. Everything else in her life might be false; but this was her true obsession.

But, as I say, nothing could persuade Caroline to admit this fact, and she kept up a pretence of being interested in other men. She even, for a time, smiled in my direction. I think she felt safe and secure with me, and we went about quite a lot. Of course it may be that Bobby was taken with me, too, and this was her way of hitting back at him – how can one know?

Soon after the application forms came from Hamburg for Caroline to fill up, and it was then that the joking began. It was Max who began it, of course: Max of the extravagant manners, who could not enter a room without permeating it with the bizarre and fantastic. He was the only queer I ever knew who could get away with so much, walking into a perfectly normal little pub with his eyebrows thickened and lipstick on, and wearing a red opera cloak – yet somehow getting away with it. He had moved into Bobby's house in the same nonchalant easy manner, and somehow we had all come to welcome the stimulation.

Max had a flair for the extravagant fantastic 'label', for making it stick, too, because it would be appropriate, even if cruel. It was he, for instance, who had once given Bobby the seemingly preposterous name of Mother; somehow in retrospect, it seemed right, for Bobby was rather maternal and did fuss about people in that sort of way.

It was the same with the nickname of 'the Baroness'. When Max first christened Caroline as such, it seemed farfetched. And yet, the more obsessed Caroline herself became with the impending new life, questioning everybody about conditions in Germany, recounting each bit of information in front of Bobby in some vague hope of making him jealous – the more, curiously, she took on the mantle which Max had so casually thrown around her.

Of course it helped a lot that Caroline herself could enter into the joke, particularly when she had had something to drink and was able to forget her real heartache. Then she would be gay and sophisticated, flicking her long cigarette holder and waving her wine glass, almost becoming the very Baroness that we teased her about.

'My dear,' said Max, not unkindly. 'Where is the Baron – did you forget to bring him along?'

'Oh, the Baron?' said Caroline, swaying her hips mockingly. 'Why he's back home managing the estate, of course.'

After that, there was no end to our inventions. It became a permanent game for which we had an insatiable appetite. The Baron, we agreed, was quite old and white-haired, but stiffly held, and lively for a man of his age. He kept a town house and a country estate but he spent most of his time at the latter. The Baroness, on the other hand, being wildly sophisticated and a renowned hostess, was allowed a smart flat on the Wilhelmstrasse or whatever the equivalent street in Hamburg might be. Here, of course, she entertained her handsome lieutenants and commanders, but the Baron quite understood

– yes, he was a nice understanding sort of father figure. He knew it was good for his young wife to have the flattery of flowers and escorts to parties and the theatre – oh, yes, she had a gay life, did the Baroness.

Meantime, the letters went backwards and forward, and Caroline announced that she was due to leave in three weeks' time, and there was great consternation as it was realised she would have to start making her preparations for the journey.

It was now that I began to watch Caroline and Bobby more closely. I couldn't help wondering if either of them realised what was happening, that they were about to separate, perhaps for ever.

On the very last day, when Caroline was due to catch the night train to London on the first stage of her long journey, we all met for a final evening in the pub before taking Caroline to her train. It was a strange experience. We all drank more quickly than usual, as if to cover up the inevitable awkwardness at the final moment of separation. After all we had come to know one another intimately, and somehow it was something more than just Caroline going – it was the beginning of a break-up of the group, for in a way she had held us together.

I wondered what Caroline felt, as she sat there, bright-eyed, her reddish hair brushed straight back and a black velvet band around her creamy throat. She looked almost beautiful that evening; she was talking animatedly and laughing a lot, but in between I saw she was watching Bobby. Now and then their eyes met and Bobby would give her a little intimate smile to herself – because, after all, he was very fond of her.

But I knew also that even then, even that evening, Bobby was also trying to catch other eyes, belonging to a merchant seaman sitting in the far end of the pub. I had noticed a quick look between them, I had seen Bobby suddenly perk up, and how he had manoeuvred round so that he was facing in the seaman's direction. Before long he managed to make some excuse to cross over and engage in conversation. Soon he was chatting away animatedly as if he had known the seaman all his life.

Caroline had noticed, of course. I thought maybe she would fly into a temper, or say something, maybe just weep. But she did none of these things. She just sat where she was, drinking steadily, keeping up the performance; only her eyes showed a little brighter than when we first came in. I felt somehow that she was suddenly a long way away from the pub, from us all, even from Bobby – perhaps already embarked on her lonely voyage into a new existence, another world that even if it wasn't a baroness's, was equally different to this one.

We all went to the station, and the seaman came with us, too. By then we were all merry, and the time for rowing was past: we were all woozy with goodwill. At the station there was a hold-up while the others fumbled with change to get their platform tickets. I had an odd penny, so it was I who escorted Caroline on to the platform, since the train was already signalled.

Just as she came to the ticket collector's gate she fumbled in her pocket nervously. I sensed that suddenly she was very agitated, though I could not understand why.

'It's all right,' said Caroline. 'I can manage. Don't bother. Oh! ...'

She gave an exclaimation as she dropped her ticket on the ground. Laden as she was she could not stoop, and I bent down quickly, though it seemed almost as if she tried to stop me.

A moment later I realised why: as I picked up the ticket I caught a glimpse of the printed destination ... Birmingham. A single ticket, not to Hamburg, but to Caroline's home town.

I handed the ticket back without saying anything. I don't think she realised I had noticed. A moment later the others were all around us and we were caught up in a wave of last minute gaiety as the train steamed in.

'A carriage for the Baroness!' cried out Max.

We found an empty compartment at the rear where she could rest in comfort. We piled in her suitcases and bags.

'Are you all right,' inquired Bobby solicitously, one arm encircling the sailor. 'Sure you're all right?'

Caroline looked at him quickly, her eyes softening.

'Yes ... yes, I'm all right.'

I put my hand on the window, touching hers, unable to help myself.

'Goodbye, Caroline,' I said, and my eyes must surely have spoken that extra message, I love you, Caroline, I love you.

I think that she sensed what I meant. Perhaps she even knew that I knew her secret, that she was going not to a glamorous new life, but to an empty old one – because she could no longer bear the torture of the present. She certainly looked at me as if somehow seeing me for the first time her eyes opening a little wider than usual, and my heart fluttered as I saw her loneliness.

'Goodbye,' she said to me alone, and she touched my hand gently.

In that touch, I liked to feel, was the acknowledgement of our secret, some kind of tenuous promise for the future.

I stepped back and for the last time Caroline looked at Bobby. I turned and looked, too. He was standing there bathed in the light from the station lamp, one arm around the sailor and a slightly fatuous grin on his face. How young he looked, how young and gay and indestructible ... how beautiful and unattainable.

The train began to move, there was a roar of steam and it gathered momentum. For a few seconds Caroline appeared at the window and waved – then, abruptly, she disappeared from our gaze, from the world.

We stood there still waving, feeling a little foolish, as the train snaked away out of our sight bearing Caroline on her long voyage – to Birmingham.

'Ah well,' said Max as he turned his mind to other things. 'Goodbye to the Baroness. And now Bobby – '

He paused and looked around.

'Where *is* Bobby? Oh, the naughty boy – he's off with that sailor!'

Max gave a faint tut-tut, then hesitated, looking at me calculatingly. We both burst out laughing. In my case, at least, it was an emotional release for other feelings.

'Ah well, let's go home,' said Max, and we walked off together.

'By the way,' he said thoughtfully. 'Do you *really* think Caroline will hook a Baron?'

'Yes,' I said gravely. 'Yes, I'm sure she will.'

# XIII

## The Potter's Art

Mrs Bartholomew had good taste, there was no doubt about that. It was evident in her whole background: the almost regal nature of her large Georgian house in London, the impressive variety of the various *objects d'art* which adorned every room – and also, to be fair, in the exquisite flair with which the good lady dressed her own formidable personage. Slim and elegant and soignée, with bold sensual features crowned by a rather magnificent sweep of raven dark hair that conspired to reduce the effect of her forty years – yes, it had to be admitted that here was a woman, fundamentally hard and shrewd and acquisitive, who still managed to project an image of allure and glittering beauty. Few people, that is men, found themselves able to resist Mrs Bartholomew: she always got her own way, if not by one means then by another.

Ever since the early demise of her late, very wealthy husband, an event which she had cogently foreseen when she married him, Mrs Bartholomew had been free to devote herself entirely to her favourite hobby of seeking out works of art. It was a pastime at which she had become increasingly expert, and one which she divided strictly into two categories. First, there were works of art of the inanimate or what might be termed real estate kind – these she collected and kept. And then there were works of art of a more lively, fleshly nature, which she also collected, consumed – and then discarded.

In this way the beautiful Mrs Bartholomew had picked her way through a surprisingly varied selection of painters, sculptors, writers, actors and so forth. But she had never had a real, live potter before. Indeed, the thought probably would never have occurred to her. Pottery, yes – upon her Chippendale writing bureau there stood a much prized Ming vase: on the mantlepiece of her drawing room two very rare Dresden shepherdesses: scattered about the house a number of other valuable pots including, for Mrs Bartholomew was nothing if she was not up-to-date, a Bernard Leach and a Lucie Rie.

But potters themselves – Mrs Bartholomew had not really spared them a thought. Until that fateful afternoon when, wandering through the cobbled streets of a tiny Cornish fishing village, she came upon the dark-haired lad in blue jeans and sweater, bent intently over an old potter's kick-wheel. His name was a very long Cornish one which began with the syllable, Pen, and ever afterwards Mrs Bartholomew called him just that – Pen. Somehow she felt it struck just the right note of impending intimacy.

Mrs Bartholomew found her Pen almost accidentally, at the far end of a long, low fish-cellar which she might have passed by if she had not heard the whirring sound of the kick-wheel in action. Intrigued, she stepped down the stone steps and into the semi-gloom of the interior, relieved a little at the far end where a small window let in some afternoon sunshine. By this vague light she saw outlined the shadowy shape of what at first seemed a young boy, bent forward and engrossed, indeed seemingly welded to the movement of the wheel. On approaching closer Mrs Bartholomew saw that it was not a young boy but a young man – a powerfully built young man wearing an open-necked shirt behind which could be sensed the ripple of strong muscles. And this positive and virile being was not so much welded into the rhythm of the wheel but, more interestingly, directing its mood and movement.

What immediately seized Mrs Bartholomew's attention – then, and as it happened forever more – was what the whole thing was really all about: the young man's sinewy sun-bronzed hands, hovering delicately over the small, spinning cast-iron wheel – hovering and then suddenly plunging forward and enveloping, with impressive confidence, the whirling lump of raw red clay. While Mrs Bartholomew watched, spell-bound, the wheel whirled round faster and faster, the hands increased their subterranean pressure, fingers alive with tension, and at last, subtly, the ball of clay began to take shape and life of its own ... at first spreading out messily, then miraculously assembling into some sort of order and form – at last rising, like the phoenix, into cylindrical triumph. Higher and higher the column rose, until it even began to tremble so that Mrs Bartholomew held her breath in anguish ... but all was well: the expert touch was eased slightly, the cylinder returned to its former, more solid shape ... and all at once, so abruptly that Mrs Bartholomew gave a gasp of surprise, the wheel stopped moving, and there was the clay, virgin pure, a definite, living shape.

It was then that the young potter turned round, and Mrs Bartholomew was pleasantly surprised to see a dark, almost Spanish type of face, sullen and handsome and crowned by a mop of curly dark hair – the whole completed, now, by an engagingly youthful grin. This, Mrs Bartholomew decided, was going to be quite interesting. She moved more into the young man's line of vision, draped herself decoratively over a low bench, and smiled brilliantly.

'You must,' she said softly, 'Be very clever. I mean to handle the clay like that.' She paused, and then said warmly. 'Please go on ... I like to watch.' She gave a pearly laugh, opening her wide mouth, showing white teeth, and the tip of a rapacious tongue. 'I think it's fascinating – absolutely fascinating.'

Mrs Bartholomew, always an opportunist, altered her holiday plan. Instead of travelling about Cornwall she took a room in the local hotel and spent most of her time in the little fish-cellar, watching Pen at work. He didn't seem to mind: indeed, why should he have done? He was, she surmised, flattered by her elegant presence, perhaps even a little awed. All the same, she judged, he was no fool, no country bumpkin ... no, that was made pretty clear by the shrewd way he appraised her sometimes, the almost impudent gloss of his smile.

To do her justice, Mrs Bartholomew really was fascinated

by the potter's art. She loved the way the inanimate red clay was taken hold of, pushed and pummelled, slapped down on the wheel – and all at once, as if by magic, transformed from something dead into something incredibly alive. And above all, she liked to watch the way Pen did it – the way his strong, sensuous hands splayed out purposefully, applying pressure here, now there, touching delicately one part, stabbing fiercely into another. Yes, it was really the hands that fascinated most of all, Mrs Bartholomew had to admit. They seemed in a way to become almost apart, an entity in their own right, those hands: young, strong, meaningful – indeed, beautiful. And day after day she found herself strangely content to come and sit in a corner of the cellar, just watching and waiting ... for those hands to spring into life, to seize upon the clay, claw it into being – and, in the end, it often seemed, consummate it.

It would have been interesting to have known what Pen made of it all in those early days: what thoughts crossed that untroubled young mind. Perhaps there were none, for he was – as Mrs Bartholomew herself would have been the first to admit – very much a creature of the moment, very much a physical being. You did not really feel that the intellect was a strong point. And after all, did that really matter? Not really, reflected Mrs Bartholomew, as day after day she sat and watched, the tip of her red tongue poking out, her lips drawn back in vicarious delight, her eyes fixed bright and burning upon the endless restless movements of those hands. Yes, she had never before realised how interesting the potter's art could be.

As for Pen, his feelings remained, as you might say, incognite. He acknowledged Mrs Bartholomew's somewhat unusual interest with appropriate appreciation: he answered her questions politely, sometimes animatedly, no matter how probing they sometimes seemed: he was ever ready to demonstrate for her every aspect of the fascinating potter's art ... and when finally, unable to contain herself any longer, Mrs Bartholomew leaned forward and seized the two, by now beloved hands in her own and pressed them sensually against her own throbbing breast – well, Pen showed himself as surprisingly able to cope with the ensuing and inevitable developments: indeed, delightfully so.

Now that, most pleasurably, she had succeeded in making her point, establishing the routine so to speak, Mrs Bartholomew was full of her usual ambitious plans. Pen must not stay in this dingy hole, in this remote village, a moment longer – he must bring himself and his potter's art into the full limelight. She would set him up in a pottery of his own, no expense spared, in the heart of fashionable London. What's more, she would see to it that his work became properly appreciated by the people who really mattered. She'd organise an exhibition of his work. And invite all the critics. And ... and ...

It was true that in her single-mindedness Mrs Bartholomew had not exactly appreciated how complicated the removal of a pottery might be: that there were other items besides the potter and his wheel. It might, alas, have been in her own interest to have paid more attention now when, with surprising vehemence, Pen explained how strongly he felt about the other processes of pottery – and in particular, the ultimate art of glazing. 'It's the glazing, you see, that makes the pot ... why, it's an art in itself. And that's really what spurs a potter on. All my life, I've been seeking a glaze that would be unique, my own creation – just perfect.'

He looked at her with sudden earnestness to which, unhappily, she was impervious, and repeated, slowly.

'Imagine – my own glaze, something quite unique.'

'Yes, yes, dear boy. Mmmh. You'll have plenty of time for all that when you're set up in London.'

Well, to give her her due, Mrs Bartholomew did the boy proud, not only converting a large section of her house into a full-scale professional pottery, but installing all the most modern equipment – including, wonder of wonders, possibly the largest studio kiln which Pen had ever seen.

'Why – it's big enough to live in!' he said jocularly, in reality hiding a faint sense of irritation. It was, after all, preposterous to buy a kiln of that size for a single potter. Why it would take him weeks, months even, to accumulate enough stock for a single firing.

All the same, he wasn't one to look a gift horse in the face. He did really care about his art, except that in his eyes it was, more mundanely, a craft, and he really did welcome the opportunity to experiment and expand. What's more his work did have a definite quality about it which perhaps in the remoteness of a Cornish fishing village might have passed unseen – but which now, under the umbrella of Mrs Bartholomew's formidable patronage, soon began to attract attention. Indeed, before long Pen's pottery was definitely a with-it item on the ever changing panorama of London art life.

Perhaps out of a certain gratitude to his benefactress Pen endeavoured to repay her for her assistance in the manner to which she was obviously most accustomed ... but truth to tell he found it increasingly exhausting and, sad to say, even displeasing. The fact was that not only was Mrs Bartholomew without any of the native earthiness which Pen really appreciated, but she was, he had to admit, a good deal older than he had imagined – a very good deal older. And somehow, as time went on and his own success obviated more and more the need for her support, this factor began to loom larger and larger, so that he was hard put to it to hide his unwillingness, and even, finally, his disgust.

It was no doubt most unfortunate that around this time, in response to the obvious hard facts of a potter's life, equipped with a very large kiln, Pen took on an assistant ... and that assistant happened to be a young girl student by the name of Miranda. If Mrs Bartholomew had not by now been so completely obsessed by her relationship with the young potter and his tantalising hands she might have done well to ponder on the significance of the appearance of the buxom, fleshly and youthful damsel – and above all upon the fact that she was a pottery enthusiast, with the same all-consuming interest in the craft as Pen himself.

As it was, Mrs Bartholomew continued upon her imperious, selfish and self-centred way, as she had done all through her life ... with the inevitable result that might be expected. Her protégé's patience turned to impatience, his tolerance to intolerance, his acceptance to rejection.

What really clinched things was the exciting discovery of a true compatability between himself and Miranda. Not only did they find real physical pleasure in each other's company, not only did her quicksilver mental powers seem to rejuvenate his own rather sleepy ones – but, incredibly, they had the same all-pervading interest. And not only that, but like himself Miranda appreciated the supreme challenge of finding the perfect glaze. Together they could work for it in complete harmony.

Unfortunately for herself Mrs Bartholomew could not bear to allow this. Coming upon the two of them in an unmistakably compromising position one day she flew into a rage and ordered the girl out of the house. As she departed in tears, an ominous, dark glowering look appeared upon Pen's face – a look that should have filled Mrs Bartholomew with apprehension, had she not been so consumed by her own rage. Like the rest of the Cornish race, Pen was slow to rouse, hard to appease.

That evening Pen had planned a firing of his large kiln. Unusually, as the evening progressed, he was to be found removing rows of finished pots out of the kiln. At last they were all out, and the huge kiln stood quite empty. For a while Pen stood back, eyeing the kiln speculatively: then he went across and checked the instruments. Only when he was quite satisfied that everything was working did he go to the door and call out, in a soft, almost wheedling voice, for Mrs Bartholomew.

She – who had been wandering aimlessly about the house, regretting her spleen, miserably haunted by memories of those exquisite hands and all the pleasures they could inflict upon her sensual being – came running at once.

'What is it, my dear? Oh, I'm so glad you called – do let's be friends again.'

'Yes, of course,' said Pen softly. 'Friends again. Here, come and see what I've been doing. I've something that will interest you, I think.'

He then escorted the unsuspecting Mrs Bartholomew into the pottery workroom and carefully locked the door after him. Exactly what happened immediately afterwards is a matter for conjecture. Let us hope, out of generosity, that at least Pen granted Mrs Bartholomew once more the pleasure of a last luxurious caress of those beloved hands ... But that much apart, the next somewhat grimmer development was that he neatly stunned the lady, trussed her up in a most undignified fashion, and, not without a good deal of huffing and puffing lifted her up and placed her into the large potter's kiln. Then he firmly closed the door, bunged up the eye-socket – and switched on the kiln.

There is no need to dwell on the less pleasant side of the next few hours. Things that had to be done and disposed of were done and disposed of: but a certain important residue was not disposed of, but carefully gathered in a deep pottery urn ... and later, after certain excited experiments, mixed with various other chemical ingredients to produce a most unusual glaze. In due course the excited Pen applied this to a number of test pots and placed them in the kiln for a firing.

Some time later, arm round his beloved Miranda, he stood holding open the doors of the kiln, staring in reverent wonder at what was revealed. The pots shone bright and metallic, aglow with a mysterious sheen never before seen.

'Why, look,' cried out the girl. 'What a marvellous glaze. Blood-red – why, it's fantastic.' She turned and looked at him marvellingly. 'Why, it must be unique.'

For a moment Pen did not speak. He took a cloth and picked up one of the pots, holding it up to the light so that it shone and sparkled like – like something alive. For a moment, almost sadly, he wished that Mrs Bartholomew was there to share the triumph: he hoped, at least, wherever she was she might have some sort of appreciation of what had happened. After all, it was most certainly due to her. What a pity – what a pity that the glaze was going to be in very such short supply. Ah well: he sighed, and turned to the girl beside him, looking forward amiably to the pleasurable future together.

'Yes, indeed,' he said. 'It's quite unique.'

# XIV

## The Secret Place

The flats were begun as some planner's dreamchild, flanking the very edge of the sands, each with a magnificent view over the wide blue waters of Trevenna Bay. I can still remember the excitement of that first day when the builders arrived to start pulling down the tumbledown remains of the old fish cellars. We lived in a small guest house nearby and life there was sufficiently placid and regular to make such a day really eventful. I ran out on to the beach and stood for a long time watching the work of planned destruction, until one of the burly Cornish workmen ruffled my hair and sent me off to play out of harm's way down by the water.

After that the flats became something of the focus of my daily life. It was holiday time – a long, languorous, Cornish summer, and my parents were kept busy in the house, so I had plenty of time to wander along and watch the builders erecting their scaffolding and hauling up their breeze blocks. They worked hard and long hours, and soon the gaunt skeleton of the flats reared up into the sky and the men began work on the interior. And then – I never knew quite why – work seemed to slacken. I suppose the firm had temporarily switched their workers to another job – anyway, the result was that as empty day followed empty day, the flats took on a sad, unfinished air, more like an incomplete monument than a symbol of private enterprise.

I suppose it was then I began to really know the flats. I used to climb in one of the unfinished windows and wander about from one room to another – some of them mere shells, others almost complete, except for a door or window. It was almost like having another home, I suppose – until, suddenly, one day I became subtly aware that if it was another home, it was no longer just mine.

For now, as I wondered from room to room, my footsteps echoing hollowly against the concrete background, I was in some way aware of – well, I can only say a sense of companionship. Nothing I could exactly pin down, but a definite awareness of some other presence or perhaps presences.

I didn't feel frightened, though: curious, rather than frightened. I didn't say anything, either, perhaps because I was frightened of being ridiculed, or, more likely, because this was a secret I wanted to keep to myself. It was only at night, when I was safely up in my little bedroom, at the top of the house, that I would really relax and savour my secret knowledge – when I would lean out of the dormer window that looked over the beach and wonder about the flats, and the secret life going on there.

Then, one such evening, staring over at the flats, I suddenly caught a glimpse of two silent shadows melting from one of the darkened structure. I held my breath and watched tensely as the two shapes seemed to spin round and round in the darkness, like released spirits – and then all at once dart away towards the distant phosphorescent glow of the sea.

I can remember now how I felt no fear – only a tremendous curiosity. I waited for what seemed an eternity, until the two shadows could be seen coming back across the beach, and then I crept silently out of my room and round to the sands – just in time to see the shadows merging into the entrance of the flats. Agog with excitement, I crept after them into the silent building. Whereas anyone else would have been at a loss, I knew the lay-out like the back of my hand, and it was easy for me to follow the faint crunch of footsteps up the stairs and along the wide top floor.

At last, rounding a corner, I came on a faint flicker of light, and realised it was a candle, carefully shielded, and placed in the corner of the room. By its flickering light I could just make out the profiles of the two shadows – children, like myself, a small boy and a taller girl, the latter with long hair hanging down over her shoulders.

I was so startled, that I must have given an involuntary gasp. At once the candle was blown out, and an unreal, tense silence fell.

'It's all right,' I called out at last. 'It's only me.'

'Who's me?' whispered a tremulous girl's voice.

'The boy next door.' Then, sensing their uncertainty, and in some way conscious of committing myself to something irrevocable, I hissed conspiratorially: 'Don't worry; I won't tell ...'

I could almost feel the tension relaxing, and a moment later the candle flickered into life again. By its light I surveyed the two strangers – the girl, with her long, dark hair and rather white face, dominated by bright, black eyes; the boy, much younger, younger even than me, rather round-faced and curly-haired. They looked somehow a little lost and forlorn, and the girl had her arm protectively around the boy.

'Hullo,' I said awkwardly. 'I – saw you on the beach.'

'Yes,' said the girl. 'We go out and play when it's dark.' She hesitated, and then said shyly: 'We live here now.'

Strange how clearly I remember over all the years the way she spoke those words, her pale face tilted up to the candlelight, so that she looked much older than her years. No wonder, perhaps, that she was called Emily – there was something about her reminiscent of that other Emily who still haunts the Haworth moors – this, too, I sensed, was an Emily whose fragility hid a steely strength, whose spirit would be as impossible to capture.

'How long have you lived here?' I said, wonderingly.

'Two days. We came the night before last. We hide all through the day and then we come out at night.' Emily turned her dark eyes upon me. 'We're *very* hungry ...'

'We haven't eaten all day!' piped up the little boy.

Thus simply was our relationship established. Soon I was creeping back over the sands and silently entering the kitchen at the rear of our house. In the larder I found the ham which my mother had bought, and laboriously cut off some slices, then I took half a loaf and some cheese and a couple of apples. Bearing my gifts triumphantly, I crept back into the darkness and up into the secrecy of the flats. Then I settled back into a corner and watched in a mood of possessive satisfaction as Emily and her brother Alan fell upon the food wolfishly.

I stayed about an hour that first night before, reluctantly, I crept back to my bedroom. When I awoke in the morning I was conscious mysteriously that this was not just another day, not just any old day, but the first day in a new kind of existence. Even before I had had my breakfast I was out on the beach, hovering outside the flats, hoping for a glimpse of my new friends. But all looked silent and desolate – so much so that, foolishly, no doubt, I clambered up and made my way to the top room. I think I was secretly afraid that the previous night had been no more than a dream, that my imagination had invented the girl and her brother. But no, there they were, still curled up in each other's arms, and asleep in a corner – now starting into life with looks of alarm.

'Shhh!' I held up my finger warningly, then smiled. 'It's all right,' I repeated, swallowing hard. 'You can trust me – always.'

Then I was gone, in case my movements should attract any unwanted attention. And for the rest of the day I kept well away from the flats, physically, at least. But in spirit – ah, in spirit, that day, and the next, and the day after that, I was with them all the time in their hiding place: I was up there with Emily and Alan, wondering what they were doing, what they were feeling, what they were thinking ...

At night I took them some more food.

'We watched you today,' said Emily, as she ate.

'Yes,' said Alan. 'We wished we could have come, too.'

'Why – ?' I began.

As if divining my thoughts, Emily said, emphatically:

'We have to hide, you see. We've run away from home. If we don't hide, they might find us.'

'Oh,' I said, not quite clear who 'they' were, but assuming Emily meant her parents. I tried to imagine myself running away from my own father and mother, and somehow couldn't.

'Are they – are they cruel to you?' I hazarded.

'Who, Mummy and Daddy?' Emily shook her head firmly. 'No. But they quarrel all the time; they say dreadful things to each other ... so Alan and I decided to run away.'

After such a simple and reasonable explanation, I understood their need for complete secrecy, and was even more careful in my comings and goings. Looking back, I was amazed that my purloinings from the larder were not noticed; I suppose it was partly because my mother and father were kept busy at the time – and, after all, why should they suspect that every night, after they had gone to bed, and the house was still, their small son was creeping about, raiding the larder, and then bearing the loot over to the apparently deserted flats ...?

By now I had learned isolated facts about Emily and Alan how their home was twenty miles the other side of the county, how they had got a lift on one of the sand lorries; how they had spent their last pennies on ice creams; how – but it didn't seem to matter, really. Nothing seemed to matter any more except this strange and secretive world: Emily and her much younger brother, whom she watched over like a mother – and me. Each time we met and talked we seemed curiously bound together, as if each meeting was a strand in the web: soon I would feel I had known them all my life.

I suppose, in the way of children, it never occurred to any of us that time might have a stop, the world an ending. Perhaps that is why I always remember, with strange poignancy, that night – the last night as it happened – when there was a full moon high over Trevenna Beach, its silver light shining tantalisingly on the slow, oncoming waves. We had been sitting crouched by the parapet of the flats, but now, as if by common instinct, we hurried down and began scampering across the sands.

'Let's have a swim. Let's have a swim!' called Alan. For a moment we paused to throw off our clothes, and then we ran on and on, feeling the night air warm and exhilarating about our bodies. Splash! – Splash! – Splash! – and we were into the sea, frothing and flailing the water, playing about in the vast ocean, like elfins or goblins ... or mermaids ...

Mermaid ... the image suddenly came into my mind and stayed there as, looking round, I saw Emily, who had left Alan playing at the edge, now wading further out towards the oncoming white-crested waves. With her long hair hanging about her shoulders, and her slim, white body glistening in the moonlight – why, perhaps she was really a mermaid?

I don't know, but under the magic spell of that moment I could have believed anything, as I watched her slipping further and further into the sea's embrace – until suddenly I grew afraid, and ran after her.

'Emily! Come back, Emily!'

She stopped and turned, waiting, and I saw her hand held out towards me as she called softly:

'Don't worry, I'll wait for you. I'll wait – *always.*'

It seems silly, after all those years, I suppose, but I can't help feeling she was remembering how I had once said: 'You can trust me – *always,*' and that she meant what she said, just as truly as I had meant that. Standing there in the moonlight, holding hands, clasped tightly as we turned to run laughing into the waves – that was, surely, a moment of truth in our lives?

I don't remember much more about the evening, except that later we huddled together up in the flats and Alan fell asleep while Emily hummed a tune, and then, for a while, we just sat there, the two of us, half dreaming, until at last, unwillingly, I said: 'I must go now.'

Perhaps Emily had a premonition, for I can remember her calling out softly, rather sadly: 'Goodnight ...'

The next morning I had not been up long before I heard quite a commotion from the flats. I ran out on to the beach, just in time to see a group of people hurrying into the building, headed by a policeman, among them, no doubt, Emily and Alan's parents. I never saw, but I could imagine only too well how they would enter at last that secret corner, perhaps to find Emily and Alan still peacefully asleep. For one wild moment I contemplated crying out a warning. But in my heart of hearts I knew it was too late, ah, too late ...

Later that day my mother and father were full of the affair. They could not understand how it had been possible for two small children to hide away in the flats for so long. Anyway, it was a good thing they had been re-united with their parents. They had seen them together, and they all looked happy again. Still, it *was* rather puzzling.

'Fancy,' said my mother, in her comfortable, middle-aged way, turning to me, as an afterthought, 'I'd have thought at least *you* would have noticed something?'

I shook my head painfully. 'No, mother, I never did.'

I only went into the flats once after that. They were big and empty and hollow, full of haunting echoes, brimming with other lives.

I was glad, a little while after, when the builders resumed work on the flats. Today, of course, they look – well, just like any other block of flats.

# XV

## The Rival

Forbes first saw the boat one evening when he and Wanda took a late stroll around the edge of the harbour beach. It was almost the end of their honeymoon holiday on the Scillies. They had walked around Pendinnis Head and ventured as far as the Giant's Castle; they had crossed to Tresco and wandered among the tall tropical trees in an atmosphere heavy with exotic scents; and they had travelled in the long low passenger launches to the other offshore islands, Bryher and St Agnes and St Martin's ... spending quiet days on deserted white shell beaches and dreamy evenings leaning over the harbour wall and staring out upon the jumble of green tipped islands. It had been a period of tentative revelation, of growing together. Now that it was coming to an end they were both conscious of the uncertainty of the future, back in the ordinary everyday world of London where Forbes worked as a copywriter and Wanda taught in a school.

The boat lay there in the slanting evening sunlight on a still, greeny-blue sea, almost as if a statue carved out by some loving creator ... its slender curved prow nibbling gently at the chain, a movement that reminded Forbes of a young mare tossing its fretful head.

'Isn't it beautiful?' he said.

Afterwards he was to remember that Wanda had made no reply but stared out at the boat with an expression that remained quite enigmatic – almost as if perhaps she did not see anything.

But at the time he remained captivated by what he, at least, could see. The boat was nearly thirty feet long, a sturdy fisherman with high sloping decks and a roomy wheelhouse: a small red mizzen sail fluttering at the stern helped to lend a touch of gaiety, even of youth. The boat was young and strong and clean – Forbes felt suddenly that he had never in all his life seen anything quite so lovely.

'I wish – ' He made a strange helpless gesture. 'I wish – '

Somehow he could not put his feelings into words: but he took the recurring yearning images back with him, closeting them away in the secret recesses of his mind. Some time in the middle of the dark night, when Wanda was sleeping peacefully, he lay awake staring into the shadows, trying to recapture the marvellous vision.

'Just imagine,' he said enthusiastically at breakfast the next morning, 'If we owned a boat like that – if it was our very own!'

He looked with shining eyes at Wanda. She had dressed with great care that morning, the last of their stay. She wore slim white jeans which clung to her boyish limbs provocatively, and a striped green and white linen shirt which set off perfectly the green of her bright glowing eyes and the suntanned brown of her soft skin. In the depths of the night, like a mermaid out of the deep sea, she had come to Forbes, the shimmer of sleep helping to unloosen the inhibitions which still conditioned their love making ... and momentarily they had tasted the fleeting intimacy of married life. All this he had experienced, and remembered – how could he not? And yet ...

'What do you think?' He broached the subject almost casually. 'If we had a boat like that and lived here ... I could write, perhaps you could do some teaching – we could manage.' He smiled rather engagingly and took her hand. 'Away from it all.'

He paused again and she sensed he was really a long way away, not seeing her despite all her perfection.

'If only we had the boat ...'

They went home on the *Scillonian*, taking the low water passage out of St Mary's Sound so that they passed Pendinnis. As the steamer backed out of the harbour Forbes leaned over the railings staring across to where the faint red sail of the boat fluttered in the breeze. He said nothing but stared back fixedly until gradually the passage of the boat took them out of the Sound, cutting off the image. Forever and ever, Wanda found herself hoping, with a strange, fierce longing.

But somehow it was not like that. Back in London they took up their new domestic life in a flat off Fulham Road, and went back to their old working life in advertising and teaching. It was not an effective compromise: each made unexpected encroachments on the other. In seeking adjustments they encountered inevitable difficulties. And sometimes, in the middle of it all, Forbes would find a part of him suddenly lost, born away like a feather on the wind ... and he would be leaning over the harbour wall at St Mary's, looking out upon a beautiful sight.

'Do you know, its a funny thing,' he said one evening in the grey mediocrity of their Fulham home. 'But I often think ...'

There was no need for him to explain what he often thought. She was only too well aware. It was one of the delights, as well as the pains, of their intensifying relationship that the regions of the secret and unexplored were yielding one by one. It was possibly not wise to explore too far: but she found great difficulty in restraint. An open and generous spirit herself she could hardly conceive that Forbes would wish to keep anything from her.

And indeed in regard to the boat he wished only to share with her the whole tantalising experience. But this was not at all what Wanda wanted: the boat was no secret to her, she felt no strange possessive longing.

'Perhaps one day ... ?' said Forbes tentatively, another evening.

Wanda said nothing. He remembered uneasily the way she had not replied once before, as they stood by the harbour wall looking out upon the vision. But how silly, he told himself, she was as happy there as I was. Surely then – if it was possible?

Doggedly, over the next year, he worked to make it possible. At first she was dubious, actively opposed even: then, seeing he had set his heart on the matter, she relented. Or appeared to relent ... It was the first time in the course of their marriage that she had had to pretend, and it made her unhappy.

Curiously, the mood of unhappiness induced about her a strange pouting, almost lustful appearance, so that Forbes was drawn to her quite passionately, as when he first met her. There was about her a dark sultriness that he could not remember since those early days on the golden isles.

'Let's go,' he said suddenly. 'Let's pack up everything and go.'

It was not impossible, nor even impracticable. He had free-lance writing he could do, she had a contact with a correspondence school who would give her examination papers to mark ... In a matter of a few days they had made all the arrangements: he gave in his notice and she fixed to finish at the end of her term. It was just a question of time.

But when they made their momentous journey back she was under no delusions as to its purpose. Hardly had they landed at St Mary's again and dumped their belongings at the furnished cottage they had taken on a long let, and Forbes was off down to the harbour. She pleaded housework, the need to get settled in, as her excuse for not accompanying him: and could not help noticing, in passing, that he did not really attempt to persuade her further.

When he returned nearly an hour later his eyes were shining, his face open and expressive – he was like a young child who had received an unexpected treat. And now he wanted to share it with her.

'The boat's still there. What do you think? I've made some inquiries.' He paused, looking at her expectantly, and she felt a muddle of emotions: fear, apprehension, even a kind of hatred.

'It's for sale!' he said jubilantly. And repeated, almost as if he was presenting her with some incomparable gift.

'The boat's for sale – do you understand?'

She felt, somehow, she could not fully understand. Otherwise, surely, it would have been easy to make a joke of it all, or perhaps at the worst to have joined in with his excited anticipation ... and now with his almost maniacal application to the final possession. Nearly all their savings were required to clinch the deal, but he seemed to have no misgiving. Within a few days the legal matters had been settled, he came to her brandishing the papers in his hand as if they were magic.

From that moment, it seemed to her, she began to lose him. Not obviously, not all at once – just imperceptibly, in a deadly, inevitable way. And yet all the time he professed their common purpose: the boats was theirs.

'*Ours*,' he said with a strange inflection of intimacy which could both thrill and pain her, putting an arm round her shoulder so that she felt warm and a part of him. And then a moment later he babbled on:

'She'll want stripping down, of course. A new coat of paint – or no, two or three. Maybe we should burn the paint off first – that's what an old fisherman said. 'It's best in the long run.'

The long run. She wondered what on earth that might mean. Day after day they devoted every spare moment to the boat. It was kept on the same mooring as before but was now, importantly, theirs. Whenever the tide went out Forbes wanted to be down at work; willy-nilly, if she wanted to be with him she had to make the same journey. To her, when the boat was out of the water it looked ungainly, almost ugly ... but to Forbes, apparently, it acquired even greater aspects of beauty. Often he would walk round the long hull, occasionally running his hand lovingly along the rough wooden planks, and the gesture was such an intimate one that Wanda had to control her anger.

'Look at the lines,' Forbes would say admiringly. 'Just look at the way she's built.'

Such technicalities meant nothing to Wanda, but she was aware of the need for caution; it would be unwise to reveal too much distaste, or even a lack of interest. Under Forbes' enthusiastic direction she participated in the laborious task of first stripping down the old layers of paint and then applying the glossy new coats. At first they worked standing on the sandy beach, but after the hull was finished they moved up on to the deck. She could see that Forbes was visibly moved to be walking about the deck of his own boat – *strutting*, she thought scornfully.

When they were not working on the boat, he continued to worry about its safety. Every morning he was up early and hurrying down to check on the ropes. And if there was one of those sudden storms peculiar to the Scillies, great winds from the west whipping up the waves to that they came crashing against the harbour walls – then he was likely to be away for hours in the middle of the night, watching over his precious child.

Once on such an occasion, after tossing and turning restlessly on her lonely bed, Wanda got up and dressed and followed him down to the beach. Although it was a wild sort of night, clouds racing across the windy sky, there was a bright silvery moon breaking through – by its intermittent light she could see Forbes quite clearly, standing anxiously at the edge of the water. Noiselessly she crept over the shell-strewn sands and halted a little distance away.

Following the line of his strained, almost fearful gaze Wanda began to watch the boat, out in the centre. It was the first time she had seen it under such circumstances. Before it had always lain placidly at anchor, or immobile on the smooth white sands. Now everything was different: the boat tossed up and down, swaying from side to side, sometimes disappearing under a cloud of spray blown from huge waves breaking on the wall. It was only now, like a revelation, that she realised the boat was in fact a living thing … a pulsating, active feeling creature.

The knowledge acted upon her with strange compulsion, so that she suddenly stumbled forward and put her arms round Forbes' bent shoulders in a kind of hopeless supplication. Startled, he turned and, seeing her look of concern, misunderstood its meaning.

'It's all right,' he said comfortingly. 'She's safe enough.'

It was then, acting by some blind instinct, that Wanda gave a shiver and, almost angrily, pulled his arms around her. Afterwards she could never be sure of the real motive for her actions: but she was as vividly conscious as Forbes of the sudden contact of their flesh, of his fingers, worn hard from working on the boat, rough and warm against the soft skin of her bare shoulders. She began to tremble.

'Darling,' he whispered suddenly. 'Darling ...'

She said nothing, remaining as still and statuesque as so often she had seen the blue boat ... and all the time, as if uncontrollable, his hands began wandering about her body, touching, feeling, stroking, caressing.

'Darling ... darling ...'

Like the wind whipping over the cliffs and blowing clouds across the moon so his sudden passion began to overwhelm not only her but himself, so that there was suddenly a vast drowning darkness in which all else, even the boat, was obliterated ... and even Wanda was startled by the strange fire of sensuality unleashed by their rough and almost angry love-making, there on the lonely beach.

The next day, at Forbes' suggestion, they made their first trip in the boat. Wanda had awoken to see the clear blue sky and feel the warmth of early sunshine and, her body still aglow from the night's magic, had felt a sense of new hope. But somehow the moment Forbes spoke she felt uncertain of herself again. It was like living with a third person always hovering over her shoulder ... she felt, dispirited, she had no strength to cope.

And yet later, after they had started the motor and chugged easily across the Sound to Tresco, anchoring below Cromwell Castle – much later, when they had gone ashore and climbed high up on the purple-heathered cliffs, finding a tiny copse that was like an enclosed world of its own, without even a distant view of the boat – then, guided again perhaps by rough instinct, she surprised herself. This time Forbes was sleepy in the mid-day sun, but the impulse in her was wild and active, a tantalising one. She would not leave him alone: she ruffled his hair, she ran her hand under his shirt, she nibbled at his ear, stroked his hot forehead, laid her cheek against his bare chest, smelling the familiar moisture.

'Make love,' she whispered urgently. 'Make love ...'

And again she was able to forget everything else in the savage ecstasy of the moment. And yet – was it real? Or imagination? She could never be sure. She only knew that later as they came down the long cliff path and saw the boat waiting there she began to feel inferior again, as if everything that had taken place had been merely, for him, a passage of time.

After that they began making trips in the boat almost every day, setting off for one or other of the many half deserted islands, anchoring the boat and rowing ashore in the tiny dinghy, then wandering off into the cool interior. And always, somehow, perhaps without planning or even anticipation, they found themselves plunging into the dark labyrinths of their new love-making, at once ardent and exciting, and yet curiously disturbing, without peace. Why, she thought to herself, I'm behaving like a prostitute. And indeed there was a kind of prostitution in her method of deliberate abandonment, throwing away all her natural restraint. It was something, she was aware, that repelled even as it excited him, so that each time she felt compelled to display more ardour, more sensuality, losing them both in a fathomless whirlpool of sexuality, but little love.

It went on with a fearsome kind of inevitability the whole of the long sun-drenched summer. Work, domesticity, social life, nothing else seemed to exist: there was only the two of them – or rather, the three of them. She and Forbes, caught up in wilder and wilder pursuits of the unattainable: while always waiting placidly at the rippling water's edge, safely at anchor, lay the boat.

In some desperation she began encouraging Forbes to take them out even on the roughest days, perhaps hoping in some subterranean way that unforeseen disaster might break the cord that bound them together. She would not have minded really – she reflected sometimes, clinging to the bulwarks as they tossed and bucked in some big swell from the Atlantic – if they went down to their doom together, the three of them. No, in a way that would have seemed almost a victory.

But even in this sphere the boat was too strong for her. Its slim lines masked a tremendous strength; it seemed able to withstand the roughest weather, its bow breasting the heaviest seas ... and she lay back helplessly, watching with curious resignation the man at the wheel, eyes bright, face aglow, as he struggled against all the wild elements to protect his precious possession.

At such times, despite all their intimacies, she felt he remained a stranger. It was a painful almost unbearable knowledge that she nurtured to herself, trying to forget, or at least to ameliorate, to hide away ... but somehow it would not be forgotten, it loomed larger and larger ... until at last, in a mood of dull despair, she gave up the struggle.

'I don't think I'll come today,' she said flatly, one bright morning. 'You go alone.'

At first he was full of protests ... but finally, seeing she was resolute, he shrugged, and went off. She could not bear to watch, but she imagined him in her mind's eye, going across the beach, unfastening the ropes and setting off across the sky-blue sea to some distant lonely island. She wondered about him intermittently during the early part of the day ... but then somehow she grew tired of it all, and thought blissfully about nothing. By the time he came back in the early evening, tired and not a little irritable, she was placid and unconcerned.

'Did you have a nice trip?'

'Yes.' He hesitated. 'I wished you'd come, though.'

She shrugged, and said, with no animosity:

'You don't need me.'

It appeared to be true. Day after day, at first after half-heartedly appealing to her but later without even making the attempt, he went off in the boat, and she was left alone. Perversely, she began to enjoy the experience, the freedom from having to consider anyone else. She took to going for long walks out of St Mary's, along quiet leafy lanes, or up to one of the craggy summits. She would sit there for hours dreamily staring out upon the vast expanse of green waters, thinking about nothing in particular. She could almost feel herself becoming a separate, self-contained person again.

One day, quite a long time after she had taken to these

outings, her eye was caught by the flash of a bright red sail and she realised it must be Forbes and the boat, sailing between two of the far islands. She watched detachedly, without any real interest. When he came back that evening it was only as an afterthought that she said dispassionately:

'I saw you today sailing, by Sampson.'

'Did you?' He spoke eagerly, grateful for the crumb of her apparent interest. 'Did you really?'

'Yes.' She paused, feeling she should say something else – but what else was there to say?

The next day, unusually, he found himself too busy to take the boat out. She was surprised, but said nothing. He pottered about in the garden for most of the day. In the afternoon they strolled about together, not speaking much, but at peace.

The next day, soon after the time he usually went out in the boat, she found him up in his room, at the typewriter.

'Not going out?'

'No.' He looked at her as if eager for approval. I've got some ideas for an article, I'm going to work on it.'

After that it seemed there was constantly one excuse or another. Once he did manage to take the boat out, but returned quite early. And then he stayed home day after day.

At first she felt almost peeved at this intrusion upon her new privacy. Then, becoming aware of a pleasant lack of strain, she began to welcome his company, even allowing him with her on some of the afternoon walks.

One afternoon the sun beat down almost unbearably – even the roadstones under their feet were burning hot. They left the road and climbed up to one of the old granite carns, a mysterious place where time had vanished, and they might have been peoples of another age. Both were made aware hauntingly of the brooding presence of eternity, the brief span of life.

'Wanda,' he said, troubled. 'Wanda ...'

Suddenly he pulled her with him down on to a cool stretch of grass, and began making love. But it was not as before. His movements were gentle and tender, there was a shyness, a caring, about them that communicated ... They had not made love for a long time, but now it was curiously fresh, almost like beginning all over again. She had thought to feel all kinds of things, a harshness, a distaste, indifference even: but she was deeply touched by what she really felt. It was a kind of motherly, protective feeling. She held his head against her breasts and felt strangely, deliriously happy.

The sun shone. The sky was blue. The grass was green. The air hummed with the sweet sounds of summer. After a while she stood up, laughing, her cheeks flushed, her eyes bright. She felt she wanted to cry out, to express a wonderful sense of fulfilment.

'Look!' she exclaimed, pointing. 'Look, there's the boat.'

Forbes looked down, from a vast distance, upon the tiny inconsequential speck of blue and red. In the still, calm sea it was not moving at all: it might almost have been dead. Beautiful, he thought wistfully, but dead.

They began walking down the hillside, aware of a tremulous feeling of life beginning.

'You know,' said Forbes thoughtfully, 'I think maybe I'll sell the boat. It's ...' He shrugged, unable somehow to finish the sentence.

They went on down the hill, holding hands.

# XVI

## The Old Man of the Towans

I suppose most people think of Cornwall as a wild rugged place, a panorama of fierce jagged rocks and towering cliffs, of curving bays and, in the background, majestic hills. So it can be, of course. But here and there, scattered around the long coastline, you may sometimes come across a different sort of landscape. Instead of rocks, a wide sweep of sands; instead of high cliffs, a pathetic array of squashed sand-dunes stretching back inland.

Sometimes, indeed, these dunes seem almost to be positioned like sentinels, designed hopefully but inadequately to block the advance of the moving sand and sea.

Every now and then a gale blows ... when the wind has subsided the thin grass reeds on top of the dunes look even more lonely, the massive slopes of sand have pushed a little further inland. Looking over the expanse it is easy to envisage the sand swallowing up not only the humps, but the fields and the houses and the people behind – and perhaps afterwards the sea flooding forward in some final tremendous deluge.

There is about these downs, or 'towans' as we call them in Cornwall, an impression of doom and decay, of impermanence. I was never more aware of this than when I spent a holiday along the North Coast and acquired the habit in the afternoons of leaving the village and walking down to the shore and out along the miles and miles of desolate towans. I was very conscious of being no more safe and secure than a grain of sand, blown hither and thither by the winds. Looking about me, I was reminded of old Cornish legends about chapels, and indeed whole villages, sunk under the sands.

All the same, I wasn't quite prepared for my own strange discovery, coming over a rise among the dunes and suddenly catching sight of the forlorn posts and broken girders still rearing up against the sky. It wasn't an old chapel, nor a village; but a building of some sort, a long, enormous building structure, or what was left of it from the past ... just the bare, skeleton-like frame.

It was a strange discovery and yet I had a queer feeling that the building's unknown history had impressed a strong influence upon the whole towans. It was too large to have been a house. Who, anyway, would have wanted to live in a hollow between sand-dunes? I stared at the empty shell. It seemed as impenetrable and mysterious as the sands or the sea. I felt it belonged already to a ghost world of which I was barely conscious. Yet at the same time I was possessed by curiosity.

It was then, almost as if in answer to my unspoken queries, that I heard the sound of a dog whimpering. Turning, I saw a large Alsatian dog approaching, straining at the end of a leash held by a little old man in a black beret and a flapping raincoat. I supposed it was not unreasonable that the old man should be taking his dog for an afternoon walk. All the same, their sudden appearance startled me.

Perhaps something of this showed on my face for, as he drew level, the old man paused and nodded, as if to give me reassurance.

'Nice afternoon,' he said.

He was a tiny figure of a human being. He might have been sixty or so – it was impossible to say, everything about him seemed so shrivelled up and shrunken, almost as if he were a mere effigy. He had a pert little face, a sharp nose, bright black eyes that darted about as he spoke – yet none of these aspects removed a faint air of unreality.

I had the strong impression that the old man was looking for something, or someone. I had the same feeling about the dog. It wasn't small and shrivelled like its master – it was a strong, burly animal with a glossy coat – but the eyes held the same look of perpetual enquiry. All the time, I felt, neither of them was looking at me – but beyond.

'Suppose you're wondering about that?' said the little man, with a nod of his bird-like head towards the building.

'Well, yes, as a matter of fact. It seems a strange place to find out here.'

'That's what most folk do think. Mind you, there's nothing strange about it to me.' A queer smile flickered over the wizened face. 'I'm used to it, see. I comes along here every day – every single day, summer and winter, rain and shine.'

He eyed me expectantly.

'Suppose you thinks that a bit queer, eh?'

'No, of course not.' But I eyed him a little uneasily. 'Perhaps you could tell me – ?'

The old man clasped his hands together over the stick he was carrying and leaned forward. As he spoke he looked across at the building. I was sure he was seeing it as something alive, not of the past.

'Munitions factory, it was. Built at the time of the last war. Camouflage, you know. That was the idea. Hidden among the sand ...'

'A good idea,' I said.

'Think so? Maybe it was, maybe.'

The old man sighed. Beside him the dog, too, parted his fanged teeth and let out a hiss of air. It was almost as if he knew the story as well as the old man.

'My daughter, Loveday, used to work there. Beautiful girl she was. Everyone said so, real beautiful. I didn't like her working there. It wasn't right. Too dangerous for a girl. There were notices everywhere. Don't smoke. Don't touch. Don't do this and don't do that. Somebody was bound to forget something one day.

'I tried to stop her going. I had a sort of premonition, you see. Each day she went I feared it would be the last. Something dreadful would happen, I knew.'

The dog whimpered. The old man stretched out a bony hand and stroked the sleek head.

'I was right, too. One morning the whole place blew up. Terrible noise it made, like the end of the world. They say they heard it as far away as Truro.'

I looked shocked.

'And the people inside?'

'Blown to pieces,' said the old man. He sighed and poked aimlessly at the sand with the end of his stick.

'And your girl – was she killed, too?'

The old man flicked his stick out of the sand, scattering a shower of white over the dog's back. In a moment he seemed to have changed, to have withdrawn into some secret self. When he looked up at me again his eyes were sly.

'Oh, no, no – she wasn't killed. Not my Loveday. Oh, no, no.'

He bent forward, so close to me that I could see the gaunt outline of the bone structure of his face, the skin so withered as to be almost transparent. He was almost like a skeleton, I thought.

'They pretended she was, of course. Don't be silly, they said to me, She went with the rest, they said. But they didn't fool me. I *knew*. I knew she was just hiding.'

He drew himself up. His sharp little face swivelled from side to side.

'Yes, you may be sure – she's hiding somewhere, is my Loveday. It probably frightened her a bit, you know, the explosion.' He looked at me slyly. 'Been trying to find her ever since, you know. Nigh on twenty years. It's a long time ... Mind you, I've never told anyone. They'd only make fun.'

He bent down and patted the dog.

'But we'll find her, won't we boy? We'll find her.'

He peered round again. The sky was beginning to dull with the approach of evening. It had a sombre, rather unreal look. Suddenly in a quavering voice, the old man cried out:

'Loveday! Loveday! Loveday, my dear – where are you?'

It seemed almost like a signal. The great Alsatian sprang to its feet and leaped forward, dragging the old man along. In a moment the two of them had disappeared behind the next sand-dune. But for a long time I could still hear the crying voice and the dog's whimpering howling. I *think*. I heard the old man's voice ...

I never went out on the towans again, although I stayed

some time in the village. I had an uneasy feeling that if I went, I might enter too far into a world that was perhaps not meant for me.

But I did, naturally enough, enquire among the local people if the story about the munitions factory blowing up was a true one. It was. The publican at the village inn remembered the occasion clearly. And he remembered the girl, Loveday.

'A lovely girl, she was,' he said reminiscently. 'A real Cornish beauty.'

Then he eyed me curiously.

'But who told you about her?'

'Well, it was one day when I was out on the towans. I met an old – an old man with a dog. He told me.'

The publican eyed me queerly.

'Was the dog a big Alsatian?'

'Yes, that's right. It kept whimpering and howling most of the time.'

The publican nodded, but did not speak for awhile. Then he leaned forward confidingly.

'If I were you, I'd just forget about it, see? You're liable to imagine all kinds of strange things out on the towans, take my word for it.'

'Do you think I could invent an old man and a dog?'

'I don't think anything,' said the publican. He rubbed a cloth around the inside edge of a glass.

'I just know that there's been an Alsatian dog wandering about the towans for some time, and that same dog belonged to the old man who was once Loveday's father. I expect in fact the dog's been searching for its master.

'But somehow I don't think you can have seen the old man himself. You see, he's been dead and buried the best part of the past twelve months ... so you can hardly have seen him on the towans, can you?'

The publican and I looked at one another reflectively. At last he shrugged his shoulders.

'Then again, perhaps you did. Who knows?'

# XVII

## A Woman of Talent

Lizzie Tregaskin had no intention of killing off her husband like that, or, indeed, in any other fashion. After all, it was only a few months since she had married the poor man in Trevelyan Chapel, and she had been relying on him to love, honour and obey her for quite a few years more.

It was all on account of the clay, the red, clammy local Cornish clay which she collected in the valley and washed and sieved and kneaded, and then pinched into fantastic shapes: gnomes and goblins, ghoulies and – and the Cornish put it – 'things that go bump in the night'. After she had baked them in a home-made kiln, they were put on show in the window of Miss Couch's gift shop, and there weren't many visitors who left Trevelyan without buying one of Lizzie Tregaskin's quaint little figures.

Somehow, though, she had never made a human head before. Just never thought about it until Peter Paul came along, a big, ox-like figure of a man, one of the most hardworking of the local fishermen – and also about the most silent! Lizzie had been glad to accept him, for she was nearly forty and had looked like being a spinster for the rest of her life.

That was why she had begun making the clay model of Peter Paul, head and shoulders. She was grateful to the dear fellow for falling in love with her, and she wanted to give him something made with her own hands. Lizzie often remembered, afterwards, the afternoon when she first took the lump of raw clay between her deft fingers and began kneading it into the general shape of Peter Paul's massive head and huge shoulders. He had been dozing in the armchair at the time, tired after a morning's fishing, and at first she had not looked at him as she concentrated on her vigorous squeezing and pinching.

Suddenly, however, she was startled by a terrifying groan. Looking up, she saw that Peter Paul had come out of his doze and was sitting forward, rocking his head from side to side.

'Oh, oh, my poor old head. It do hurt somethin' terrible, all of a sudden.'

Lizzie had been so concerned that she had put aside her work and rushed over with womanly comfort that seemed, gradually, to alleviate Peter Paul's distress.

She would have been more concerned if she had been with Peter Paul that same night down at the Miner's Arms, when he got taken queer. But as it happened, she was at home, curled up by the fire, working on her surprise present for her husband. With one finger she shaped out the two ears, and with her thumb she stove a hole in for the eyes, pressing and pummelling with great vigour. Finally she put her fingers around the neck of the model and began squeezing away the surplus clay, an effort that required considerable strength – but then Lizzie's fingers were powerful and supple from years of modelling.

That was about the time – come to think of it – exactly the time when big Peter Paul, who had alarmed his friends in the pub by a succession of heart-rending groans and shrieks, suddenly went blue and then purple in the face, then abruptly toppled over on to the floor. When they picked him up he was quite, if unexpectedly, dead.

It was all so upsetting and confusing, what with the inquest and the funeral and all that – Lizzie hardly had time to stop and think. The doctor was greatly puzzled, and took another opinion, and even a third. But nobody could explain satisfactorily why Peter Paul, in full view of the usual twenty or so inmates of the Miner's Arms, had apparently been strangled.

Of course, strangled was hardly the word. It must have been some sort of accident, like swallowing something, or breathing the wrong way, or ... something ... or other ...

Nobody could understand it, least of all Lizzie Tregaskin. No, she just couldn't understand it at all ... Until one day, when the funeral was over, and she was sitting by the window with nothing much to do, and she picked up that bit of clay and looked at the effigy of Peter Paul on which she had been working. Somehow – yes, somehow it almost seemed as if those hollow eyes were alive with an angry light, a sort of complaining look.

'No ...' whispered Lizzie, flinching as in her heart she began to suspect the truth. 'No, it can't be!'

Well, of course, that's not the sort of thing anyone wants to contemplate, or most certainly broadcast, the possibility that by some sort of supernatural power you had caused the very painful death of your own husband.

Very firmly, Lizzie put away the clay model, locking it in a drawer and throwing away the key, and hoping that might be the end of the matter. Naturally enough, like any other woman, Lizzie found her curiosity quite insatiable. For days, even for a week or two, she managed to pretend to avoid thinking about the forbidden subject. Yet all the time one of those small, but by no means still voices, which lurk in every human being, was piping the questions. Did I really kill Peter Paul? Just by pressing a lump of clay?

And supposing I did it again – would it kill someone, anyone – just like that?

She was quite resolved to have nothing more to do with such thinking. And, indeed, quite possibly she wouldn't have done – if it hadn't been for Mr Nicholas.

Mr Nicholas was the local baker, a stout, but exceedingly surly man, with a sour look and a sour tongue. When his large, unfriendly, complaining figure actually had the sauce to present himself at her front door and demand his money, Lizzie Tregaskin found that she had suddenly lost all her good intentions.

That evening she sat in the porch of her trim little cottage, basking in the evening sunshine, her fingers busily engaged in pinching and shaping the raw red clay. She was making a model, a new model ... a large, plump model.

It was, after all, an experiment in the cause of scientific development, Lizzie told herself. After all, until she tried again she could never be quite sure. She went on moulding the vast shape of Mr Nicholas's over-fed belly. She finished the shaping, held up the model for a critical inspection; and then, with her forefinger, gave the belly a savage jab, and then another – and another.

The next morning something unheard of happened. The people of Trevelyan were without their daily bread. Nobody could understand it, until word came that Mr Nicholas had been rushed off to hospital the previous evening with acute appendicitis.

Go and ring up the hospital, someone said. The message was brought back, round-eyed:

'You'll never believe it – he's dead! Died on the operating table, our Mr Nicholas.'

Lizzie heard the news without surprise. It was annoying to be without bread, but apart from that, she couldn't really say she was sorry. After all, perhaps it was possible that she had been given this extraordinary power in order to do some good in the world, by clearing it of such miseries as Mr Nicholas.

It was a fascinating line of thought. After all, there must be other people, even in her own district, who were not exactly assets to the community?

For some time Lizzie Tregaskin looked around and about, very, very carefully. Little did many a personality of Trevalan and district realise the full implications of the long, lingering look cast upon him or her by the widow of Peter Paul, the fisherman.

There was Mr Emmens, the churchwarden, an estimable man, so most people thought – but then they'd never seen him carrying on with Mavis Troon up on the cliffs. And there was Charlie Hosking, the part-time postman, who was always sniffing open people's letters with his curious long nose. Maybe he deserved swift justice. And then there was Roberts the Dairy. Everyone knew he watered his milk. Hadn't he been up in court for it? If Roberts the Dairy had had the misfortune just once at this time to deliver watered milk to Lizzie Tregaskin, then the people of Trevalyan would suddenly have been without milk.

Oh, Lizzie had a fine old time of an evening, drawing up long lists of potential victims, and crossing off the names, one by one, sometimes with a regretful pursing of the lips. Sometimes she almost made up her mind and reached for a piece of clay, and once she even began working on a model of Stan Rowe, the plumber, who had left her pipes blocked for ten days, causing a flood on her best carpet. The next day Mrs Rowe was heard telling in the post office how the previous evening her Stan had been taken proper queer – but then, just when she thought she had better get the doctor, he seemed to brighten up again.

No, somehow Lizzie could never quite make up her mind. The trouble was, she knew the people around her too well; she knew all their little failings, and was always making excuses for them. Meantime, the weeks were slipping by, and she hadn't used her power once. Oh, yes just once, that time when the bus conductor had been so insolent to her. Fairly mad with rage she had been, all the way home, keeping her head down against the wind and her eyes closed, so that she shouldn't forget the cheeky man's face ...

And the next morning the bus driver had a strange story to tell, how his mate had dropped dead over a cup of coffee in the canteen.

But apart from this, Lizzie was only too well aware that she was, so to speak, wasting her talents. The fact was, she had devoted a lot of time and trouble to studying her neighbours, and somehow none of them quite fitted her deathly bill.

On the other hand, in the wide world beyond the ken of Trevelyan, surely there must be many people – oh, ever so many people – who were, alas, only too deserving of the supple-fingered attention of Lizzie Tregaskin ...

Yes, indeed. The more she thought it over, the clearer became her duty. And that was why, one day in the spring, the people of Trevelyan were startled to see the removal van arriving at Lizzie Tregaskin's cottage.

'But you can't be leaving us?'

'Whatever will you do, maid?'

But to all and sundry, Lizzie gave the same answer. She was sorry, but she had a job to do – an important job. In fact, a job of national importance, you might say.

And then she patted on her old straw hat, humped up her shoulders, and got quickly into the old taxi … Then, a moment later, popped out again and scurried away into the cottage; to reappear clutching to her bosom a large brown package.

'My clay! I nearly forgot my clay.'

And then, with something like a wink – which, fortunately, or perhaps unfortunately, the people of Trevelyan didn't fully understand – Lizzie Tregaskin was whisked off in the taxi, never to be seen again in Trevelyan. Some say she caught the train to Plymouth; and others say she went all the way to London. The only thing certain is that somewhere, maybe here or maybe there – but somewhere, mark my words, there's a little old Cornish lady, called Lizzie Tregaskin, sitting placidly with a lump of clay between her fingers … and so be careful – you and you – just how you behave. Don't forget to love your neighbour as you love yourself, and don't be unkind or cruel to anyone, especially little children – or … well, you never know. Lizzie Tregaskin's fingers are just itching to get at that clay again.

# XVIII

## Beyond the Dump

Ransome noticed the Dump when he first entered the town many years ago, walking carelessly along the neat pavements, being absorbed into the restless flow of shoppers that swept in and out of the glittering arcades. Looking across the hollow of sunken grey roofs he saw a black tip protruding into the sky, like a man's clenched fist raised in a despairing gesture ... it was undignified, almost obscene, something that should have remained hidden away but insisted on announcing itself – an ever present shadow over the hum and bustle of the town.

At first the sight of it worried him, pricking at some lurking conscience; then he forgot all about it as he was plunged into the mechanised routine of the town. But the memory came back later, when his feet were blistering from endless tramping up and down hard pavements, when the edges of his trousers were tattered and a stubble of dark hair framed his face because he had no money to afford to shave.

The shops were as gaudy as ever with tinsel decorations and silvery streamers, windows filled with rich foods and clothing and houseware, stacked high with bright cellophaned packages. Everywhere there was the same purposeful bustle of life and prosperity, people hurrying about, money flowing, taxis hooting, banknotes fluttering from hand to hand, everywhere there was a roaring rushing sweep of people backwards and forwards, jostling anxiously in their efforts to keep pace with the endless rhythm of sound and movement. But Ransome suddenly, obstinately, wished to move in some other direction he was hurled and buffeted about, thrown exhausted by the wayside. And as he persisted in struggling his loneliness became worse: until there was no money in his pockets, a lightness in his stomach, a weary ache in his bones. Wherever he turned he was aware of hastening movements, of blank masks, of deaf ears; he felt himself tossed about like a raft on the sea, and as meaninglessly. It was as an act of desperation that at last he broke away from the mesmerising centre, away from the eternal flickerings of red and green and amber and red and green and amber, away from the absorbed business men and the artificially lit shops, away from the neat red-rowed suburbs – forcing himself onwards by a tremendous effort of will, until he found the out-of-place, pot-holed gravel lane leading up to the dark splodge of the Dump.

He came because he had been told that this was where all the town's refuse and unwanted rubbish was cast away, and among the flotsam there must surely be the scraps – of food and shelter – to keep a man alive. He had kept this flicker of hope deep within him, nursing it resolutely through the long, aching tramp, but now as he climbed on to the top he felt the hope dying, a great tiredness sweeping over him like a pain. It seemed impossible that anything could flourish here except death and decay. He could see how the Dump had started as a small flat heap, perhaps no more than a few rusty pots and pans, and how it had swelled upwards and outwards, an ever-expanding scar. Now it was a small hill, its sides bulging outwards, until they crumbled away in treacherous slopes of sand and soot, thick gravel stones and dead logs of wood, here and there a rotting motor car tyre or an old armchair half grown over with weeds.

Everywhere along the slopes of these artificial cliffs strange silhouettes protruded like the hulls of shipwrecks out of the sea: long iron bars, the corners of bedsteads, the bonnet of an old car, the legs of a table, the fluffy shroud of a mattress, the skeleton wheel of a bicycle, and the rotting corpse of a once genteel drawing-room couch. Where he stood, at the top, a narrow platform had been hammered out by the churning of lorry wheels, and all around its boundaries were heaps of silver cans and glass bottles newly tipped out from the dustvans. Sometimes the faint glow of sunshine reflected off the globular bottles, creating little blazes of colour and brightness that seemed false and brittle in such surroundings.

Ransome trod the ground carefully, remembering that under him lay the stewing, sweltering mountain of years and years of the town's castaway salvage. As his feet moved they stirred up a tiny fog of sooty dust and he felt the dirt seeping into his hands, breathing into his lungs. Coughing, he walked to one corner and peered over. He was surprised to see in the space beyond a pattern of flat brown earth lined by distant green trees – as if the Dump marked the boundary of one world, the gatepost of another. Then, looking downwards, he was shocked to see moving among the crumbling slopes, clutching and pecking into the sides like hungry birds, a few crouched shapes ... the bent figure of an old man, several younger men, in the distance a woman with a handkerchief round her head.

For a time he watched, thinking of himself as a spectator witnessing some degrading private revelation. Then, almost with surprise, he remembered that he was not a spectator but had come to join these strange pickers of stranger fruit. And with that realisation he lost the sense of fastidious distaste, and was only aware of relief to know that he was not alone here with the rusting irons and the barren sootiness, that there was the waving warmth of other human beings. He kicked aside some cans and began climbing down the side of the Dump.

The name of the old man was Macey. He was small and wiry, had a wrinkled face with bright brown eyes, a crop of neat grey hair, a humorous twist at one corner of his mouth. The tattered stump of a cigarette dangled at the other corner. It jumped up and down precariously as he spoke to Ransome.

'Not much luck today. A lot of gravel and strong soot, a few strips of tin, an old saucepan with a leak, a sack half full of lime – that's about the lot so far. Other days it'll be better. Much better. Only yesterday I found a deck-chair that would have done merit to anyone's garden. I did indeed.'

'Have you been here long?'

'Oh, quite a time. It has been hard work. And always dry.

There's something about it all that seems to dry things up, an aridness.'

'Yes. I felt it.'

'And, of course, there's the stench, from old decaying things. Rats, too. It's not what you might regard as pleasant, at first. But you'll be surprised how much can be found. The Dump can be just a heap of dirt, or it can be an oasis in a desert. It depends if one looks hard enough.'

Macey's two bushy eyebrows lifted sideways in a sharp look.

'Mmph. You've had a tiring journey, I can see.'

Ransome nodded, suddenly conscious of his weakness.

'From the town, of course?'

'Yes.'

Macey straightened.

'Well ... At least I can offer you a cup of tea. No, it's all right really. I have it on the boil over here.'

He led Ransome down to the foot of the slope and across a patch of grass to where a small elm-tree formed a small square of shade. There was a fire burning in a brazier, a kettle steaming on top. Macey started preparing the tea.

Ransome lay down, letting his whole body go limp, sinking gratefully into the comparative softness of the grass. He felt as if he had been travelling not for a day, but for ever; over the face of an endless, town-filled world, a world of streets and shops and bright lights and clanging bells and shouts and strident hooters. Now there was silence and a breathlessness, a peace. He gave himself up to it luxuriously until Macey called. With an effort he raised himself on one elbow. He drank the tea gratefully, swilling the sweet hot tea around his mouth so that it flooded every desert corner.

Macey did not speak until he had finished the drink.

'You haven't any money, I suppose?'

Ransome shook his head miserably.

'It wouldn't be much use to you now you've come here.'

Macey chuckled. 'For that matter, if we looked hard enough I've no doubt we'd find some money. A forgotten penny, a lost threepenny piece – even sixpences. You'd be amazed at what people throw away. Not only money, but precious jewellery, valuable clothes – even wireless sets. It may sound incredible, but it is the case.'

'And food?'

'Not so liberal, not so varied. But there is food, if one looks hard enough. Bread, vegetables, potatoes, scrapings of fruit. Always something left amongst the tins. Sardines, pork, perhaps a drop of fruit juice. Coffee – often one finds some good coffee at the bottom of the tin ... And there are other things, like cigarettes. People are careless with cigarette ends. Incidentally, allow me to offer you one. Quite half size at the least.'

Ransome lit it from Macey's own cigarette. It was the first smoke he had had for four days. He breathed at it sensually.

'You had a – difficult time?' said Macey abruptly.

Ransome watched the smoke.

'Yes I came to the town when I was quite young. I had great ambitions. I was strong, enthusiastic, full of ideals. I wanted to make the town beautiful, a happy joyful place. But no one would listen to me. No one had time to bother with me, not among all the whirl and bustle. Who was I? I did not belong among the scintillating glitter of the shops, in the teeming banks and the counting houses. I did not fit in. I was not quite the right colour, perhaps. Not exactly the correct shape and specification. I had the wrong ideas, I was out of joint. So there was to be no place of me, I tried hard. I wanted only work, to keep myself. I asked little more. But there was no work, no money, not even a roof. And no one would help. Of course, I realise it was my own doing ... I had only to accept their beliefs, their conventions, and there would have been an end to my troubles. But I couldn't. I felt only that I must get away before I was somehow persuaded, starved perhaps, into submission. I thought it was too late. But somehow I managed to come.'

Macey smiled.

'You are very welcome. It is a difficult journey. Not many attempt it. It requires courage, faith. To the people in the town the Dump is the end of the world. Whereas, as you can now see, the whole world lies beyond, waiting.'

Ransome stirred worriedly.

'I ought to be making a start. I have nothing at all. I must find food and shelter. Do you think I will find material enough to make a roof?'

'Oh, yes, I think so. Look.' Macey pointed away to the far end of the field, along by the line of trees.

'We have most of us built homes there. We are quite a colony now.'

Ransome picked out little huddles of corrugated iron hut, canvas awnings, some wooden planks. At one point there was a large tent.

'You have built all this from the Dump?'

'Yes. And more. We have forced the Dump to provide us with Life instead of Death. Destitute, we have found food and clothing and shelter out of its apparent barrenness. A sort of miracle, if you believe in miracles. From the beginning we have been able to develop, make things, grow things. Soon we hope to be self-supporting ... But, of course, we have only done so by working together. It would have been impossible to carry on separately. Some of us are old, others are not so strong. The very young have not the patience, the understanding. And then some, not all, are very weak when they come. Weak and exhausted though they do not perhaps realise it.'

Macey took hold of Ransome's elbow quietly.

'It requires a short time to gain strength again, friend. We will walk over to the huts, and you shall have something to eat.'

Ransome frowned.

'But – '

'Come.'

Macey led the way across the field. Ransome noticed that they followed a precise path. On either side what had once been hard unbroken earth had been ploughed up and sown. The early plants were now beginning to burst through.

'Potatoes,' said Macey. 'We have hopes of a good crop. Then we shall plant lettuces, tomatoes. There is much that can be done. There are some products that we have even grown on the side of the dump. It is surprising what perseverance will achieve. We dried our own seeds from thrown away vegetables. Now we are planting on quite a large scale.'

As they approached nearer Ransome saw that though the huts were built of flimsy materials, they were securely erected. Smoke curled out of one or two tiny chimneys. He heard the sound of wood being sawn. A group of children ran out to meet them. Their clothes were tattered and worn thin and there was a pathetic urchin look about them. But their eyes were surprisingly clear, and they were smiling.

At the shrill babel of their voices, at the sound of their welcoming calls and laughter, Ransome felt a lump in his throat.

'We will eat now,' said Macey gently. 'And then you shall sleep. There will be time enough for your work tomorrow.'

The next morning, refreshed, Ransome went to the Dump to begin his search. He found the other men already there, dotted about the rough landscape. It was a hot day and some of them worked stripped to the waist, their skin shining with sweat. Their bodies were brown from long hours in the sun, and the muscles rippled easily as though long used to the steady rhythm.

They greeted him with friendly waves. He had met many of them the previous evening, when they gathered around the bonfire that was lit outside Macey's hut. There were about twenty, two of them brothers, the other solitary figures like himself who had somehow climbed out of the empty skeleton of the town and achieved the last weary march to the Dump. Some had brought their wives and children with them, and these women and their daughters cooked meals and shared the work of looking after the huts and the tents. The married men were in their forties, but most of the others were quite young. Like himself they wore clothes that were worn and tattered, and there was a conventional appearance of poverty about them. But he was impressed by the way they carried themselves. There was a freshness in their step and their eyes were open and unshadowed. For a time he watched how they went about work, the expert manner in which they sifted through the layers of soot. Then he selected an unoccupied part of the Dump and, digging his feet deep into the crumbling sootiness, began seeking for the pieces with which he might build himself a shelter.

All through the day he toiled until he could hardly bend for the pain in his back, nor scrape his hands through the soot for the soreness of them. At mid-day he ate some sandwiches which Macey had put in his pocket: were it not for them he would never have been able to carry on. Even so when, in the late afternoon, he tried to drag his materials over to the camp, he stumbled and fell. Groaning, he tried to pick himself up; before he could do so the other men came running over. One of them lifted him up and insisted on helping him over to the huts. Looking over his shoulder he saw the others clustering around the pile, and then they walked after them, each carrying an article. While, protesting, he was made to rest in the shade of a tree, the others cleared a space of ground and began laying a floor of wooden boards. Before it was dark they had erected, by a mixture of ingenuity and enthusiasm, a serviceable lean-to shelter, and Ransome had a roof over his head.

That evening he talked to the men again. They were a mixed collection. It was almost as if each had been chosen from a different walk of life: farmer, lorry driver, teacher, sailor, salesman ... Each had made his own journey, each with his own problems and sufferings. Ransome felt a special respect for the married ones, for they had brought with them women and children. About the women, indeed about everyone, he observed a common quality of unexpected serenity, of courage and confidence. Strange that it should be found here, at what would seem the very end of everything to most people – here by the stinking side of the Dump, with its dust-frothing refuse, its cast-aways from the sophisticated townspeople.

'Yes, it must seem strange at first,' said Mills, the teacher. 'I remember when I came towards the Dump I felt as if I was entering the very kingdom of Hell. It was a day in winter, there were still white fringes of snow along the roads. The vans from the town had just emptied a load on top, and the men had lit a large bonfire to keep themselves warm. The flames and smoke seemed to spring up from the bowels of the place. I nearly turned and ran – I suppose that is what so many have done. But instead I hid until the vans had gone, and then I went on. And I had my first reward. The fire was still burning and I was able to get warm for the first time for weeks. That fire made all the difference. By the time it was out I felt a new man. I had strength to go on, to find some scraps of food, to build a shelter. Later I found Macey and the others. Since then the time has swept by. I have been absorbed.'

'But why did you leave the town?'

'I had to get away. The town was throttling me. I felt it throttling everyone. At the school where I taught, it seemed to gather around all the pupils, like a monster, stultifying them all with its false values, its artificial behaviours. I tried to tear through all these, to expose them so that at least the next generation would break away. It was useless. I couldn't make them understand. And, of course, I was stopped. I was too risky to be allowed to influence "impressionable young people". Irony!'

'But why have you stopped here, by the Dump?'

'Why,' said Mills, 'because there is no need to travel further. I have found what I wanted.'

When the sun had gone in the night air came cool, and supper was eaten sitting around a fire built up of old pieces of wood and clumps of dried twigs. Ellen Wilkes, the stout wife of the grocer, served out the meal, hot potato soup with hunks of brown bread, afterwards more bread and some tinned cheese, after that black coffee.

It was by no means a luxury meal, but it was warm and solid. Ransome felt it sinking into him comfortably. Afterwards, stimulated by the coffee they talked and argued among themselves, until Diane, the daughter of the farmer, was called for to give some songs. Ransome did not know the songs, but they had an easy lilt, and gradually, rather to his surprise, he found himself joining the choruses. The men sang the background and Diane and Len, the lorry driver, contributed the solos. The sounds, then ran away and were lost forever in the night air: but while they remained, they were warm and uplifting.

As the others went to bed, Ransome stayed by the fire, listening to Len.

'It was a funny thing how I came here, yes. For I was actually driving a lorry up to the Dump from the town. I'd never been before, mind you. No, my run was long distance journeys up and down the country. I was hardly ever in the town. But this day there was no relief man, so I had to make the trip. Now, always before, I'd been able to drive in the open, to breathe fresh air. But this time, winding in and out of those streets, under the endless roofs of smoke, seeing the tiny little slum tenements, row after row – and the rails around the doors, and the broken windows – and everywhere people looking out with grey anxious faces – and the tramlines and the trolley-bus wires – oh, it fair got under my skin. I suddenly felt a terror at the thought of what was behind me, of the town and its smoke and its dirt and its dried-up torturous life. I felt like I daren't go back. I felt it was something evil.

'Do you know what I did? A crazy thing really. I drove to the top of the Dump, where the lorries turn round. I faced her back the way we'd come from, I started the engine and let in the clutch and – hey presto, off she went. I suppose I had some fantastic idea that the lorry would crash straight back into the centre of the town or something. A sort of gesture. But, of course, she didn't get that far. Careered about a bit, and in the end smashed into a tree. There wasn't much left ... The funny thing really was that no one seemed to bother about it. Or me, for that matter. Of course, I wasn't surprised, on reflection. A town has no heart, only an evil tongue. I suppose it seems a crazy thing to have done?'

'I don't think so,' said Ransome slowly.

'I was glad afterwards. When I climbed over the Dump, and found the others. They were good to me. Macey, Ellen,

Wilkes, the rest. It was, sort of ... you know ...'

Ransome's hut was built at the back of Macey's. He sensed without actually seeing, that the old man was keeping a benevolent eye upon his welfare. He imagined that Macey should be well satisfied, for within a few days he felt himself more of a whole being than for years. It was partly the atmosphere and the kindness, partly no doubt the existence of a steady routine to take himself out of himself. He discovered that work on the Dump did not always last through the whole day, unless a new load had been brought. Periods were given over to digging and planting in the fields, or attending to some poultry and goats that had gradually been acquired. He liked being out in the field, a spade in his hand, working steadily down the line of the furrow. It was clean and fresh, after hacking away into the dust and soot of the Dump. The field, like the town, lay below the Dump. Yet he was not conscious of the same sense of uneasiness as when in the town. The clenched fist formed by the Dump seemed to curl backwards, not lunging out further.

At other times the men shared duties of cutting wood, mending any breakages, improvising labour-saving instruments. Now Ransome found an outlet for himself. He had always been useful in this way, with his hands. He ferreted about the dump for screws and bolts and levers. As the weeks went by he produced racks for plates, a drying frame for clothes, a renovated gramophone. Then he turned his hand to chairs, taking the parts of two or three wrecked ones, cutting and shaping them into a complete chair. It gave him an immense satisfaction to work on these, to complete his planned product and present it for someone's use.

He began to mix more freely with the others, to feel himself more their equal. He liked them all, but in different ways. He liked Len for his cheerful good humour, his spontaneity. He liked the grocer because he always seemed contented, because he worked painstakingly himself, never grumbled at anyone else. He liked Mills because in mind he fancied he came nearest to himself, and he felt he understood things as Mills understood them. Then he liked Diane, the farmer's daughter, because she was forever a sight of pleasure, a slender young flower breaking into bloom with a freshness and innocence that seemed wonderlike against the sombre background of the Dump.

Diane was little more than a girl, perhaps sixteen, perhaps seventeen. He used to go for walks around the boundaries of the field with her and her father, a dark, rough little man with eyes keen grey from scanning wide spaces. He envied them their lives that had been spent among fields and hills, with the music of birds and sheep.

'How did you ever come to be here?'

'Ah,' said the farmer. 'Well you might ask. My fault I fear. Once we lived on an outlying hill farm. Sheep and hills were all we saw from one end of the year to another. 'Twas a fine life, you'd think. I know Diane was happy enough and her mother too. But I had other thoughts those days. I had a craving for lights, people, bustle, for more money, for the trappings of so-called civilised life. I was a fool. But give a fool his head ... When Diane's mother died, I sold the farm and brought her with me to the town. Going to have a good time, I promised her.'

'Anyway, it was exciting at first,' said Diane.

'Aye, p'raps. But it didn't take us long to see through it. There we were rushing about all over the place, just like one of those town cars, until our heads were reeling. And the noise! It was like living with thousands of braying sheep – and not on a farm, but cooped up in narrow streets. Well, at any rate, I came to my senses at last – didn't I, Diane?'

'You did, father. We packed our bags and off we went. We had nowhere to go, but we knew we must get away from the town. So we walked and walked ... and in the end we came to the Dump.'

Ransome looked at the girl, marvelling at her youth and her fresh innocence, yet sad to think of her perched on the edge of all the world's drabness and sordidness. Knowing what he had seen of the world of the town he could have cried to think that Diane might have to endure it again.

'But won't you go back to the farm?'

They both looked at him.

'Why should we? This is happiness, here.'

It was true. He knew it, deeply and convincingly. It seemed incredible, but the knowledge would flood upon him time and again – as he was bent down groping among the bones and blood of the Dump, as he squatted in the evenings by the firelight, singing. When he lay in his little make-shift hut at night, on a bed of straw with a length of matting over it, he would look out through a crack and see, beyond the black shape of the Dump, a glow from the artificial lights of the town beyond. And at the sight he would feel a much greater glow in himself, of relief and gratitude that he was here, on this side of the Dump.

As the weeks went by and he settled into the routine, Ransome could hardly imagine there had been another life. With O'Rory, the sailor, he shared the task of milking the goats that were tethered at the corner of the fields. There were three goats, and they called them Flotsam, Jetsam and Scraps. O'Rory was always a little scared of the goats, so he would let Ransome do the milking while he held the ropes and patted them soothingly on their black noses.

'Sure, course a man misses the sea, me lad. There's nowhere quite like it, oi'm thinkin'.'

O'Rory wagged a meaning finger.

'But when me thoughts start to wander away like that, wistful like, oi quickly calls them back. For there's no forgettin' what things were like back in the town. Sure, it's a real deceitful place, the town. Oh, it has a foine look about it, big houses and shiny shops, and there's iv'ryone smarmy and friendly – so long as ye can pay for it. Ugh! Oi've knocked about, me lad, oh yes, but don't mind tellin' ye oi was soon parted from the money saved up all those years on the water, when it couldn't be spent. Nivver mind, says oi to meself – oi've been on hard times before. There's always someone to give a helpin' hand.'

The red face darkened.

'But the town had different ways. Iv'ry creature so busy rushin' about, catchin' trams and meetin' other people. Nivver a moment in the day when anyone dares to step movin' – no, they must always be up and down and round about – why, they even go runnin' down the movin' staircases! O'Rory was out of luck's way. A few pence to his name and not a helpin' hand anywhere.'

'So you came here?'

'Well, me boy, so oi did in the end. But that was six or seven weeks later.'

O'Rory eyed Ransome thoughtfully.

'And for what happened in those weeks there'll be no need for me to be troublin' to tell ye, now.'

'No,' said Ransome. 'No need to tell me.' There were those who had endured their six or seven weeks, and there were those who had not. That was all.

When the milking was done he would walk over to where Buckley was working on the Dump, scraping about for cogs and wheels and bolts. Buckley had been a motor car salesman back in the town. He had worn a smart cut suit and had his hair flattened with brilliantine, and smiled a fixed smile at all corners, seven hours a day, five days a week. He had been a good salesman, too, he said. He found that by concentrating every ounce of energy and thought upon the task he was able to persuade unwilling customers to purchase cars that they did not really want, or could perhaps not even afford. He achieve this by talking at them incessantly, by drowning them in a flow of high-pressure arguments. Now he hardly ever talked at all, save for abrupt but expressive monosyllables.

'I was a fool. Ten years wasted. A talking sales dummy. A human selling machine. Didn't eat properly. Seldom slept. Lived and breathed motor cars. Hardly knew there was a life besides. Bowing and scraping to stupid women. Hollow-eyed business men. Never looked at their faces properly. Pity. Would have seen my own reflected. I was getting just like them. Cared only about money, about success, about selling more motor cars. Bits of tin and iron. Fool. Woke up one day. Just put on my coat and walked out. Didn't want to do any more selling. Didn't want to do anything at all like that. It meant the bottom out of my world. But I couldn't stop myself. I had to break not only with selling motor cars, not only with selling anything – break with my whole life. That meant stepping into a vacuum. Doing nothing. Even starving. All right, I'd starve. Until I knew what was the right thing. And I was starving before I realised what was wrong – the town, of course. It was dead, deceased. You just couldn't live in the town, you could only pretend. When I realised that I began walking. The old road. Here I am.'

Now Buckley was the mechanical genius of the group. He spent all his time collecting old tools, nuts, bolts, frames of bicycles, pieces of car engines, tyres, wheels. Already he had created a make-shift tractor which had enabled them to plough up the field. Soon he hoped to complete building a small van. He had the wheels, part of the frame, a steering wheel, half an engine.

In the afternoons they all gave up separate purposes and congregated in the field, to work side by side, digging and hoeing, planting and stacking. It was a time of subtle coming together. As they worked in physical proximity, so they were conscious of an emotional meeting and merging. A couple of hours in the field, working together – it was a symbol of what bound them.

And afterwards, if there was a sun in the sky, they would go to the west side of the Dump, throw off their clothes and plunge into the small pool their own labour had hewn out of the ground. One of the brothers who had been a surveyor had devised a system of damming up a nearby stream, running it into the pond at one end and letting it out, slowly, at the other end. So there was always this small oasis of cool water, right under the shadow of the Dump. It might hardly be long enough for a proper swim, but it was cool and soft and tender, you could lean back and wallow in its luxury.

Most of all Ransome came to value the evenings. It was in the evenings when you had the chance to enter into other people's lives more closely than during the working day. He was amazed to think how little he had known about people, how superficially he had mixed with them. He was constantly surprised, as he talked with this one and that one, to know the reality of individuals, the abounding imagination and life within each human form. It seemed that immeasurable qualities and talents, long stifled, were now released in the freedom of destitution.

'That is well said,' remarked Macey. 'That is a phrase to remember.'

Macey always sat in the same spot, and the rest of them formed a semi-circle fanning outwards from him. With this thick white hair and his wise face, his gentle brown eyes, Macey carried a natural air of authority. It was obvious that to him belonged the role of leader, of father of the group.

How had Macey come to be there, Ransome used to wonder. But no one knew. Macey had always been there, from the beginning. If you asked him he would never answer directly. He would say, 'I came here because I wanted.' Or, 'Someone had to be the first.' But it was not only this vagueness that lent a mystery to Macey and his presence, that surrounded him with an air that was almost unearthly. There was something altogether unexplainable about him. He had a great wisdom, you could see. He might almost be a saint.

Sometimes Macey would squat outside his hut, staring up at the Dump, seemingly oblivious of his surroundings. Outlined by the firelight his face took on a strange glow, and his lips could be seen to be moving. He would say that he was praying for the people of the town, on the other side of the Dump, praying that their eyes could be opened and their hearts cleansed, so that they might learn to escape from the prison of their lives.

Ransome used to sit at a respectful distance, crossing his legs like Macey, staring into the same direction. It was not mere vulgar imitation, but something that came upon him naturally. Closing his eyes and letting his mind go blank he would sit there for half an hour or an hour, and when he awoke he felt greatly refreshed.

One evening, as he sat dozing in the early dusk, it seemed to Ransome that a great darkness fell upon the world. Bigger and bigger loomed the darkness until he realised that it was caused by the Dump. The Dump was swelling and bulging as if all the town's vans were feverishly emptying load after load of refuse and rubbish, piling them up without heed, higher and higher. At first he feared that the Dump would grow so large that it would shut out the light of the sun, the very breath of the air. But as he watched he saw that the higher the debris was piled and further the shape of the Dump curved backwards; that, swollen and top heavy, it was beginning to lean over backwards, towards the town. Then he wanted to scream because he knew that if there was a strong wind it would blow straight upon the Dump and send its enormous shape toppling over the town. He waited in anguish suspense, fancying the wind would come howling and snarling like a revengeful tornado. But there was no tornado, only a tiny gentle puff of a summer breeze. He could almost watch it as it drifted along, tripping through the air with a tender gaiety and innocence until at last it rocked itself gently against the tip of the Dump. Oh, and then there was terror and disaster and a sight beyond words – a vast black swirling of soot and dust, the whole sky alive with spluttering smoke. Staring with frightened, unbelieving eyes, Ransome saw the Dump disintegrating in one huge sliding mass; pouring down towards the town, rushing upon the streets and the shops, the building and the park tree tops, flooding out in all directions; smothering the whole clockwork heart of the town. In agony he strained to hear the screams and the cries and the groans of the townspeople; but he heard nothing. He only saw the dark sooty mass from the Dump smothering everything in an infinite devouring fog, he only saw darkness and finality ...

He screamed then, a short high cry, and the sound of it woke him. He found himself trembling in a sweat from his nightmare.

He ran over to Macey and took his arm beseechingly, pouring out the story of what he had dreamed.

'It was dreadful. A terrible dream.'

Macey looked at him steadily.

'Yes, friend. It is a terrible dream. But you are not the first.

Every one of us here has had the dream, not once but many times. There is no escape from it. There can be no mistake about its meaning.'

Ransome put his hands to his face.

'You mean – it's true? It will happen?'

Macey looked away to the Dump. One of the town vans had driven up to the top and was now tipping out its load. They could hear the tinkling sound as the refuse crumpled and scattered about.

'What else can happen? The people of the town are obsessed not with life, but with death. They race hither and thither blind to the goodness latent among themselves, seeking always some new erotic sensation – finally craving the greatest sensation of all. Death.'

Macey stired slightly.

'Beyond the Dump lies a new life, freshness, land, a freedom for everyone. But the people of the town have no time and no sight for this. What more fitting Nemesis than the Dump with which, so carelessly erected, they blind themselves to the vision beyond?'

Ransome groaned.

'But is there no way of stopping it? Can't we save them?'

Macey looked at him sadly.

'They can only save themselves from themselves, each one of them. A few have done so. Here we are.' He sighed.

'That is why we wait here, by the Dump – because there remains always the hope that before the end comes there will be others who will join us.'

'And then?'

'Then brother, we will have to set forth and build our new world. Pray we have good fortune and humility, and we love one another.'

And after that Ransome felt he understood many things. He went about his work patiently and steadfastly. He shared his possessions with his fellows just as he shared with them his sorrows and his happiness, and they with him. Now and then there was a great stir and joyful cries and they knew that a traveller must be approaching from over the Dump. But for the most part they lived undisturbed, while all the time they were aware of the Dump growing bigger and bigger, like a black spot on the sun. Soon it got so large that they would sit in the evenings watching it, each secretly dreading the fulfilment of the dream. And all the time, desperately, they told themselves, surely there must be some way of stopping it? Surely if we went and pleaded with the people in the town? Surely they would realise? And all the time, irrevocably, they knew that there was nothing they could do, that only the townspeople could save themselves.

And the great sadness in their hearts was because now it was almost too late; now there was time only for a few more to save themselves.

# XIX

## My Son, My Son

My son Larry was always a great problem in the family. For one thing, he was the eldest. For another, the laziest. Since, however, he was also a great tactician, he usually managed to keep out of harm's way. Whenever we wanted a message run or the washing up 'volunteered' for, Larry was mysteriously absent. But if there were some sweets offered, or the suggestion of an outing to the pictures – there was Larry, his fourteen years and eight stone towering a good three inches above my wife, grubby hand held out avariciously.

Periodically, my wife and I would have acrimonious discussions about what to do with Larry. She varied between sentimentality and downright self-deception. ('What about the Foreign Office?' ... and even, once, 'Suppose he takes after his Uncle Harold and goes in for the ministry?').

My attitude was simpler, and more fixed. 'He's just a lazy so-and-so. You could hand it him on a plate, and he'd drop the plate.'

Most of the time, I tried to forget about Larry. After all, I had enough worries, trying to build up a business in the city, working all hours, desperately trying to maintain a growing family. All the same, as Larry shot higher and higher, broader and broader, ('He'll need another new pair of shoes – that's the fourth this year,' observed my wife in despair – 'What does he do, play football in them?' I snarled) – all the same, I became aware of Larry as a new kind of problem.

'He's fifteen, you know,' said my wife, one day. We were sitting at the window, looking out on the garden. Larry was sprawling on the grass, reading a book, while the other children rushed madly backwards and forwards. Now and then he would pause and yawn.

'Soon be time for him to be thinking of a job,' my wife added, with a little sigh that mothers reserve for eldest sons about to go out into the big world.

'But yes,' I thought, more joyfully, seeing an end to the perpetual bills for shoes and trousers and socks and shirts. 'Of course. Quite right, my dear. It's time Larry and I had a little talk. Get his future sorted out and all that.'

'Now, my boy,' I said, adopting the best fatherly attitude, when we were alone. 'Your mother and I have been discussing your future. I mean, you're a big lad now. I know your school reports haven't exactly set the house on fire and I don't mind admitting it's all a little disappointing. However, we feel the time has come to consider what you are going to do – I mean when you leave school.'

I paused to lend weight to my next words.

'Now, it seems to me there are a number of courses to follow. I have one or two friends in the City; no doubt they would help. I might get you into a bank, or insurance, you know, a nice comfortable office job, not too hard on the muscles for a tired lad. Or there's ...'

'That's all right, dad,' said Larry cheerfully. 'It's all fixed.'

'Fixed? What's fixed?'

'My – what do you call it? – my career.' He smiled, the bland, self-assured smile of every fifteen-year-old on the threshold. 'I'm going to be a fisherman.'

I suppose my eldest son had the wit to observe the shock and horror on his father's face, for without waiting for me to stutter out the obvious questions, he went on – I must say, pithily and to the point.

'You remember how I went fishing with Jimmy down at St Ives?'

I nodded, vaguely, not really having appreciated the exact reason for Larry's pleasing absence during most of our annual summer holidays in Cornwall.

'Well, I'm going to be a fisherman, like Jimmy. Mackerel, hake, pilchard, maybe shrimps, crabs ...'

I listened fascinated, as my eldest son rattled off facts and figures with complete aplomb.

'Why, I had no idea,' I said. 'I mean that you'd ever thought about – ' I paused, before mentioning a word which I feared might make Larry shudder, ' – *work*.'

Strangely, I don't think I took full note of his smile, then. I just remember he seemed calm and confident, and that when I nervously probed the matter, it appeared that at fifteen years he had it all taped.

'... Jimmy will let me help him to start with. Soon as I've saved up enough, I'll buy my own boat, and then – hey presto!'

'Dad,' went on Larry cheerfully. 'Can I go out in the garden?'

When he had gone, my wife peeped round the door.

'Well?'

'Well, indeed,' I said.

But the strange thing was, there wasn't too much to be done about it. I mean, you can lead a horse to the water, but you can't make it drink, not even a fifteen-year-old one. From time to time I paused in my hectic business activities to have a word with my son. It was difficult, indeed, since I rushed off soon after seven-thirty every morning to catch an early train, and Larry would still be asleep; and by the time I got home, late in the evening, he would be in a semi-doze on the couch in the sitting room. But now and then I caught his attention.

'The *professions*, Larry – don't they attract you? I mean, if you swot you might pass your exams, and then they're all open to you: medicine; the law; dentistry – I believe a lot of dentists are wanted.'

'I don't want to be a dentist, dad.' Larry looked at me with what I could only estimate as pity. 'I want to be a fisherman.'

By the time the next summer holidays came round only my wife, who had a pathetic devotion to the sanctity of academic education and the holiness of university degrees, would still occasionally worry – sitting up in bed in the middle of the night and saying with anguish: 'Larry ... a fisherman ... It doesn't make sense.'

No, it really didn't make sense, I decided. That summer holiday, I made a point of going down to the harbour, there to watch my son Larry and his friend, Jimmy. It seemed to me that they spent hours and hours just messing about with the dirty little motor boat in which, eventually, they chugged out of the harbour into the blue waters of the bay. Of course, it was all rather romantic and all that – but well, I mean to say, what was the future?

We weren't even appeased when Larry came in late and threw a couple of glistening plaice on the table and said, with a wide grin: 'Jimmy made fifty pounds today. Not bad, eh?'

I looked angrily at his mother and snorted.

'Pouff! Dead end job ...'

When he had gone to bed, though, I couldn't help stealing a look at my wife.

'Fifty pounds in a day?'

But of course, that was just one day. Probably on lots of days there was no money at all. Fortified by this thought I packed my case and went back to London. The family were staying on for the rest of the school holidays, but of course I had to get back to work. I couldn't afford to spend more than a few days on holiday, otherwise, goodness me, the business would go to rack and ruin. For me it was nose back to grindstone.

At the end of the school holidays my family made the long journey back. I was glad to see them. But one member was missing.

'Where's Larry,' I demanded. I had been spending odd moments working over dreams of courses at colleges, apprenticeships, civil service exams, all sorts of possibilities for my eldest son's future.

My wife looked embarrassed.

'He didn't think there was much point in coming back ...'

'He's a fisherman, now,' she said sadly.

I went off to work the next morning in a bad temper. When I thought of all the years I had devoted to educating that boy: the money, the care (the shoes – five pairs a year at least!) When I remembered how my wife and I had sat round the fire, in the early days of our marriage, dreaming of what would become of that tiny golden-haired creature on the hearth. Why, we had rambled through the phrases: doctor, author, statesman, politician, artist ... but never, *never* fisherman.

It used to worry me. Even though I seemed to be working all the time, now and then I would think angrily about Larry, three hundred miles away, probably just sitting in a boat and rocking gently with the tide. Yes, I could just imagine the lazy lout, one foot over the side, basking in the sun – oh, it was too bad, really, I pressed an anguished hand to my aching head and went back to adding up rows of figures.

We were busy, busy all the time. I used to rush off in the morning, and bring back work with me at night. I hardly had any other life, never saw my friends, or even, hardly, my family. My wife used to worry.

'Don't overdo things, darling, will you?'

I promised I would think about taking things easy. But truth to tell, I found myself thinking more about Larry. Why on earth had he chosen that way of life? Why, he could have lived in London, catching the city train every morning, wearing a smart suit, just like so many thousands of other smart, sophisticated young men. Why, then ...?

One day on an impulse I decided to spend a weekend down at St Ives. 'Be a break ... and I can see what Larry's up to.'

I wasn't surprised when Larry didn't meet me at the station. It was up a hill, and I couldn't imagine him wasting energy climbing all the way up when he knew I would make my way to the harbour.

I found my son there, of course. But I had a bit of a surprise, for he wasn't in Jimmy's old boat, but in another, larger, newer one. He grinned.

'Hullo, dad. What do you think of her?'

'But – ' I gesticulated. 'How – ?'

'Oh,' said Larry lazily. 'It's been a good season. I saved up, kept my eyes open. And now – I've got a boat of my own.'

He looked up, and I don't think I've ever seen such a look of sheer happiness before.

'Come on, dad. I'll take you round the bay.'

It was a cool, autumn evening, the sunshine still flooding everywhere with gentle light. Larry headed the little boat out to sea. Somehow, I don't know how, I found myself relaxing for the first time for – well, I don't know how long. It was grand, really grand, to sit back in my son's boat and feel the sea breeze on my face, fresh air in my lungs, watch the sun on the water, the white seagulls flecking about the sky.

Larry took the boat round Clodgy Point, then swung across the bay. I sat back, indolent, comfortable, at peace.

The boat droned on. Now and then we passed another small boat either fishing or laying nets; or perhaps a pleasure boat.

'In the summer I might take trippers,' called out Larry. 'It depends how the fishing goes.'

I nodded. I wasn't really listening much. I was just leaning back, drinking in the sunshine and the fresh air and the tang of the sea. Funny, but I'd never really experienced it quite like this before. And the strange thing was – it was all free.

The next day Larry took me out fishing. We were out all day, and when we headed home the hold was brimming over with our catch: mackerel, plaice, congers. Larry sold the whole lot at the quay: then we went home for a meal. That night I slept like a top – the first real sleep I'd had for months. The next day I went out again, and even enjoyed myself more: and at night I had my second wonderful sleep.

And then the day after that – well, you know, the funny thing is – that was three months ago – and I haven't been back yet; yes, I know it's disgraceful and all that, and all my business associates think I'm quite mad, and maybe you can't blame them. But the truth of the matter is I feel ten years younger and twenty years happier. And – well, do you see that new boat down there, the blue and white one with a bright red sail? That's mine – my very own. My son Larry agreed it was time I branched out. He thinks I'll make quite a good fisherman – er – in time.